Finding Ian

STELLA CAMERON

Finding Ian

KENSINGTON BOOKS
http://www.kensingtonbooks.com

KENSINGTON BOOKS are published by

Kensington Publishing Corp.
850 Third Avenue
New York, NY 10022

Copyright © 2001 by Stella Cameron

Library of Congress Card Catalogue Number: 00-103524
ISBN 1-57566-713-4

First Printing: January, 2001
10   9   8   7   6   5   4   3   2   1

Printed in the United States of America

For Mellie—wherever you are

Chapter One

One shoe box with a broken lid. One lousy shoe box held together by a knotted length of graying elastic.

Byron saw the end of the thing beneath a pile of shirts he never wore. He'd probably have thrown them out years ago—only somewhere inside him where he tried never to look hovered a warning not to go near that pile.

Ignoring the deluge of falling clothes, he pulled the box from a shelf in the walk-in closet, carried it to the bedroom, and dropped it on the bed.

It slipped to the floor. The elastic snapped.

The life of Byron and Lori Frazer spilled out.

Two years of loving scattered on a green and rust Chinese silk rug Lori never saw. Loving, and hoping, and praying, and daring to laugh—and losing. Thirteen years ago they'd lost the battle for a future together, and it hurt all over again, dammit, it hurt almost as much this morning as it had hurt then.

He went to twenty-foot-high windows overlooking a sheer drop to San Francisco Bay. Here, high up on the west side of Tiburon, he'd managed to find a kind of peace, a kind of insulation from the demands of his life that he'd rather leave either in his consulting rooms in the city, or at the TV station where he spent hours every day.

Jim Wade, the private investigator who'd worked for him for years, had obviously followed Byron's offhand invitation to finish his coffee—even though Byron had excused himself from their meeting to come up here. While Byron watched, Wade slowly emerged from the two-story house and sauntered to his inconspicuous brown Honda.

An inconspicuous car for an inconspicuous man who made his living watching, while not being watched. And he was good at it. Jim Wade was the perfect, unremarkable face in any crowd.

He glanced toward a cloudless blue sky, and the water that shimmered beneath an early March sun. Blue, on blue, on blue. Shaded bowls of blue, their rims dissolving into each other. Bougainvillaea in colors of ripe oranges, red, and a luminous purple billowed over white stucco walls edging the steep cliffs. The twisted limbs of stunted pines backed the wall and made jigsaw pieces of the horizon.

Wade threw a battered black briefcase and the jacket of his brown and beige striped seersucker suit into the Honda, climbed in, and drove away from the parking area at the back of the house.

Then he was gone.

Wade was gone, and Byron was left with no one but himself to make the decisions he'd hoped would never have to be made. Not that the fault for what had happened could be set at anyone's feet but his own. And he could choose to walk away from responsibility. After all, he'd turned his back on responsibility once before and been able to convince himself that what he'd done was for the best—for all concerned. And it might have been, mightn't it?

He returned to the side of the bed and went to his knees. He started gathering pieces of paper and photographs. Notes. Pressed flowers that crumbled at the slightest touch. A bracelet of colored yarn—faded now—and with Lori's name, in turquoise-colored beads, woven into the strands. Cards, Lori's, and even some of Byron's, handmade. They'd had so little money, not that he could have felt for a store-bought card what he'd felt for each of Lori's simple designs, or her words that could not have been for anyone but him. "I promise I'll never slow you down. I'll only be free if you're free. Be free, Byron. Love you, Lori."

He hadn't wanted to be free, not free of Lori, the sweetest, most honest creature ever to be part of his life.

He had owed her so much, but he'd failed her. And when he'd failed her, he'd failed himself. He had turned her concern for him into an excuse to do what he'd wanted to do—to avoid anything that might tie him down.

Hell, he didn't know anymore. He hadn't known then, but after all he'd been doing what Lori told him to do—choosing freedom at a time when to do anything else would make his way not just hard, but near impossible.

Byron Frazer had betrayed his wife.

The box should have stayed where it was.

A picture taken in Golden Gate Park. Lori clowning by a tree trunk. An insubstantial girl, with long, fine blond hair blowing away from her face, a bright grin, and gray eyes screwed up against the sun. He'd been playing his guitar and she'd leaped up to dance. She'd twirled and laughed, twirled and laughed, and he abandoned the guitar for their old point-and-shoot camera. Her slender body and well-shaped legs showed in shadow through a thin, flower-strewn, gauze dress.

His hands shook.

"Byron! Byron, are you here?" The unmistakable voice of his agent, Celeste Daily, came from the foyer. Celeste had her own key and never hesitated to use it. "Byron, darling, it's me, Celeste."

He listened to her inevitable exceedingly high heels clip on the terra-cotta tiles that covered the ground floor. She would be checking each room for him.

Celeste, his agent, and the woman who thought she owned him.

Tucking the photo of Lori into his shirt pocket, he made a rapid pile of everything else, and crammed it into the box. Then he pushed the box under the bed.

Celeste was already climbing the stairs.

What the hell was he going to do?

"Byron Frazer? Come out, come out. Be warned, I'm comin' in if you don't come out."

Some might be beguiled by her playfulness. Byron knew her too well.

The bedroom door stood open to a wide balcony that ran around the second floor. This room, decorated for him by the strangers he'd hired to make the house peaceful—his only instruction to them—echoed the cool greens and creams, and soft white used in the foyer that soared to open beams above the upper floor.

Tall, slender, elegant in putty-colored silk, her blond hair curving smoothly to chin level, Celeste appeared on the threshold. She looked at him, and frowned. "Byron? Honey, what gives? There's a studio full of people twiddling their thumbs and waiting for you over there." She looked at the phone by the bed, took obvious note of the unplugged cord.

He could lie, say he was sick, had unplugged the phone to get some rest, then overslept. Only this wasn't a time for lies. He shifted his foot slightly, and the toe of his right sneaker made contact with the shoe box.

No more lying, especially not to himself.

"For God's sake, what is it?" Celeste jiggled the car keys she held in one hand. "Oh, there isn't time now. We'll talk about it while we drive. I met Rachel outside, by the way. She's not a happy camper. She likes early morning visitors less than you do. Good housekeepers are hard to come by—you'd better smooth her feathers."

"Rachel's fine. She enjoys complaining."

He didn't have to deal with what Jim Wade had told him. For thirteen years he'd avoided doing anything—why start now? He crossed his arms and felt the photo in his pocket.

The coldness, the old coldness he'd learned to ignore, spread beneath his skin. His scalp tightened and he felt himself growing distant. Celeste's mouth moved. He watched, even shook his head a little and turned away as if dismissing her, but he couldn't hear her clearly anymore.

He drew a deep, deep breath and closed his eyes, willing himself to be calm, to stop himself from moving away, moving inside himself. It was Byron the quitter who ran away. He wasn't that man anymore. He wouldn't run again. Would he?

"Why didn't you come to the studio?" Celeste asked. "Or at least call and say you'd be late."

He struggled to concentrate. People thought him rude, arrogant, when he turned his silence on them, but he literally withdrew, just as his mother had withdrawn from his father's mental and physical battering. In the end she had gone so far away she'd never returned . . .

"Byron?"

"We're well ahead of schedule on the tapings," he said.

"That doesn't matter. You can't leave that many people standing around doing nothing just because you decide to sleep in. That's expensive. And it's not your style. You can't—"

"How do you know what my style is?" Much as he yearned to shout, he kept his voice steady. His father had been a screamer and Byron had learned to stuff down any urge to follow in good old dad's footsteps. "You don't know me, Celeste."

Her large, violet-colored eyes grew hard. "If you say so. That's a discussion that'll have to wait. Right now I need you downstairs in my car. We've got some major opportunities lining up. You're one hell of a success. I do know that about you. You're thirty-four, and you're already a media phenomenon. Dr. Byron Frazer, the country's leading popular expert on the family—and every woman's ideal man. Let's go."

"You go," he said. "I've got some things to attend to. Be a love and go buy me time, hm?" He managed a smile. The instant softening in her perfect features brought him no pleasure. So he had a face and smile that had women eating out of his hands. Big deal. They wouldn't want to come within miles if they knew what he really was. No woman worth knowing would want to.

"Byron, please—"

"I just told you I've got things to do."

"You bet you do. If we hurry, we'll at least make lunch. Buddy's talking about product tie-ins."

"We've already got product tie-ins."

"Other than tapes and videos and books."

Byron rubbed his eyes. "I'm not talking about this now."

"Because of the detective?"

He grew still, then slowly dropped his hands. "What did you say?"

Celeste walked across his bedroom to the simple teak writing table by the windows. She skirted the table and sat atop deep green corduroy cushions on a long window seat. "Rachel was outside dead-heading some flowers. Your Mr. Wade was just leaving."

"*My* Mr. Wade . . . How do you know his name?"

"He stopped and said goodbye to Rachel, and she said, 'Goodbye, Mr. Wade.' Then Rachel rolled her eyes at me and said, 'Detectives wanting coffee almost before my eyes are open.' " Celeste crossed one long leg over the other and didn't attempt to stop her skirts from slipping up her thighs.

"What's happened, Byron? Why would the police be here?"

"He's not a policeman. He's a private investigator—and my business with him is private."

She raised her silver-blond brows, got up, and bent over the writing table.

Damn, he'd forgotten about the papers Wade had brought and left spread out.

Celeste picked up a photograph and studied it. "Who's this?"

"No one you know." No one he knew—he'd made sure of that.

On that terrible day he was never going to forget, Lori had said, *"Byron, promise me you'll put this behind you if something goes wrong.*

Promise me you won't let anything stop you from doing what you want to do."

"This is what I want to do," he told her.

"But if . . . if something doesn't turn out the way we hope? You won't be stupid, will you? You won't give it all up. We both know that would never work. You wouldn't be able to manage everything."

"No, Lori, we don't both know that. You think you do. But nothing's going wrong."

"Promise me, please," Lori said. "You're going to be a great psychologist. You're going to help people like us. Like the people we were when we were kids."

"I promise you I'm always going to try to do what's right."

But afterward he'd lost his nerve.

"Nice-looking kid," Celeste said, and tossed the photograph down again. "C'mon, open up to me. What's going on?"

"Back off, Celeste."

"We've been through too much together for me to shrivel up just because you sound pissed."

"I've got to leave California for a while. Maybe quite a while." That had been the last thing he'd intended to say. But that was the answer, that's what he had to do—what was right. Finally. The pressure on his chest lightened. He'd made his decision. "Yeah, that's it. I'm going away. We've got plenty in the can at the station. If necessary they can go to reruns."

"That's the craziest suggestion you've ever made." She hurried around the table and came to him, grasped his biceps. "You're tired, that's all. Everything's gone so fast and you haven't had a real break in two years. Take a vacation. Go to Grand Cayman for a couple of weeks. You like it there."

"I don't like it there. I'm going to . . ." No, he would not tell her or anyone else where he was going. "I'm going to visit someone."

"Who?"

She never backed off, never gave up.

"My son," he told her, meeting her eyes while, inside, he began to move away again. The faint, familiar buzzing began at the center of his mind. The palms of his hands sweated—cold sweat.

Celeste dropped her hands. "*Son?* What son? You don't have—you *can't* have a son, for God's sake. What are you saying to me?" Her voice rose to a thin shriek.

"I have a son," he said, and this time the sound of it felt more real.

"No. Where is he? With his mother?"

"I'm not talking about Lori."

"Oh, my, God." Clapping her hands over her mouth, she tottered to the bed and sat down with a thump. "Lori? We've known each other for years. We've been more than business partners, Byron. But now there's a son, and *Lori?*"

"I've told you I won't talk about Lori. I've got a son who needs me." A son who might or might not need him, but Byron intended to find out for sure.

"That's him." She nodded toward the table. "The blond kid with the dog. I don't get it. How could you do this? Dr. Frazer can't have a secret kid stashed away somewhere. Or a wife, or ex-wife, or whatever. Think what that could do to your credibility. If you'd been straight about it up front, we could have made sure there was never any mess to clean up."

A mess to clean up? "Please go . . . Celeste, please give me some space. This isn't something I can talk about with you. Not with anyone. I need—"

"Oh, Byron." She surged to her feet and rushed to him, wrapped her arms around him. "I'm sorry, I'm sorry. Forgive me, please. I don't know . . . You shocked me and I've never been good at shocks. Why aren't I saying what I should be saying. This is *wonderful.* You have a son and he's beautiful. He must get the blond hair from his mother, but I bet he's got your eyes. What a beautiful boy."

"You can hardly see him in that picture. He's too far away." Wade had been warned never to intrude on Ian, to make certain the boy was never frightened.

"I don't have to see him any clearer to know he's wonderful. He's your boy. He'd have to be wonderful. A green-eyed blond. He'll soon be fighting off the girls. I want to meet him. I want to come with you."

There was only one person he'd like with him when—if—he met Ian, and she wouldn't be available. "No." He stiffened and gently disentangled himself from her. Forcing a smile, he said, "But thank you. Cover for me here, will you? Family is what I'm supposed to be about. You can say—without lying—that I've got a family emergency."

"That man—the investigator. He's working for you."

He bit back a retort. "Yes, yes he is."

"He came with all that." She waved toward the writing table. "About that boy. You've been having his mother watched, haven't you? Because you want custody?"

"You watch too much television." His voice was jocular, he made sure of that, but his pulse hammered at his temples. Somehow he had to satisfy Celeste's curiosity and keep her out of his business. "Nothing like that. Custody? Get real. What would I do with a kid? I analyze 'em, I don't live with 'em."

She smiled at that, nervously at first, then more widely and with confidence. "So why do you have to go see him?"

Blurting out his intentions about that hadn't been smart. "Just to check out that everything's okay. His situation's changed." Changed? Every shred of security had been pulled away from him and he'd been shuttled off to some relative he'd never met.

"You keep tabs on him through a private investigator. Why?"

"I don't have to go into all that with you, but it's the way it had to be." Because, when the chips were down and he'd officially turned his back on the boy, he'd been unable to put him out of his mind. Making certain Ian was safe and well cared for had felt right—essential.

9

"You don't have whatever rights a father's supposed to have in cases like this?"

She had to leave. She had to stop asking questions he didn't want to hear, much less think about.

Her eyes flickered away, then back again. Something had changed in the way she looked at him. Wary? Questioning? He could almost hear her wondering what else she didn't know about him, just how much he'd hidden behind a false face he'd perfected for the world.

"Look," he began, stepping cautiously, thinking his way through each word before he spoke, "this isn't something I ever expected. I thought the issue had been put to bed years ago. It all happened when I was a kid—twenty-one. It wasn't supposed to become an issue again."

"Ugliness has a way of not staying dead."

"There's nothing ugly—" He made himself take a breath. Of course she thought he was keeping a dirty little secret, a secret he was ashamed of. "I know what you're trying to say. I'm being absolutely honest with you, Celeste. We've been in business together a long time." An idea came to him. "Maybe you'd feel better if we severed that now—at least until I've straightened all this out and I can come back minus the baggage again."

"No, Byron!" She fluttered around him. "Let me pour you a drink."

"It's the middle of the morning."

"I could use a brandy even if you couldn't."

"Help yourself. I've got plans to make."

The heels of her cream leather pumps were of a gold metallic material. When she moved from the rug to the rosy-hued madrona floor, the heel tips made muffled thuds.

He wanted to take a closer look at the photos of Ian. Through the years he'd avoided having Wade take any shots. Without a visual image it was easier to remain detached.

Ian hadn't needed him before—not really. He'd made sure he

was well provided for, and safe. And from Wade's regular observations and reports, the boy was happy enough.

Celeste opened a cabinet fronted with etched glass, selected a decanter and brandy bubble, and poured a healthy measure of Hennessey. She drank too much but she didn't want Byron's opinion or advice on that topic.

She wandered back, a calculated, hip-swinging wander, and arranged herself in his favorite dark green leather wingback chair. She used one heel to pull the ottoman close, and stacked her feet. Celeste's legs were her most remarkable feature, not that the rest of her wasn't remarkable.

"How old is . . . Ian?"

"Thirteen."

"You haven't exactly been an active part of his life."

He hadn't been any part of his life. "No. It never worked out that way."

"So why go rushing off now? Why not get through this season's shooting and make leisurely plans to take some time off? It would be much simpler—"

"Simpler for whom? No, that won't be possible." The truth was that he only had Wade's word for it that Ian was happy, and now, with this move, there was no assurance that life wasn't very difficult for a thirteen-year-old uprooted from home and school during early adolescence.

Celeste swirled her brandy, sniffed, tipped up the glass until she could poke the very tip of her tongue into the liquor. She kept her eyes downcast, but the affectation was deliberately sexual. He regretted the brief, intimate interlude they'd shared. The cost had been too high, but it was over and would stay that way, no matter how hard Celeste tried to find her way back into his bed.

She rested her head back. "What's she like?"

"He . . . Oh." He spread his hand over the pocket with Lori's picture inside. "A wonderful woman. That's all I'm going to say. That, and we had a child. Then something happened, something too awful to be true—only it was true. I had to make a decision and it meant I gave up being part of my son's life. As long as everything was fine with Ian, it was fine with me. Now I'm not sure he is fine, and everything's changed."

"You're wonderful," she told him, drinking more brandy. "You'll forgive me for overreacting, I know you will. And I am coming with you. You need someone to look after your needs, too."

"No, Goddammit!" So much for being the expert on controlling temper. "No, Celeste. A man has to do some things alone. But I promise you I'll keep you in the picture—as much in the picture as you need to be to do a good job for our interests here. And I appreciate your concern." He went to the open door and stood there, pointedly waiting.

Uncurling her legs, Celeste got up slowly. She walked toward him until she was close enough for him to see tiny beads of moisture on her brow. The lady was thoroughly unnerved.

"It's about the woman, really, isn't it? You want to see if it's still as good as you remember."

Even the thought sounded disgusting. "You . . . You wouldn't understand someone like Lori. I don't want you to mention her again. Not ever. Do we understand each other?"

Pressing her glass into his hands, she made a silent "Oh" with peach-colored lips. "Forgive me. I didn't know you were in love with a saint."

Anger confused him. "Give my apologies," he said formally. "I will contact you—but I'm not sure when. Until then, you can say what I've told you to say: I've been called away on a family emergency."

She started to say something, but he turned his back on her and went to sit at the writing table. He touched nothing until he heard her footsteps on the stairs. She moved quickly and soon the front door slammed hard enough to rattle windowpanes. Defeat wasn't a word Celeste liked to include in her vocabulary.

Byron picked up the photo and looked closely at Ian. For the first time he allowed himself to wish he could see the boy more clearly.

Ian was bent over with his face turned aside to accept licks on his neck from the big, black lab he embraced with both arms. A thick head of blond hair and a grin. A tan from what Byron could make out.

He pulled out Lori's photo and set it on the table beside Ian's.

And he brought a fist down so hard the impact made him flinch. They should all have been playing together with the dog, laughing together. And Byron and Lori Frazer should be holding each other while they watched their boy romp, secure in his parents' love— their love for him, and for each other.

He closed his eyes and rested his forehead on his hands. He didn't want to think, not about that hospital. He didn't want to hear its sounds and smell its smells—or see what he had seen there.

Why couldn't he forget?

"It'll get better, Byron, son."

He tried to evade the doctor. "I'm not your son. I'm nobody's son, never was." He took several steps along the hospital corridor, but his legs were too heavy.

"Look," Dr. Harrison said, "this is a tough one. The toughest. My God, I want to help you. Right now you feel—"

Byron's teeth chattered. "You don't know how I feel."

Rubber wheels squeaked on the green and white tiles. The doctor caught Byron's elbow and steered him closer to one wall. An orderly in blue scrubs pushed a gurney past—to the closed door of the room Byron and Harrison had just left.

"No!" Byron yanked his arm free. "Oh, no. Not yet, please."

"Byron, why don't we take a walk."

The orderly had stopped. "Are you talking to me, sir?" He looked uncertainly at Byron, then at Dr. Harrison.

"Carry on," Harrison said.

Before Byron's stinging eyes, the corridor's beige walls rippled sluggishly as if they were under water.

He looked at Harrison, and the man with the gurney. They were all under water here, and sinking deeper.

"God's not finished with me yet," he muttered.

Harrison came closer, jutting his chin and frowning, his eyes vast and popping behind thick-lensed glasses. "You need some air," he said.

"Don't tell me what I need." Byron pointed to the room into which the orderly pushed his white-draped gurney. "She needs air. My wife needs air."

"I want you to lie down," Harrison said. "I'm going to give you a shot of something to make you feel better."

"Stop telling me something can make me feel better." Byron sidestepped to the opposite wall. He held out a hand to ward the man off.

Harrison shook his head and said, "Okay, okay. Coffee, then. I'll get us both some coffee. Come with me."

"She tried to laugh," Byron said. Tears burned his throat. "She tried to laugh and she said she didn't think she'd die today because God hadn't finished with her yet."

"Lori had spirit."

"She was twenty years old." He reached behind him to feel the cool wall.

"And you're only twenty-one." Harrison folded his arms and bowed his head. "Too damn young, both of you."

"Those people don't know her," Byron said. Breath fought its way in and out of his lungs at the same time. "I don't want"—he rubbed his eyes and tried to focus— "I don't want strangers touching her."

"Byron—"

"I don't want them seeing her like that. Putting their hands on her." He made to go back the way he'd come, but Harrison stepped into his path. "I want to take care of her. Please. I can do it. Just tell me how and I'll do it."

"Hell," Harrison said, almost to himself. "She's . . . Lori's at peace now, Byron. There isn't any pain, now. Just peace."

"She never weighed anything. I could carry her where she has to go, couldn't I?"

"No."

"Sure I . . . could. I—" With a clicking sound, his throat closed. "I want to hold her—just one more time. Please."

The doctor's hands came down on his shoulders. "If I could change this, I would. Damn it to hell, there are never any right words. You can't hold her now, Byron. Lori's dead. You've got to find a way to let her go."

"I want to die. I want to be dead, too."

The banging open of the door jarred his teeth together. He saw the orderly backing from the room.

This time the white drape covered Lori on the gurney. Webbing straps had been buckled over her body.

Laughter welled in Byron's chest. "They think"—he pointed—"they're afraid she might run away. And they're right! Lori can really run. Give her a blue sky and soft grass and she can run . . . and run."

They wheeled her past.

"Watch her," Byron called. He wiped the back of a hand over his mouth. "Watch her, you hear? She's fast."

A nurse came to stand in front of him. He remembered her face, but not her name. "Will you let me take you upstairs, Mr. Frazer?" She had a light voice. "That's where you need to be. It'll help."

"No." He shook his head, and shook and shook it. "I can't. Not now."

"Yes, you can." Her fingers closed around his left wrist. "I'll take you. For Lori, Mr. Frazer. You told her you'd be all right. Remember?"

"She wasn't supposed to die." Abruptly, the tension drained away. He just wanted to lie down. "Leave me alone."

"I don't think that's a great idea." The nurse tucked her arm firmly beneath his. "Upstairs we go. There's someone who needs you to hold him. It's time you were properly introduced to your son."

Beneath his face, Byron's crossed hands were wet. Tears? How long had it been since he'd cried? Not since that afternoon in a San Francisco hospital watching his young wife's body wheeled away?

Or had he last cried some weeks later, in the dark, in the bed they'd shared?

Yes, that had been it. And he'd turned his face to the wall and prayed he would one day believe what he'd told himself in a lawyer's office, that he'd been selfless in relinquishing his tiny baby boy to a couple who would never have children of their own.

Now that grateful husband and wife were dead and once more the boy was moving on, moving on to more strangers.

But this time Byron would do what he'd promised Lori, he'd try to do whatever was right.

Perhaps then he could stop hating himself.

Chapter Two

"*There's nothing I won't do for you.*"
That had been their promise to each other. Their final vow on their wedding day. Their final words to each other before they slept each night. And on the day when Lori had died, she had whispered them to Byron. He couldn't remember if he'd repeated them back. But today he could hear her voice, the way its timbre dropped at the end of a sentence.

He hadn't thought about it for a very long time, but today he couldn't keep it from his head. On the journey he'd made since early yesterday morning, he'd felt Lori with him. Perhaps she was making sure he didn't change his mind.

The thought brought a smile, the first in days that he remembered.

He'd flown from San Francisco and over the pole to London. Following in the footsteps of Ian Spring who had been born Ian Frazer. Boy baby Frazer. Byron had been told the adoptive parents would expect to name their new son, and he'd looked at the rumpled little face and thought "*Our son,*" and "*Matthew.*" Before his birth they hadn't known if the baby was to be a boy or a girl, but if they had a son, Lori wanted to call him Matthew because, she said, it meant, gift from God.

Byron had planned to break his journey overnight in London before renting a car and driving to Cornwall. Instead he'd set off within a couple of hours of landing at Heathrow.

He'd never driven on the left before. Secondary roads had seemed like a good idea until the first time he was all but forced into a hedge by an oncoming vehicle. "There's nothing I won't do for you," he had said aloud, and pointed the Land Rover firmly southwest. "Cornwall, here we come."

Jim Wade had been very thorough. So far all the details he'd given Byron had been correct. They had led him to a rental cottage in the tiny Cornish village of Boddinick, across the River Fowey from the town of Fowey. And together with the inquiries Byron had made for himself since his arrival, they had brought him here, to his knees in a foreign church.

One word was all it would have taken. "*No.*" Thirteen years ago, standing in the office of a San Francisco lawyer, he could have said no. If he had, then today he wouldn't be in an ancient English church, in an ancient Cornish fishing town, trying to make a decision that could change the rest of his life.

But thirteen years ago he'd said yes, yes he thought it would be better to give his baby up for adoption.

He'd never lost track of the Springs and Ian. The only request he'd made of his boy's new parents was that he be the one to put him in their arms. He'd done so, looking into their happy, yet anxious faces. And he'd managed to tell them his wife would have wanted him to make sure their boy was going to good people.

The Springs were good people, straightforward, hardworking, kind people. And when he'd made himself leave them, he'd started the long, long road back to feeling alive again.

Byron after Lori.

Back to school. A life submerged in learning, learning about people and what made them the way they were. And in time the raw places within him had hurt less, then less, and finally he'd been on his way into a successful career that became so much more than he'd ever hoped for.

He'd done the right thing for the boy. If anyone should know how important it was for a child to have loving, reliable parents—people who would always be there for you—it was Byron Frazer, and he could not have given that to a baby. So he'd told himself. Then he'd managed to think less and less about the child he'd given up. Ian had a good life—Jim Wade's semiannual reports assured Byron that was so—and disrupting it once Byron was secure would have been wrong for both of them.

But Ian's life had been disrupted now. Not just once, but twice. First his adoptive father had died, then, a matter of weeks ago, Ada Spring had also died, and with that news, Byron had stopped sleeping.

The notebook in his hand was expensive. Small, bound in soft black leather and bearing a discreet gold-tooled B.S.F., it was as elegantly expensive as almost everything he owned. He didn't need the notebook. Even if he hadn't had a photographic memory, he would have remembered every word he'd written.

In that San Francisco hospital, not far from the room where . . . He didn't want to think about the room where Lori died. Then he'd been a twenty-one-year-old student making his way on scholarships and the paltry money he made as a condominium security guard. There'd been no custom-tooled leather notebooks then. Byron flipped through pages without looking at any of them, and tucked the notebook back into the breast pocket of his sportcoat.

Propping his elbows, he rested his chin on laced fingers and closed his eyes. He could still change his mind. True, he only intended to check up on Ian, but he didn't even have to do that, not if he was uncertain about the wisdom of doing so. He was a psychologist, an expert on complex family dynamics. He belonged where he could observe other people's families and give advice based on learning, not here, not . . . He was scared. Damn, it was laughable.

He was a fraud, a scared fraud who advised, and chided, and lectured, and quoted.

The possibility of his own reality changing everything he'd accomplished ought to stop him cold.

There was nothing he could do about the boy now. He'd given up that responsibility, that right. Who did he think he was, God?

A coward.

He was a hollow man with nothing to offer to flesh and blood people, not if they actually threatened to encroach on his own well-ordered existence.

In this quiet place, centuries of history settled their weighty cloak about him. He was tired. Finally, after being unable to close his eyes for almost two days, he longed to sleep, to sleep and not to dream.

A swishing sound halted his exhausted drifting. The swish of nylon colliding with nylon. A woman drew level, then passed the pew without ever glancing in Byron's direction. Evidently the kneeling position guaranteed invisibility beneath these soaring Norman arches.

"Well, there you are!"

At the sound of the woman's voice, Byron jumped. Turning in the aisle, she faced his direction, and frowned. Red brows thinly penciled into permanent surprise drew together over bright blue eyes. Hair the same unlikely color as her brows curled tightly about a plump face.

"I told you not to dawdle, my boy."

She spoke not to Byron, but to someone behind him, someone whose metal-capped heels made an echoing clatter on tesselated gray stones.

"Whatever will the vicar say? Taking half the afternoon with the flowers. Hurry up, now."

Rather than speeding up, the footsteps dragged more slowly through the nave. Byron held his breath, fighting the urge to look back. The smell of old incense and older dust stifled him. Motes of the dust swirled in swords of colored light through stained glass windows. He shouldn't have come.

"Put them over there," the woman said.

The boy drew level. Byron felt him. Then he saw him, his arms full of some sort of greenery, silently, doggedly following the woman's directions.

"Make yourself useful, there's a good boy. I know you want to make me proud of you, you just don't know how. Mrs. Harding will be along any minute. She'll expect all that to be sorted. Separate it into piles on some newspaper." She paused, a peeling metal vase in each hand. "Can you do that, Ian?"

"Yes, ma'am."

Ian. Byron's heart pounded in his ears. He had to strain to hear.

Hair the same fair color as Lori's, but thicker. This was the three-dimensional Ian, not the Ian of the distant photographs. If he chose, Byron could get up and go to him, touch him, say his name.

This was a hellish mistake. What had he been thinking of?

Ian was tall for thirteen, and thin. Would his eyes be green? What would it feel like to look into his face and have him look back?

The boy didn't know him, wouldn't know him. Byron wished that truth didn't hurt, but it did.

"Here?" Ian turned, searching for something. "On the benches?"

Byron was too far away to see his eyes.

"No!" The woman tutted and plopped her fists on ample hips. She wore a much-washed floral apron over a sensible brown tweed skirt and matching woolen sweater. "I can't imagine what Ada can have been thinking . . ." She pressed her lips together and looked heavenward. "God rest her soul. But she should have taught you something."

"Mom taught me lots, ma'am," the boy said, and even at a distance Byron saw red stain his slender face.

"I've told you to call me Aunt Muriel."

Ian shifted from foot to foot. "My mom taught me plenty . . . Aunt Muriel."

Muriel Cadwen. Muriel Cadwen, sixty-three, retired spinster librarian, sister of Ada Spring, née Cadwen. This was the woman he'd traveled from San Francisco to see. Not necessarily to speak to, but to watch. He knew she did volunteer work at the local library. The man he'd spoken to on the phone there had been quick to tell Byron that Muriel and "the boy" would be at the church this afternoon.

She sniffed and planted her brown lace-up shoes firmly apart. "Of course Ada taught you things. She was my sister, you know. But she should have made sure you knew how to behave in church. And they're pews, not benches. Separate the ferns from the teasels and the ivy and put them in piles on the floor in front of the chancel rail." She pointed to the crossing in front of the nave.

The boy looked dubiously at the bundle in his arms.

"On newspaper, mind." Muriel turned away.

Ian stared at her back a moment then started dragging newspaper over the floor with a toe.

Byron itched to get up and offer to help. He mustn't. He mustn't do anything. Not yet. Maybe never. *Go to Cornwall and take a look at the boy.* That's what he'd promised himself. Make sure he's all right. Do it for Lori because she would have wanted that. Celeste, who now knew where he was, had been charged with putting out the story that Dr. Byron Frazer, behavioral psychologist and family life guru, needed a sabbatical from his office and the TV cameras. So—if he could make peace here—he'd stick around for a few weeks, maybe get some writing done, then go home to San Francisco.

Simple. Charting logical courses for humans was his forté.

So why was his heart still thundering? And why did his throat feel as if he'd swallowed a golf ball?

More footsteps approached from behind him, these with the squish, squish of rubber soles.

Muriel, who had disappeared through a door at one side of the altar steps, popped her head out again. Hitching her apron, she bustled forward. "Afternoon, Effie. Running a bit late, I'm afraid." She raised her formidable brows and inclined her head meaningfully toward Ian. "Lot more on my hands these days. If you know what I mean."

"Yes, well, I shouldn't worry." The new arrival, a weathered, gray little woman, put a basket of roses on a pew. "You're a saint, Muriel. We all say so. I can't imagine how you're managing knowing . . . well, you'll get your reward. You know that."

In the shadow of a cold pillar, beneath an unlit candle sconce, Byron edged deeper into shadow. This wasn't going to be simple. He would have to decide. Was Ian okay or not? And if he wasn't, what could be done? What did Byron want to do?

Ian kept his head bowed. He worked a branch free, then seemed undecided where to set it.

"You'll have to be quicker than that," Muriel said, and to Effie, "I thought I'd give him something to do. He obviously hasn't had any guidance. A month he's been here and he's still reading the first book I got him from the library. Comics, he came with. And those funny skates. Wheels all in a line."

"I wouldn't have any of that. Those comics. They give children bad ideas. Violent." Effie, inches shorter than Ian, pulled the cut greens from his arms and started to sort. "You're right to give him things to do. Keep him out of trouble. And with his history . . ." She sighed.

Muriel gave an echoing sigh and trudged into a partitioned area at the entrance to a side chapel. The faded sign on a screen read CHILDREN'S READING ROOM.

Byron seethed. He realized he'd curled his fingers until his nails cut into his palms and he made an effort to relax. The two women spoke about the boy as if he weren't present. *His history*. What would they do if Byron leaped up and said, "I know his history. There's no one who knows it as well as I do. Ian Spring doesn't remember me, but he's here because of what I did"?

Light glinted on Ian's short-cropped straight hair. TWINS emblazoned the front of a white sweatshirt, and his hands had found the pockets of well-worn jeans. The all-American kid from Minneapolis, Minnesota. And every miserable line in his handsome young face said he'd jump at the chance to be right back where he'd come from.

Effie scuttled around Ian. "Sit down somewhere," she said, impatient but not unkind. "Keep out of the way, there's a good boy."

Byron closed his eyes. He had no right to interfere. *He shouldn't have come.*

"Here you are." Muriel's voice snapped Byron's eyes open again. "The text is too young, but the pictures are beautiful. Sit over there and look at it like a good boy."

Ian stared at the book Muriel had given him. He didn't move.

"Oh, you aren't trying," Muriel said, puffing with exasperation. She snatched back the book. "Go outside. Children need plenty of fresh air. They sleep better."

His face expressionless, Ian started down the aisle.

"And don't step on any graves, mind. And don't go too far. I don't want to have to look for you."

Muriel's voice followed Ian. The heavy wooden door opened, then closed with a solid thunk.

"He still doesn't say much," Effie said. She'd finished sorting. With a practiced hand, she selected roses from her basket. "I'd have thought he'd at least try to fit in."

"I'm doing my best," Muriel said. "I talked to May. Thought with her having brought up two children of her own she'd have some ideas, but you know May." She shrugged eloquently. "She does suffer so."

"Yes, poor dear. Funny how different you three sisters are. You always busy and making the best of everything. May delicate like she is and such a homebody, and Ada!" Effie rolled her eyes upward. "God rest her soul. But Ada was the wild one. Running off and marrying that American. Then living over there. And so many years between visits. When you told me she'd been widowed, I thought she'd come home then. But no. Who'd have thought she'd pass on so young? Only fifty-two."

"Ada was independent," Muriel said, her voice oddly soft. "She was never wild, not our Ada. Pretty and independent. And we got along well. That's why the boy came to me. She'd have visited more often if it didn't cost so much."

He hardly knew that he'd risen to his feet and moved to a side aisle. Almost noiseless in his boat shoes, he left the building.

Standing by an ivy-covered wall, he took in a deep breath of fresh, early June air and blinked while his eyes adjusted to pale sunlight. Set on a hill above the port town of Fowey, the church commanded a view over crooked stone roofs and steep, narrow streets, to the harbor and the English Channel beyond. In the distance and farther inland, across the slender, sparkling inlet from the sea, lay Bodinnick. With his travel agent's help, Byron had taken a summer's lease on a cottage. He wouldn't need it more than a few weeks, but the owners didn't rent for periods shorter than two months, so Byron had paid for the whole time in advance. He'd leave when he was ready.

Now he saw Ian. Sitting on a bench, almost hidden behind the gnarled trunk of a huge chestnut tree, only his right sleeve showed . . . and moved. Byron put his hands into the pockets of his own jeans and picked a path between gravestones.

The arm moved and a steady plink, plink sounded as pebbles glanced off a gray marble statue.

Byron grinned. The least he could do was divert Ian from being a "bad boy," before Muriel caught him.

If he approached from behind, he'd startle him. Backtracking, Byron made a circle, slowing down to read markers as he went.

He stopped on the other side of the statue Ian had been using for target practice and pretended to study the inscription at its base.

He looked up at Ian and smiled. "Hello."

The eyes were brown, not green. Dark brown and heavy-lashed and wary. "Hi." The blond hair dramatized those dark eyes.

No feeling Byron had experienced could have been like this. His hands were numb. Ian, the boy who had been a baby the last time they'd been together, was looking at him with no inkling that they shared a past.

Stillness shrouded Byron. It began to suffocate him. He cleared his throat and said, "Nice day."

"Yeah, I guess so." The boy was too thin, his expression too guarded with a deep weariness that had nothing to do with being tired.

"You're from the States."

Denim scraped as Ian shifted on the wooden seat. "Yeah. How d'you know?"

"Wild guess." Byron laughed. He'd never felt less confident—not for a very long time. "Minnesota?"

Ian sat forward. "How'd you know *that?*"

Byron laughed again, indicating the sweatshirt. "Twins." He noted that Ian wore new, very shiny black lace-up shoes rather than the expected sneakers. "On your shirt."

"Oh, yeah." Ian plucked at the rubberized letters. A spark of animation entered his eyes. "You're from the States, too?"

The boy must have felt the immediate kinship of shared nationality. "Yes," Byron said. "San Francisco." He took a couple more steps closer.

"Yeah? I'd like to go there sometime. If I ever get out of here."

How much did Ian know about his past? "Cornwall's nice."

Ian leaned to scrabble for another handful of pebbles. "I hate it." He resumed his attack on the statue.

Careful, Byron warned himself. "Where do you live?"

"Down there." Ian nodded toward the town. "Not far from Place. You know about that?"

Byron looked at the square towers of a huge house crammed into the middle of Fowey. "Yes. Like a castle. Pretty fantastic, huh?" He also knew Muriel Cadwen lived at 4 The Rise. In the gray hours of early morning he'd stood across the street and stared at the pretty terrace house with its profusion of flowering hanging baskets.

Another rock found its mark on a cherubic cheek. "Pretty weird, calling your house Place and nothing else. This whole town and everything is so old."

Byron searched for the next question. He should have shown surprise at Ian living in England, but the slip didn't appear to have been noticed. "So you live here now?"

"Yeah."

"And you don't like it?"

"No. I don't have much choice though, not yet."

Byron didn't have to ask what was meant by that. Already Ian was planning his escape. Feeling a rush of something close to pleasure and pride was wrong, but Byron hadn't forgotten his own drive to get away from an impossible childhood, or the fact that he'd eventually made his dreams come true.

"What's so bad about Fowey?" he asked.

Ian tossed down the rest of the rocks and turned his face up to Byron's. "Everything."

The tilt of the head, the way the faint breeze ruffled fair hair to show darker tints, the pointed chin and slender neck, lightly tanned skin—all familiar. Byron's stomach made a slow, painful revolution. "Want to talk about it?" He was a stranger. Regardless of the part he'd once played, he was a total stranger and he was dealing with this all wrong. "I'm a great listener."

"Nah."

"Okay." Why would a boy bare his soul to a man he didn't know?

"My dad died five years ago," Ian said suddenly. "In the winter. His car skidded on ice."

"That's rotten." The thudding in Byron's chest started again. "My father died when I was pretty young, too. Fifteen." Not that he'd mourned the event.

Ian crossed his ankles, seemed to notice his feet and immediately stuffed them under the bench. "My mom died, too. A couple of months ago. Cancer."

"I'm really sorry." Would the boy talk to anyone this way or had he felt some bond—other than through the country they both came from? The unreality of the moment, the situation, disoriented Byron.

"Anyway, I don't have any family in the States to take me, so I was sent here. My mom's family lives here."

"I see."

Silence fell between them. Ian's hands were long and slender, but with blunt fingertips. Again Byron's insides twisted.

"You on vacation?"

"Sort of," he said. He could see the boy from time to time. Casually. Make sure their paths crossed in an easygoing way. There'd be nothing wrong with that. "Have you been to Bodinnick?"

Ian immediately looked in the direction of the village across the river. "Over there?"

"Yes. I'm staying at Ferryneath Cottage. Near the ferry and the pub." The Old Ferry Inn, a whitewashed sixteenth-century building, stood out even at a distance. It nestled at the bottom of an almost perpendicular road lined with cottages.

"I haven't been there. If you can't drive around, you have to take the ferry."

A passenger and eight-car barge wallowed laboriously back and forth all day. "That's right. You might like it over there. Good hiking. D'you like to hike?"

Ian looked dubious. "Probably. I never did any. Anything would be better than here. I never get to do anything." He flushed crimson. "I got left to my aunt. She doesn't have any kids so I guess she isn't too sure what kids do."

Byron felt a swelling sensation. Ian was under siege, facing the biggest crisis of his life, but he could still be objective enough to try to find excuses for Muriel. "Probably. What exactly do you mean by 'got left'?"

"In my mom's will." He snorted. "Kind of like a house or something. Only Mom asked Aunt Muriel if she'd take me and she said she would."

So that's how it had worked. Jim Wade was good, but the lawyer's secretary he'd wined and dined had only been persuaded to tell him where Ian had gone and to whom—not the legal aspects of the arrangement.

"When do you go back home?"

Byron started. There was wistfulness in Ian's brown eyes. "Not for a while. Probably not 'til September." Damn, he had to think before he spoke.

Ian turned sideways. "Yeah? That's a long vacation."

"I'll be doing some work here." If he could concentrate. Why had he said he'd stay that long? It didn't matter, they weren't going to get close enough for the boy to care.

"What kind of work do you do?" Ian asked.

"Writing. Stuff like that." He took a deep breath. "Why don't you come over and visit? I could take you for a hike on Hall Walk. That's where—"

"Yeah, I know. Aunt Muriel told me about a king who got shot over there in 1644 or something."

"Shot at," Byron corrected. "King Charles I. But it was a fisherman who died."

"She wouldn't let me visit."

"Sure she would." Now he sounded too eager. It was a wonder the boy wasn't already figuring him for a pervert. "Well, you're probably right. But if your aunt gives you some time off, ask if you can come over."

Ian got up. "I could. D'you like baseball?"

He hated it. "Love it."

"Football?"

"The season's finally getting almost long enough." And he was a liar. "More bowl games every year."

"You said it! Isn't it great? I guess you're for the 49ers?"

Byron's brain scrambled. "Er, yes." Inspiration hit. "I've always kind of liked the Vikings." This was where research paid off.

"Yeah?"

"Oh, yeah. They're cool."

"Cool! That's my team. Maybe I could ask my aunt if I could take the ferry over sometime and we could talk ball."

"Do you play sports at school?"

Ian made a wry grimace. "Nah. I was on the swim team back home is all. But I liked fooling around with my friends. We had pickup games all the time. Everyone plays soccer here. I guess that's okay, only I'm not any good at it."

"What do you like to do for a hobby?" He couldn't detain the boy much longer, yet he dreaded ending the conversation.

Ian used the toe of a shoe to make patterns in the dust. "Nothing much. I like music." He glanced up and Byron held the breath he'd taken. Naked longing shone in the boy's face. "I used to play the guitar," he said.

Byron felt the breeze, smelled freshly cut grass, and sensed the sky's blue at the edges of his vision. All he could concentrate on was the desperation in Ian Spring's brown eyes. Fate could be damn mean-spirited. Why did the kid have to be crazy about the one thing that brought Byron true peace—music, in particular the music he made himself—on the guitar? And why did he have to deal with the clear vision of Lori playing, Lori who had played better than anyone he'd ever known?

"My mom and dad paid for me to have lessons," Ian continued. "And after Dad died, my mom said he would have wanted me to go on having them, even though we didn't have a lot of money."

"So you did go on," Byron said and cleared his throat.

"Yeah."

"You must be pretty good."

Ian jerked the corners of his mouth down. "I used to be."

Seconds slid by, and Byron's too-vivid memory threatened to hurtle back to places he didn't want to go. "You mean you're a bit rusty at the moment?"

"Maybe. Aunt Muriel doesn't like any noise in the house." He shrugged. "So I don't play much."

An idea sprang instantly to life. "You could take lessons again. That would give you a chance to play."

"She said there's no one here to teach me. Then there's—" He brought his lips together and looked away. Byron saw him swallow.

"What?"

"Oh, money, I guess."

"I'll teach you." Byron's gut contracted. "I've never given lessons, but I've played for years. I picked it up myself, then finally got some instruction when I was in college." Despite the bitter-sweetness of the memories, he grinned. "Actually I got a lot of instruction in college. I met a girl who played the guitar like no one you ever heard. She wasn't so hot at math. I helped her get through her courses. She taught me to play a pretty mean guitar. Fair, huh?"

Ian wrinkled his nose. "I guess. Would you really teach me?"

The way Byron's spirits lifted was nothing but bad news. "Sure I would." Getting involved here wasn't what he'd planned. "And we could spend some time just jamming as well. Sometimes that's the best part, huh?"

"Oh, yeah. Boy, that would be great." The longing was there again. "But it probably won't happen. She won't go for it."

Byron wanted to argue. A bad idea. "Here." He reached for his notebook, tore out a page and scribbled. "This is my name. Byron Frazer. And my telephone number. Your aunt can call me there. Or you can." He stood up and handed the sheet to Ian. "At least give it a try and ask."

"Maybe." The paper was tucked into a pocket. "I'm gonna see if it's time to go back to her house."

31

Not home. *Her house.*

Byron fell in beside Ian and they walked in silence toward the church. The scent of carnations and hyacinth wafted by in drifts. Overhead the occasional mound of puffy cloud broke an otherwise clear cerulean sky.

"My name's Ian. Ian Spring." He kept his eyes on the ground.

"Okay, Ian."

"Just in case I do call."

Byron could hear how badly he wanted to come, if only to talk to someone from home. "Right." *Dammit*—what if Muriel Cadwen knew his name? After the initial meeting with the Springs, the adoption had become closed, though they had met him and heard his name.

"You going into the church?"

He hadn't thought where he was going. "I left my glasses in there," he improvised. For some reason he wasn't ready to leave. The door stood open now and Byron followed Ian into the gloom. Ian immediately slipped into the nearest pew. Byron hesitated, then headed around to the side aisle again. He'd have to at least appear to be looking for the glasses that were already in his pocket.

"That about does it." The woman called Effie trotted through the door beside the sanctuary. "Very nice, too. I don't know how we'd do without the vicar's roses."

"Not nearly as well," Muriel said, appearing and shutting the door. "Oh, dear. I'd better find that boy."

Effie stopped in the act of pulling on a pink cardigan. "We worry about you," she said. "Even Reverend Alvaston seems quite in a dither about it all."

"You don't have to worry about me," Muriel said, but her voice took on a thinner note.

Byron stood still and glanced back to where Ian sat. There was no question that he'd be able to clearly hear whatever the women said.

"We do anyway," Effie continued in an enthusiastic tone. "It's one thing when you know what you've got to deal with. You don't. And that's too much. Ada should never have left you with such a burden." Her eyes turned predictably in an overhead direction. "God rest her soul."

"Yes. But I promised I would look after him if something happened." Muriel took off her apron and folded it. "I'm managing."

Effie puffed up her chest. "Of course you are. You're the kind who always does. And there aren't enough like you. But after all, who knows what kind of background a boy like that really had?"

A boy like that. Byron felt glued in place. His blood seemed to stop pumping. He dared not look at Ian again.

"I told you I'm managing," Muriel repeated. "If he was good enough for Ada, he's good enough for me."

"That's all very well," Effie said. "But the chances are there's bad stock there. For all you know his mother wasn't . . . well, you know . . . she got into trouble. That kind of thing comes out in the end."

Muriel picked up a black purse and pulled its double handles over her wrist. "You're probably right. I only hope I'll know what to do if it does."

"But should you have to?" Effie's weathered-apple face took on an even more pinched appearance.

"I have to do what my sister wanted." Muriel's chin jutted. "She adopted the boy and she loved him without knowing any more about him than I do. He wasn't wanted, that was all. We Cadwens stick together. I'll see it through—I'll keep him until he doesn't need a family anymore. I couldn't live with myself if I didn't."

Byron spun around, his throat so tight he felt sick.

The back pew was empty.

So much for worrying about Muriel recognizing the name Byron had written down for Ian. At least that was something.

Effie finished putting on her cardigan. "You Cadwens may stick together. But I hope you don't regret this. After all, *he* isn't a Cadwen. It isn't as if he's even blood."

Ignoring any effect he might have on the two women, Byron sprinted outside and strode downhill, looking left and right. There was no sign of Ian.

The gate to the churchyard stood open and Byron guessed the boy had left, run off, either to "her house" or to some other place where he could be alone with his thoughts.

If he hunted, he'd eventually find him.

A few yards down the hill toward Fowey, Byron stopped. He wasn't ready to talk to Ian again. Before he did, he must think very carefully about what he ought to do.

What would the boy say if Byron decided to take that step he'd never planned to take? How would a thirteen-year-old respond to being told, *"Ian, your real mother was my wife"*? Byron scrubbed at his face. How did you tell a boy, *"I'm the one who signed away his right to be your father"*?

Chapter Three

Whistling, Jade Perron sorted through a jumble of keys in a box wedged between the seats of her van. She found the one she needed and hopped out onto the cobbled yard beside Ferryneath Cottage.

"Here we are, Rose," she said to the very small five-year-old buckled into the passenger seat. "Sit tight, sweetheart, and I'll get you. Don't forget your bag."

Jade walked around and lifted Rose out. The child wrapped her arms around Jade's neck and looked into her face. "Daddy says you're our angel," she said, lisping through a space where she'd lost a baby front tooth. She gave a big smile that wrinkled her nose. "He says you won't go away from me."

Rose's daddy knew only too well that she would repeat whatever he said about Jade. Did he think she was fool enough not to know what he wanted? Despite the affair he'd had while they were married, the one that had produced Rose, he'd begun angling to get her back. She hugged Rose tighter and inhaled the scent of baby shampoo on her hair.

"You won't go away from me, will you?" Rose said.

Jade closed her eyes and said, "No, of course I won't, sweetheart. I live in Fowey and so do you. I'm there for keeps."

"Keeps?"

"Forever." Jade almost choked on the word. She loved her hometown, but she didn't love her life there. She didn't *have* a life there and part of that was the fault of Doug Lyman, Rose's daddy and Jade's ex-husband.

No, she had to be honest or she had nothing left of who she really was—or who she'd hoped to become. In their younger school years, they'd been friends. Friendship had progressed into a teenage romance and Jade had been thrilled to be the center of handsome Doug Lyman's attention. He'd wanted to marry right out of school and Jade's parents had thought that a fine idea, but she wanted to go to a trade school, and she held fast to her plans. By the time she started work, she was ready to do what most young women in the area didn't do, work and provide for herself. Jade wanted to be independent.

"I'm glad Mrs. Tilly couldn't take me today," Rose said of the lady who ran a small day-care facility in the town. "I love it when I can come and help you."

Jade smiled at that. "I love it, too. You're a good helper."

It had taken Doug four years to beat down Jade's objections to becoming his wife, but he'd managed and she'd regretted giving in almost from the day he'd put a ring on her finger. Doug didn't want a ring himself. *Daft for men to wear rings. It embarrasses them in front of their mates.* Why hadn't she heeded all the signs that they were going to fail together?

Why hadn't they at least had a child to show for six years of marriage? Of course she loved Rose. Of course she'd never leave her as long as the child needed her around sometimes. But Jade wanted her own baby, her own toddler, her own growing child. She couldn't be sure she'd ever had a talent for making a man happy, or for being fulfilled by a man, but she did know she'd make a wonderful mother.

She wanted to be a mother.

She wanted her child to have a father.

She wanted her child to know, without question, that her parents loved each other and would never part.

She wanted to be free to grow and to be all she could be.

She didn't know how long she could go on exactly as she was but she didn't think it would be too much longer. Somehow she would find a way to look at men again—look at them as potential loves, potential lovers, as friends to be trusted, and as people who could help make a family too strong to be breached.

Almost every penny she made went into the bank. If she found someone who wanted what she wanted, and they decided to go forward together, Jade intended to bring a solid monetary contribution into the partnership. And she'd always manage to do her share so that she could insist she keep her own bank account, rather than repeating the old nightmare Doug had demanded. Everything they'd had, he put into an account in his name. Jade had suffered through the frustration of having to ask for what she needed.

She'd cuddled Rose long enough for now. "Down you go, missie. Time for me to get to work."

The child trailed a worn, plush Winnie the Pooh backpack by its straps and looked up at Jade. "Dog's coming too, isn't she?" she said.

"She's coming," Jade assured her. "Come on, Dog," she called into the van's recesses, and waited for her random-bred sidekick to scrabble her way out into the dawn of what promised to be a great day.

Rose tossed down her backpack, sat on the cobbles, and wrapped her arms round Dog's neck. If dogs could roll their eyes, Dog would be doing just that, but she sat, too, and submitted to being adored.

Pink-washed Ferryneath Cottage perched above the water like a cheerful, if peeling, old lady wearing a hat made of crooked stone slabs. A fairy tale cottage, Jade had always thought. Jade cast a critical eye over window boxes and trim badly in need of a fresh coat of white paint. Dealing with any leaks would be the first priority.

She went to the kitchen door and let herself in—and stopped on the threshold.

A man about to pour coffee into a mug also stopped.

Jade held the door handle firmly, gauging how long it might take her to grab Rose and make it back into the van. "Who are you?" she asked.

He set down the coffeepot and strolled to the table. "Do you usually unlock other people's front doors at dawn and walk in?"

What did they call people who took over houses that didn't belong to them? Squatters? "Who are you?" she repeated.

"Who are *you?*"

The tone of his voice wasn't exactly threatening, but it was tough enough to make Jade nervous. He didn't look like someone who might wander into a vacant cottage in search of a free bed. True, his dark curly hair stood on end and heavy beard stubble covered a good deal of his face, but he was a well-built man and certainly a confident man—even if he was dressed only in white boxer shorts he'd obviously slept in.

Jade weighed her responsibility to the owners of Ferryneath Cottage against potential risk to her own safety. This man looked fit, but so was she, and she'd bet on herself to make it into the middle of Bodinnick's main street—lane—and yell for help before he caught her. And unlike in those big places in other parts of England, around here people looked after each other.

He surprised her by smiling and batting the side of his head with the heel of his right hand. "They forgot to tell you when I was arriving, right? You're the maid. I'm sorry, but I guess I'm not clicking over too swiftly yet. I'm glad to see you. This place could use a good cleaning."

She was a woman in overalls and that made her a maid? "What are you doing here?"

"I'm living here. For now."

He wasn't from around here. He was different, American perhaps. If she'd seen him before, she wouldn't forget him. Very nice looking. He was certainly comfortable wearing nothing but underwear in front of a strange female.

"Did you hear what I said, ma'am?"

"Er, no." She tore her eyes from the shorts and smiled brightly, then frowned. "I'm not the maid. What do you mean, you're living here?"

"I suppose there's been a mistake," he said, and snapped his fingers. "You've got keys. Did they rent the place to you, too?"

Jade studied his lean face checking for signs of lingering intoxication. "Are you saying you've rented Ferryneath?" His green eyes were clear. He appeared perfectly sober.

"Exactly," he said, crossing his arms over a broad chest covered with curly, dark hair. "For the summer. At least two months, anyway. They don't rent for shorter periods. I've already paid a security deposit, paid up the two months, and signed a lease."

Jade digested that before saying, "Well, we'll just have to make the best of it, I suppose. I expect you'll be out a lot anyway."

He gave a short laugh. "Something tells me we aren't communicating. This isn't a boardinghouse. It's a single-family lease property and *I'm* the current single tenant."

"Well, I suppose that's something." Jade glanced around. Pale green wallpaper dotted with assorted grinning teapots gaped at the seams. "At least I won't be wasting time falling over a bunch of people. I'm used to doing things my own way. I expect to be here about four weeks, unless something comes up to keep me longer."

"Really?" He smirked; there was no other word for it. "Perhaps we'd better stop talking in code and find out exactly what's going on here. Are you telling me you've rented this cottage for four weeks?"

Jade raised her eyebrows. "Rented? Good grief, no." She indicated her white overalls. "I'm here to redo the place—completely. A top-to-bottom, everything-inside-and-out, job. If the owners weren't so cheap, I'd have taken care of a good deal of things last year and there wouldn't be such a mess to deal with now." She shrugged. "But what can I tell you? They are cheap. This time they're so cheap they've rented the place out to you so they won't lose money while I'm working on it. It doesn't help much that the winter was so hard. The trim's going to need burning off."

He screwed up his eyes at her, half turned away, and turned back again. "Let's get this straight. You think you're going to do something or other to the paint around here?"

"Yes," she said patiently. "I'm a painter and decorator and I do a lot of work for Curtis. That's the rental agency you used, right?"

"Right." He glanced in the direction of his very long, very muscular legs and finally seemed to register that he was talking to a woman he didn't know, early in the morning, in his underwear. "Wait here. I'll be right back."

Jade couldn't recall seeing a better pair of male legs.

Two long strides took him from the room and Jade heard his feet thunder up the stairs. A glance outside showed Rose and Dog in much the place as she'd left them. Then Jade barely had time to peer into a cupboard—where a jumbled assortment of groceries confirmed the man's occupancy story—before the footsteps sounded again and he arrived back in the kitchen zipping up a pair of faded jeans. He hadn't bothered with a shirt.

"Completely redone? Is that what you said?"

"Yes. That's exactly what I said," Jade told him.

Dog, who had an uncanny habit of timing her appearances for maximum effect, chose that moment to slide into sight on her short, probably basset hound legs. She shook herself, sending water flying, and flopped down on the floor. Rose must have turned on the hose.

"From what I've seen so far this morning," Jade said to distract the man's attention from the dog, "I've got a fairly good idea what needs doing. Everything."

"But—" He came around the table until he stood, looking down upon her. "But why wasn't I told?"

It had been years since Jade had stood in a kitchen with a man, early in the morning. There was an intimacy about the moment. She'd like to enjoy it, to enjoy something she'd never had—the conviction she was with someone strong and independent, exciting perhaps, but honorable.

This was turning into an amazing morning. Now she'd started weaving dreamy scenarios around a total stranger. She'd better do something about the need that showed signs of beating its way out of her.

"I asked," Byron said, faint color rising in his face, "why I wasn't told you were supposed to come."

Dog shook herself again, spraying both Jade and the man. He stared at his damp jeans, then at Jade again and said, "Well?"

"I don't suppose they thought it was necessary. If they thought about it at all. My schedule's always fixed a year ahead. Never changes much."

"A year ahead?"

"Always."

"That's ridiculous."

"It works for me."

He brushed absently at his jeans. "Outside with you," he said to Dog. "Go home."

"She belongs to me," Jade said. "Her home is wherever I am."

"You bring a dog to work?" He managed to make everything about her sound outrageous.

This was wasting precious time. "Excuse me. I need to start bringing in supplies."

"Just a minute." He put himself between Jade and the door. "Let's talk about this. There's got to be something that can be done to rearrange your schedule."

Behind him, the door opened a little wider. With a squelch, squelch coming from her purple plastic sandals, Rose ventured into the kitchen, leaving soggy prints on the linoleum as she came. Jade barely stopped herself from grimacing.

"I'm Byron," the man said. "Byron Frazer. I'm from California. Tiburon. Just out of San Francisco."

"Nice to meet you. I'm Jade."

At last he heard Rose's squelching sandals and turned around. A vast quantity of long, dark red curls sprouted in all directions around Rose's small, pale face. Rose had her Winnie the Pooh backpack by the straps again and she held it before her while she frowned up at Byron Frazer.

"This is Rose," Jade said quickly. "A very good friend of mine. Come on in, sweetheart."

"Hello, Rose." Frazer turned amazed green eyes on Jade. "Does she go everywhere you go, too?"

His tone brought out her stubborn streak. "When she needs to. School's out today and the day-care place didn't have room for her." Doug Lyman had started an affair with Rose's mother some months before Jade found out. By that time the woman was pregnant. Jade detested Doug, but he tried to be a good father and she gave him credit for that.

Frazer spread his hands. "Didn't you tell me you don't like any-thing—anybody getting in your way?"

Jade didn't answer.

"How many more little helpers are we expecting?"

Jade ignored him again. "Let me get my equipment in, Rose, then I'll find you somewhere nice to play." She left and went to the van to start carrying in supplies.

"Look"—Frazer followed her outside—"there's been a mistake."

"I agree. Why don't you call up Rube at Curtis's and ask to be moved." The idea of an occasional glimpse of a very attractive man held some appeal, but not if he didn't want her around. "The sea-son hasn't really started yet. There's bound to be a vacancy some-where."

He stepped back to allow her to pass with two buckets of paint and almost tripped over Dog, who had trotted after Jade. "Hell! I'm *not* moving. Let me carry those for you."

"Thanks, but it's not necessary," she said, but she liked the offer just the same.

"Yeah, well, they're too heavy for you."

Jade didn't tell him he was no judge of what was too heavy for a woman, even a small, rather insignificant-looking woman. What was there about a man showing basic protective instincts that made some females glow inside? Jade was glowing—just a little.

"Okay." He strode along beside her, taking one step to every two or three of hers. "This is how it is. I just got settled and nowhere else is going to have the view of the river and harbor I've got from here."

"I know." Jade carried the buckets into the kitchen. "It's my favorite. How long have you been here?"

Once more Ferryneath's annoyed tenant faced her across the table. "I arrived five days ago. Look—"

"Isn't the view of the harbor super at night? With the lights on the water?" He'd get used to the idea of her being here.

"Yes. Look—"

"I'm going to get the bedrooms done first. Then the outside. Then I'll move back inside. I've got the weather patterns around here down to a fine art. July's often rainy. I will have to check the windows for leaks sometime today." She headed back outside and dragged a dolly from the back of the van. On this she loaded her toolbox, paste, brushes, and the wallpaper Curtis had selected for one of the bedrooms. On top she balanced the collapsed table she used for sizing and pasting the paper.

When she got back into the cottage, pausing to heft the dolly over the threshold, she found the man—wearing wire-rimmed glasses—poring over a sheaf of papers on one of the counters. Rose stood beside him and he ruffled her curls absently.

"I'm calling the rental agency," he said. "They didn't mean you to come. I think there's been a mistake."

"There hasn't," Jade assured him. "Take it from me. This is the right day." And Curtis knew better than to meddle with the

timetable for Fowey's busiest and most reliable painting and deco-
rating firm.

"There *is* a mistake." He marked a spot at the top of a page and
reached to haul the phone closer. "You said your name's Jade?"

"Yes, Jade." The glasses suited him.

"Who did you say you were from?"

She stopped and looked at him—more or less. "I didn't. I'm from
Perron and Son."

He frowned at her. "Perron? Haven't I heard that name before?"

"If you've been here five days, you must have. It's a very common
name in these parts."

Dog stretched her considerable length on the white linoleum
and yawned. Rose whooped, and dashed to lie down beside the dog.

"Jade, right?" the man said, looking slightly wild-eyed. "That is
what you said?"

"Mm. Several times."

He glanced at her and frowned. "You've got blue eyes—dark
blue—not green."

She stared at him incredulously. "Most babies are named at
birth. I was."

He said, "Yes," as if he didn't know what she was talking about.

"Newborn infants' eye color usually changes anyway."

"In other words, why would your name have anything to do with
your eyes?" He jabbed at the paper. "Will I get these people at the
St. Austell number?"

"Probably. Are you sleeping in the front bedroom?"

"Yes."

"I'll start in the other one."

"No!"

Jade almost dropped the hammer she was holding.

He smiled an almost sheepish smile. "Sorry. Didn't mean to
shout. But this is exactly what I *don't* need right now. Would you
mind if we had a little chat?"

What had they been having for the last thirty minutes? "I suppose not." Experience had taught her that the reasonable approach invariably won out over aggression. But she'd listened to an angry man's raised voice too often, and even though this was different, it frightened her. She dropped to her haunches and gathered Rose into one arm. With the other hand she stroked Dog's bristly, black and brown spotted white fur. "I am on kind of a tight schedule, I'm afraid. But I can spare a few minutes."

"You do understand that it isn't you, specifically, that I object to?"

She drew a blank in the answer department. This was already becoming a sensory overload, especially since she was out of practice interacting with a man on almost any level.

"It's just that this is a tense time for me. I came here for a few weeks of absolute peace and quiet. You can understand someone needing that, can't you?"

"Oh, yes." The fact that most people she knew rarely had the luxury of even a few days off wouldn't interest him.

"So you won't be offended if I arrange to get your schedule changed?"

Jade let Dog take the hammer between her teeth.

"Nice dog." He sounded awkward.

Let him suffer. "Thanks. I usually get comments about unfortunate canine liaisons, but I've always preferred mutts."

"What's his name?"

"Her. Dog."

He worried his lower lip. "Yes. Does she have a name?"

"Dog. That's her name."

"Ah," he nodded. "Cute. Rose is lovely, but I don't have to tell you that." He smiled at the child and Jade could tell the smile was effortless.

"Is it okay if I get started while you make your call, sir?"

"I guess so. It's Byron."

"Come along Rose." She picked up the toolbox and made a move toward the hall. The man stood between Jade and the door.

"You're sure you're going to do this?"

"I have to. Is it all right if Rose plays in the sitting room? She won't make a mess?"

"It'll be a waste of time to start, then have to stop again."

"That won't happen, sir." Holding Rose's hand, she took another step toward him.

He took off his glasses. His eyes slanted slightly upward. Jade liked that. There were traces of gray in his hair. The lines around his eyes were deep. He'd laughed a lot—frowned a lot?

"I'll make that call then."

"You do that. It'll make you feel better. More settled."

He turned aside, but not far enough to allow her to pass with ease. "After I get through to them, I'll come and let you know what they say."

"You do that." Standing close to him, Jade had to raise her chin to meet his eyes. Up close, she saw black and yellow flecks in the irises. His pupils dilated . . . and his lips parted. It had been a long time since she noticed a man this minutely. Maybe she never had, but this was one peculiar day.

She edged a little farther past. "The front bedroom, you said." Now she could smell him—clean, with a hint of soap and fresh linen. And she could feel his warmth.

He didn't respond.

"You said you were sleeping in the front bedroom?"

"Yes." His gaze dropped to her mouth.

A thought struck hard. "Oh, dear. Is . . . um, is someone still asleep?"

He looked blank.

Dog chose that moment to drop the hammer and sit back to scratch a floppy ear. Jade set down the toolbox and bent over—and her face collided with a hard shoulder as the man also stooped to retrieve the hammer.

"Sorry." He caught her forearm and held on until he'd rescued the tool. "Who would still be asleep?"

His biceps were hard, his skin smooth. "Oh, I don't know, it was just a thought."

A faint smile twitched at his lips. "I'm all on my own here."

Jade felt hot, and foolish. "Ah." This was dumb. She was actually responding to a man she'd only just met—a stranger who wouldn't notice her if she weren't pushed into his space, a stranger who was doing his best to get rid of her. "I'll just go on up then."

"Mm." He still held her forearm.

"Okay." Jade drew in a deep breath and immediately wished she hadn't. His glance moved lower. She usually tried not to draw attention to her meager stature. Her insignificant face wasn't something she could disguise. "Anyway, you make your call."

She eased past, drawing her arm from his hand, and led Rose into the tiny, dim hall. When she looked back, Byron Frazer was watching her, an oddly speculative expression on his face. He bent over to pick up the toolbox she'd forgotten to retrieve, and handed it to her.

Her own vulnerability had made her careless, and stupid. She kept a firm hold on Rose's hand and, instead of putting her in the sitting room alone, led her to the stairs and started up. Dog fell in behind.

The man's presence was something she felt even before she stopped and turned. He leaned against a doorjamb—watching her again. No trace of a smile softened his face.

With a thudding heart, Jade nodded, and continued up the stairs, forcing herself not to rush. Her cell phone was in the tool box. Apparently he'd lost interest in checking up on her. Jade would get herself and Rose into as safe a place as possible, then find out just how much danger they might be in from Byron Frazer.

Chapter Four

Perplexed, Byron had watched this Jade Perron climb the stairs. A small person with masses of extraordinary long, black hair, she clutched the child's hand while the incredibly ugly dog leaped upward in hot pursuit—leaped as well as a dog could on very short legs and splayed feet.

When Jade had glanced back and seen him, she looked closed and suspicious. He really did get the feeling she expected to win the battle and send him packing. He smiled faintly. She was part of the narrow world he'd found in this insular Cornish place. All of the locals seemed to dismiss any world outside their own, and he was a "foreigner" and therefore not to be taken seriously.

The wary, blue-eyed lady had managed to make him hunt for words. Quite a feat considering she was dealing with the famed "Tell Dr. Frazer," the psychologist guaranteed to shoot from the hip, no punches pulled, while he mesmerized millions with his silver-tongued, but hard-line advice.

All that seemed far away and long ago—and vaguely embarrassing when viewed from the position he was in now.

In the kitchen once more, he closed the door and phoned the rental agency in St. Austell. Only minutes later he hung up again.

"Hell," he muttered, his teeth on edge from talking to Jade's "Rube." "These people make laid-back sound like hyperactive." Good old Rube had assured him she'd do her best to find him alternate accommodations, if that's what he decided he wanted, but it might be that he'd have to pay more, and didn't he want to think about that? In other words, he could go if he liked (other than request a refund), but Jade stayed put—although if he wanted to call the outfit she worked for, well, that was his business.

The phone rang. He snatched the receiver, preparing to tell Rube she had the order of things all wrong.

"Is that you, Byron?"

Celeste. Damn, he'd told his secretary not to tell *anyone* where he'd gone, not even his indefatigable dynamo of an agent. Especially not her. But he should have known Celeste Daily would browbeat poor Angela until she caved in.

"Byron? Answer me."

"Yes, Celeste." Carrying the phone, he dropped into a chair. "I'm not in the mood to talk to you. I left a message to say I'd contact you when I was ready."

"What way is that to treat me, darling?" She was shrieking now. Byron hated it when Celeste—or anyone else—shrieked. "I'm your *agent*, for God's sake. Your *best* friend. Is this any way to treat a best friend? Sneaking off in the night like a thief and leaving me to spend an entire *week* searching for you. I've been *beside* myself, I tell you. *Beside* myself!"

Beside herself worrying that she might be losing money on the appearances he'd canceled. As his finances went, so went Celeste's. She'd virtually made his career her life's work. "I thought I'd made it clear that this was something I had to do. If I didn't, I will now. I have to do this, Celeste. This isn't a good time for us to talk. Why don't I get in touch with you later?" Much later.

"No, Byron. Absolutely not. Don't you dare try to close me out of whatever's going on. When you said you had to leave California, you didn't say you were heading for some godforsaken little hole in

Cornwall, England. I've got to look after you. You're either in some sort of personal trouble you're afraid of, or you're having a breakdown. This is a crisis. I'm already in Seattle. I'm catching the next flight over the pole. I'll be in Heathrow by midafternoon tomorrow. I'll give you the flight number. Meet me, darling. Promise you will. We'll spend a few days in London and have a wonderful time together. We don't even have to talk business for a day or two if you don't want to. Then I'll take you—"

"I won't meet you. Don't come."

The only sound for seconds was the faint crackle of the overseas line.

"You missed the lecture in Chicago," Celeste said finally.

"I gave them a week's notice. And I told you to put everything on hold until I made contact with you."

"A *week? A week*, you say. As if you didn't know how far ahead these things are scheduled. This is too much, Byron, really too much."

"Have you informed everyone else who needs warning that I can't appear in the near future?"

"You can't do this," Celeste shouted. "You can't just drop out of sight without an explanation."

"I have no problem with you putting out a press release stating that a personal crisis has intervened."

"They'd *crucify* us. Oh, my God. Think how people would speculate. What's the matter with you? You have to be squeaky clean, you know that. They'll come up with a million sleazy rumors."

He didn't answer.

"I'm coming, I tell you. This isn't like you and I want to know what's going on. You can't rush halfway around the world without telling me first."

"The hell I can't, I—" A slight sound made him look around. Jade was trying to tiptoe past. She held Rose's hand again, and the dog trotted at her side. He met those blue eyes again. She raised delicate brows and pointed first at her dolly, then hooked a thumb toward the door to the rest of the house. Byron shook his head emphatically. He covered the receiver and said, "Please wait here. This won't take long."

"Byron, darling. *Please*."

"Don't push, Celeste."

"Don't *push?*" She expelled a hard breath. "You have a public. You have responsibilities to that public, and to your practice."

"I'm way ahead on my taping schedule. My practice is my concern, not yours. My patients have been given the option to see a colleague or, if they feel able, to wait for my return. I'll also deal with emergencies by phone."

He found, even as he spoke to Celeste, that he couldn't take his eyes off Jade Perron. She had dropped to sit cross-legged on the floor beside the dog. Her springy black curls arched away from a point in the center of a high forehead. She had a perfect, heart-shaped face. He'd never seen anything quite so intriguing—other than in paintings of Victorian girls who hadn't yet put their hair up. She was very pale-skinned, and men who went for flamboyant beauty would find her too subtle. He could hear her whispering softly to the mutt while she kept an arm around Rose.

"I'm coming," Celeste said, controlling her voice this time. "And I'm going to bring you back with me. That's that."

"No, it's not." He should have put his foot down with overbearing Celeste years ago. "As I've already explained—several times—there's something I have to do here and that isn't negotiable."

"*There?*" The rattle of papers sounded. "Bodinnick-by-Fowey, Cornwall. Not even a published population count on the Net, for God's sake."

So, she'd already done her research. How like Celeste. She'd go into shock if she had any idea what had been running through his mind in the past two days, even if he was totally unsure what he intended to do about it. He was in a strange place and in a strange mood. He was completely unsettled. When he thought deeply about the steps he'd taken, he scared even himself, but he wasn't prepared to leave without completing what he promised himself he'd do. Ian grew in importance to him with every hour. He had to make sure the boy would survive here and come through without being crippled by an environment that seemed impossible.

"What could you possibly have to do in a place like that?" Celeste said. "How did you find it?"

"I found it. You wouldn't be interested how. And Bodinnick may be small, but linked to Fowey, it isn't *that* small."

"Try me. Interest me."

Mollify, his defense mechanism advised. "Celeste, we've been together a long time."

"I thought for a moment you might have forgotten that."

To hell with mollifying the barracuda. Her bossiness had long ago failed to divert him. "But maybe we've been working together too long. Maybe it's time for you to use your talents on someone up-and-coming who'll be more of a challenge," he paused for an instant, then added, "and willing to be controlled."

"My God! How can you be so damnably ungrateful? How can you even suggest this? Are you trying to fire me, because if you are, you'll have a war on your hands. I'll fight you to the wall, baby. And I may be a lady, but I can fight dirty when I have to."

He swallowed the temptation to give Celeste his description of a lady, but he said, "I'll just bet you would fight dirty. Back off, Celeste."

"That private detective is mixed up in all this. Since he's the one who sent you on this wild trip, he can do the rest of whatever needs doing. Tell him to get there and deal with things. You're too expensive to be wasting time like this."

She just didn't know how to give up. "No one but me can do what has to be done. End of topic. Now back off."

"I will not let you push me aside."

Jade Perron's pale face had lifted again. She regarded him with interest. Her full mouth held a permanent, quite sexy pout. If he didn't have a clear impression that she wouldn't know how to be other than her natural self, he'd say the pout had to be practiced. In Jade's case the mouth undoubtedly came that way. She was really quite beautiful, an ethereal, somewhat undersized vision even in the unflattering overalls.

"Byron? Did you hear what I said?" Celeste said loudly. "I won't be pushed aside because you've found someone more interesting— so you think. Take it from me, it won't be a good idea for you to cross me in public." She softened her voice. "I'd have thought you'd remember how far we go back, what we've meant to each other."

"How could I forget?" Cooling things down would be for the best, at least until he got himself sorted out. "Now I'm asking you to trust me. And to cover for me . . . darling." He detested theatrical largess. "This is something I really need. This time away in total isolation. Will you trust me? If I promise to call you in a few days, say in a week? Next Monday? Please, Celeste?"

"Well." Her tone was still wounded, but more gentle, and he almost felt ashamed of his own manipulation—almost. "Byron, darling. You aren't sick, are you?"

"I've never felt better." A lie, but the reason for his feeling rotten had nothing to do with his physical condition. "I would tell you if I was ill," he added, anticipating her next question.

By the time he finally hung up, Celeste had promised to return to San Francisco to await his call next week. She'd deal with any inquiries that came in about appearances, putting people off where necessary. Byron knew he'd need a very convincing story to appease her on Monday.

He smiled at Jade. "My agent," he said, suddenly awkward that she'd had to listen to the conversation. "Sometimes agents and their clients have different views on what's important."

"Oh."

"She doesn't think I deserve a vacation." He laughed, coughed. "Not that this is a vacation. Not really."

She bounced to her feet and looked at her watch. "May I get started now?"

"Um. I called the rental people. They offered to move me." At least she didn't give a triumphant grin. "They did say I could call your company to make sure your calendar isn't mixed up. They didn't seem to want to take the time to look up the number for me. I'm sure if I talk to your people, they'll confirm there's a mixup."

"Could be." Her smile took him totally by surprise. It intensified the tilt of her eyes and drove dimples into her cheeks. "These big outfits tend not to keep very good tabs on all the little people on their staffs. This is the number." She fished a card from behind a row of pens pocketed in her overalls bib. "There's an answering machine. Leave a message. I really must get on."

Glancing at the card he said, "Perron and Son. You said that. Same name as yours."

"Uh-huh. Perron in Cornwall is like Smith in some places."

He pulled his bottom lip between his teeth. He had the impression the lady might be enjoying some private joke.

She left with Rose perched on the loaded dolly with the equipment. He could have sworn Dog shot him a grin as she pranced behind. The situation here was getting to him. He had to keep a tight hold on himself.

Byron remained at the table and drummed his fingers on a yellow pad he'd been using to make notes for the book he already had a contract to write. Who was he fooling? How could he write anything on the inner self that might make sense when his own inner self was in turmoil?

Since Saturday he'd found three reasons to take the orange ferry boat across the smooth, silver water between Bodinnick and Fowey. He'd trailed the quaint streets, some so narrow that pedestrians had to stand on doorsteps to allow cars to pass, searching for a glimpse of Ian. 4 The Rise was a skinny terraced cottage with faintly bulging leaded windows and a riot of flowers blooming in boxes and hanging baskets. Ian hadn't come or gone from the shiny black door. But Byron discovered that the children still had a number of weeks in school before summer vacation. And they didn't get out as early each day here as they did in the States. Twice he'd strolled past the school just as students streamed out on their way home and had "accidentally" run into Ian. They'd walked a block or two together, chatting, mostly about the States, before Byron made himself turn away.

He got up and went from the kitchen into the sitting room and his own leaded-paned windows. Bodinnick eyed Fowey across the estuary, so close the ferry took only minutes to make the trip.

What should he do about Ian?

The instant a move was made to interfere with the boy's current home situation, Ian's life would be forever changed and Byron couldn't know if that was right. He couldn't know if it would be the right step for himself. His own life would also be turned upside down—particularly if he decided to do what might be necessary, and get into a legal wrangle for custody.

Overhead something scraped. And Byron winced. The scraping came again, making the light that hung from a wire in the middle of the room swing.

She was such an insubstantial creature. The idea of women doing what used to be considered purely men's jobs—and heavy work—didn't surprise him . . . except when he was confronted by someone who probably didn't reach his shoulder, someone with a face that belonged in commercials for natural soaps.

Stretching out on a puffy, rose-colored velvet sofa, he hauled an ancient black phone onto his chest and dialed the number on the card she'd given him.

"Perron and Son. This is Jade Perron. I'm sorry to miss your call. Please leave a message. I'll get back to you as soon as possible. Thank you."

So, the lady was the boss—or closely related to the boss. Which was undoubtedly why she'd insisted she knew the timetable for repairs around here was correct.

He left a message and set the receiver down gently. Sure she'd had her little piece of fun with him and he should be irritated, but he was unable to repress a smile. No wonder she'd looked so amused. He'd treated her as his inferior, and now he thought about it, that made him ashamed. He's committed the sin of putting someone in the box he'd automatically judged appropriate, and done so with very little information to go on.

Jade Perron had a very nice, husky voice, very nice indeed. Particularly on the phone. He could almost imagine her saying: "Gotcha!"

Chapter Five

"Must be nice to be able to flit around the world taking summer-long holidays," Jade mumbled to Rose. "Not for the likes of you and me, girl. Poor working types, we are." She wasn't about to remark to the child that Byron Frazer's life sounded too complicated for the simple likes of them.

At least her telephone call to Rube, she-who-knew-everything, put Jade's mind at ease about Frazer's character. He did come from a place called Tiburon, in California and close to San Francisco. He was a doctor of some kind and he wrote books. Rube thought it funny that Jade wondered if she should be afraid of him. "Clobber him with your hammer if he makes any moves on you. I never met a man who would be a match for you if you got your knickers in a twist."

Sitting on the kitchen floor and listening to him argue with his agent had revealed a few other details to Jade. He was the kind of doctor who saw patients, and gave lectures to people. An important man from the way it sounded. In other words, she wasn't in personal jeopardy.

Jade wedged herself between the wall and the head of the bed. "Too bad I don't have a little more weight to put into this." With her back against the headboard, she walked her feet up the wall, knees almost touching her chest, and pushed. The bed was old and made of very heavy mahogany. A couple more inches of progress was all she made.

"Waste of time." After a moment's rest, she crab-walked up the ghastly cabbage-rose wallpaper again, took a huge breath, let it out, and heaved.

Rose stood beside her, spread her little hands on the headboard, and pushed. She held her breath until her face turned red and Jade had to fight down laughter.

"Can I do something to help?"

Propped more or less horizontal, two feet from the floor, Jade went rigid.

"You'll hurt yourself doing that. Why didn't you call me?"

Frazer walked into her line of vision, carrying the rest of the rolls of paper she'd left on the dolly at the foot of the stairs. Dog moved close to Jade and growled, a faint rumble that meant little but usually had the desired effect. Dog wasn't fond of men, especially men she sensed were troublesome to Jade.

If the man noticed the noise at all, he showed no sign. "Please. If you'd let me help you up, I'm sure I could . . . we could do this together in a minute. The bed's catching up on the rug."

She felt a complete fool. Relaxing her leg muscles, she attempted to stand up. Instead she slammed—bottom first—to the floor, jarring her neck. "Ouch! Damn it all, anyway. Damn—" Oh, great. "Complete fool" didn't cover this. She was swearing in front of Rose, whom she tried to cushion from anything unpleasant, Rose whose eyes were huge and worried. Jade kissed a finger and tapped the little one's nose, and watched her relax almost instantly.

"I know how you feel." Frazer's voice really was nice. Soft but deep and very, very clear. He offered her a hand. "Up you get."

Unable to do otherwise unless she wanted to appear any more foolish, she put her hand in his and let him haul her to her feet. "Thanks."

"You're welcome."

She hadn't met many Americans, but those she had met all said that. *You're welcome*, and *Have a nice day*. Like some button had been pushed.

"I called your office."

She blushed, something she didn't do often these days. "Yes." That had been childish on her part. She ought to be ashamed. She was. "Sorry about that."

"Why be sorry? I left a message."

"Good." This was turning into the most frustrating morning in recent memory. She loathed getting off schedule, although he was certainly something worth spending time looking at . . . if she were still into looking at knock-em-dead men. But she'd given up the habit.

No, she hadn't. No, not one bit of it, not anymore. She wasn't about to start looking for handsome men, but she was going to allow herself to think about an occasional date with someone who didn't make her feel threatened—maybe. That would be a start.

She was going to do something about changing her life, not that Byron Frazer—Dr. Byron Frazer—entered into the picture other than playing a small part in forcing her to start examining what she'd allowed herself to become: a boring, unfulfilled woman who was going nowhere, was unhappy, and who—as of today—had decided to stop wasting time.

Jade realized she was staring at him, and he was waiting patiently for her to say something. "I'd appreciate your help with this bed. Mahogany is very heavy."

"Would you like to know what I said in my message?"

Jade pretended to turn her attention to the bed. "I should have told you who you'd be leaving your message for. Forgive me, please. Mornings aren't my best time." Now she was spilling her uninteresting personal hangups. "They bring out my evil side."

"Mine too—sometimes. Let's get this bed moved. Then I'll tell you what I said."

Did he think that by being so darned nice he could divert her?

Well, he could divert her. Very easily. She took a shaky breath and recognized the almost forgotten sensation of being vulnerable, of wishing she was more attractive, and in this case that this man were interested in her other than as a problem to be eliminated.

She'd made rapid progress in changing her attitude toward men . . .

The sleeves of the blue denim shirt he'd put on were rolled up over muscular forearms. He smoothed Rose's cheek, earning himself the fluttering, plainly trustful touch of her fingers on the back of his hand. He smiled, and Rose smiled. Then he pushed the wretched bed into the middle of the room as if it were a piece of doll furniture.

Rose said, "He's strong like my daddy," with evident awe.

"Thank you," said Jade.

"You're welcome."

You're welcome. Oh, he could definitely divert her any old time. Yet again she caught speculation in his dark green eyes.

He smiled, crossed his arms, and stood with his bare feet planted apart. "What exactly are you supposed to do in here?"

"Everything," she told him. He had the kind of legs that must have inspired whoever had invented jeans: having seen him without the jeans, she should know. "The designer paper goes. And the brown paint around the windows."

"Sound like good moves to me." He screwed up his eyes and surveyed the room critically. "Pretty dreadful the way it is."

"They want me to use acoustical tile on the ceiling. I don't like the way the stuff looks. I don't like it anywhere, but in a lovely old place like this it would be a sin. I'd rather sand the beams and oil them, then texture the plaster between."

"You've got great instincts. If you want me to put in a word for your idea, I will."

He was trying to win her over. But for what? Jade glanced at his wide mouth and decided his ploy was working . . . and she was nuts.

Byron Frazer had no reason to care about her in any way. "It was very nice of you to help with the bed."

"You're welcome."

She bit the inside of her mouth to stop a laugh. He stared at her and smiled once more. Such a nice smile. Such a nice face. Better than nice.

"What else can I do to help?"

"Nothing, thanks."

When he smiled, the laugh lines at the corners of his eyes deepened, so did grooves beside his mouth. His tan suggested that, unlike Jade, he didn't spend most of his life indoors or hidden under the type of hat she used for outside work.

"Would you like me to tell you what I said on your answering machine?"

"If you like." He certainly was a big man. She liked big men. Her father was big, if stooped now, and her brother, Peter . . . and Doug.

"Do you live in Fowey?"

She hesitated. "Yes."

"Have you lived there a long time?"

"All my life."

"Is Perron your husband?"

"No. My father." She'd thought he was the one who was about to tell *her* something.

"Did you grow up helping him?"

A true third-degree. "No. I didn't come into the business until after I'd been to trade school. Then I apprenticed to my father." Would he have any idea what she was talking about?

For the first time he seemed stalled for a question. "Do you like it in Cornwall?"

"I don't think I'd live anywhere else." She'd change a lot of things in her life, erase some of the mistakes she'd made, but Cornwall was in her blood. True she thought she'd decided to broaden her horizons—move to another town, maybe—but that town didn't have to be in another county. And she had to be where she could see Rose easily, at least until she was old enough to understand that someone moving away didn't mean they didn't care about you anymore.

"Um, do you live with your, er, parents?"

"No." She'd swear he was interested in her. That was nutty. Why would a man like him, obviously successful and wealthy, pay any attention to a simple Cornish tradeswoman? "I live in a flat over a secondhand shop," she said impulsively, unsure why she suddenly felt like volunteering personal information.

"Sounds interesting. Is it a big place?"

Jade frowned. "It's very small. Dog and I don't need a lot of room. But it's comfortable, and I love it there."

He puffed out through pursed lips, and ran a hand over his hair. "I see. You'll have made it a special place."

"Thanks."

"You're welcome."

She shook her head. "I'll go and get the rest of my things."

"What about my message?"

"What about it?"

"You don't know very much about me. Don't you think you should if we're going to be sharing a cottage?"

Sharing a cottage? "I know you're a busy man with the kind of career that means you have to have someone help you run it." And she wished she were more sophisticated so she wouldn't feel intimidated by him in some areas. "I don't think I need to know much more."

She'd pinned his age at thirty-something, his height at six-something, and the rest of him at definitely more than worth looking at. And she'd like to know him. She blushed at the thought.

He had a way of tilting his head and looking her directly in the eye, so directly she had to look away. If he noticed her discomfort, he was polite enough not to react.

"I told the machine I'm planning to spend the summer here. I'm going to be catching up on some work I've put off for too long because . . . I need to recharge a bit."

Was he someone famous enough to be known even in England? He could be. She didn't have much opportunity to keep up on celebrities, which would excuse her for never having seen him.

"I said I've been hoping for some peace. Quiet. You know?"

As in no banging and all the other things that went with her occupation. "I'll do my best to keep the noise to a minimum. This job really has been scheduled for a long time and it can't be changed now—not without disrupting my business, and forcing me to reschedule work for other people. I could lose that work if I make them upset. The work and the money. I've also got men who work for me and they don't expect sudden changes. It's not fair to them." She did sound reasonable, didn't she?

"I'm sure you will try to be helpful. And I'll try to adjust, but if it gets too much, I'll have to talk to the leasing agency again."

She raised her brows. "That's your prerogative."

"I also asked a question on the answering machine."

Jade wiped her hands on her overalls. She was unaccountably hot. "I'll be sure and listen when I get back to the office."

"Oh, I might as well repeat it in person. I rarely do impulsive things, but I'm new around here and could use some help."

"Help?"

"Yes. I want to learn as much as I can about the area. On the machine I asked if Jade Perron would consider having a drink with me on Friday evening. A drink and conversation. No strings attached."

Chapter Six

There were times when Shirley Hill's prying went too far. "I don't know anything about Byron Frazer," Jade told her, making a valiant effort to edge away from her landlady.

"Oh, you must know *something*," Shirley said. Thick, tow-colored braids slithered back and forth with the knowing waggle of her head. "You've been working in the *same* house with him for days."

"*Two* days," Jade said impatiently. "And working in the same house, but not *with* him." She liked Shirley, but frequently wished it wasn't necessary to pass through the cluttered showroom of "New to You" on the way to the flat.

"Sam says he's *really* famous. Someone on one of the yachts in the harbor—some American—saw this Byron Frazer and recognized him. He's on the telly, Jade. He's *really* big in the States."

Jade sighed. Shirley and Sam Hill were an unlikely couple. Thin, devoid of makeup, and a militant vegetarian, in her long floral skirts and shapeless gauze shirts, Shirley resembled an aging flower child. Sam Hill was a ruddy-faced ex-heavyweight boxer who was said to consume his body weight in beer in an average month. He swore good-naturedly, argued incessantly—if good-naturedly—and ran a water taxi between Fowey and the many yachts that anchored in the harbor.

"Does he hold wild parties over there?"

Jade sighed and crossed her arms. Shirley wouldn't give up without a fight for what she wanted. Jade was so tired, and so muddled up in the confusion that reigned in her head. She said, "Dr. Frazer is a very quiet and private man. He's here to work." She searched for a way to end speculation. "He's writing a book."

"A book?" Shirley's brown eyes became round. "He's a . . . He's a behavioral psychologist. That's it. I bet he's writing a book on sex!"

Jade barely contained the urge to tell Shirley she was an irritating gossip. "All the things I've seen around the cottage are about families and children. Now, I've got to get upstairs."

"Does he talk to you?"

"He's—" She should have refused to have a drink with him on Friday. The invitation must have been issued on an impulse because he didn't know anyone locally yet. He'd said as much. "We have talked a few times. He's very nice." Her acceptance had also been impulsive, but she wanted to go. She wanted to go because it would be an opportunity to be with a really interesting man of a type she'd never expected to meet, much less receive any attention from.

Jade shivered although she wasn't cold. Today he'd greeted her pleasantly, but as if he had a lot on his mind. Then he'd gone out, and still been out when she knocked off for the day.

And she'd watched for him.

She felt desperate to get away from Shirley. "I'd better get upstairs. Dog's hungry." She had watched for Byron, looked from the windows at the slightest noise, and left the cottage feeling deeply disappointed. Like a plain teenage girl mooning over the most popular boy in the school. She disgusted herself.

"Is he good-looking?" Shirley asked, watching her too closely.

Only the best-looking man she'd ever seen. "I suppose some

people would think so." He was probably regretting having asked her out. She should make an excuse and renege.

Shirley started to hum, a sign her attention had wandered as it so frequently did. She turned sideways to squeeze between tables crowded with merchandise of every description—from plastic jewelry to antique tea sets—and went behind the counter.

"Night then, Shirley."

"You're wasting yourself," Shirley said. "You know that, don't you?"

Jade bowed her head. "I'm very tired, Shirley."

"You need a man in your life—and that doesn't mean you ought to let that Doug Lyman wheedle his way in with you again."

"That will never happen," Jade said quietly. She picked up an almost new Paddington Bear wearing yellow welly boots. "I've been looking for one of these for Rose. I'll buy him."

"It's working," Shirley said, her tone grim. She reached Jade and took the bear. With her mouth pursed and her elbows sawing the air, she wrapped Paddington in several sheets of much-used tissue and fastened the paper shut with a row of star and moon stickers. "He's using that girl to get to you. What kind of man calls his ex-wife to fill in as a baby-sitter. Especially when his child is his by the woman he played around with when he was married? You answer me that, Jade. You're lonely. That's what it's all about. I'm going to find a way to get you out of that."

"Please don't say any more," Jade said, horrified to discover she was trembling. "I'm smarter than you think. I know what Doug's trying to do and it won't work. But I do love Rose and I'll be there for her when I can."

Shirley handed over the package. "A pound," she said.

"Oh, it's got to be more than that. It's almost new."

"I said it's a pound." Shirley sounded angry enough to shock Jade. "I love Rose, too. The difference between you and me is I love Rose but it's because she's a lovely little girl. And although we were never blessed with children, I don't start imagining some nice kid who comes my way is really my kid."

Jade located a pound in her pocket and handed it to Shirley. "Thank you," she said. "I don't pretend Rose is mine. That's what you're suggesting and it's not true. I need to get upstairs."

Shirley turned abruptly away and skirted loaded tables to get to the counter, where she began moving piles of books for no evident reason, banging them down and raising clouds of dust.

With escape in sight, Jade made for the door leading from the shop to a store room and the steps to her flat.

Dog overtook her on the dim landing and raced to wait at the slightly crooked door to what had been Jade's home for five years. "That's the girl," she said, bending to rub a short, bristly muzzle. "Guard the castle." Every day brought the same ritual and Jade took pleasure in coming home to a place where she could do as she chose without deferring to anyone else. Life might not be great, but it had been worse.

She unlocked the door and walked into the four-room flat her mother never missed an opportunity to refer to as "that chicken coop." The living room, bedroom, bathroom, and kitchen were indeed tiny, but they fitted Jade like a glove of her own making. Brilliant yellows made the small areas bright. Puffy cushions the color of sunflowers and striped or polka-dotted with red heaped a rattan couch and chairs. Polished yellow cotton drapes were drawn back from a bay window over Lostwithiel Street and early evening light cast warm shafts over the pots of fresh flowers provided from Art Perron's garden. For Jade's supposedly retired father, gaining a reputation as Fowey's premier gardener had become an obsession.

She tossed her keys onto the yellow lacquered chest that served as a coffee table and bent to unlace a tennis shoe.

"Jade!" Shirley's high voice accompanied thumping footsteps on the stairs. "Jade! Are you there?"

"No," she muttered. "That was a ghost you just told off."

"Really," Shirley said breathlessly as she entered the room, a bulging paper bag in each arm. "If my head wasn't screwed on, I'd lose it. Sam says I've got nothing between the ears but alfalfa sprouts."

Secretly, Jade thought Shirley's husband might have made a valid discovery.

Shirley cleared her throat and said, "You won't hold it against me, will you? What I said? I care about what happens to you is all. But it is past time you found yourself another man, you know."

In the act of pulling off a shoe, Jade paused, wobbling on one foot. "Don't start on that again, please."

"You can't go on punishing every male member of the species just because of Doug Lyman."

Jade almost overbalanced. "My ex-husband's history as far as I'm concerned. I don't even want to hear his name."

"Does this Dr. Frazer turn you on?"

"Shirley!"

"No, don't get mad at me. I mean it. Does he? Turn you on, I mean?"

"Shirley!"

"Oh, don't give me that shocked rubbish. I'm just being sensible. You know what they say, it's as easy to get turned on by someone rich as someone poor. And Sam says Dr. Frazer's *really*—"

"Rich? And he's really famous and who knows what else he *really* is? I can't believe you're talking like this about someone you don't even know."

"He's here, isn't he?"

"Yes, but—"

"And he's on his own, isn't he?"

"Yes, but—"

"And you're on your own—more or less—aren't you?"

"Except for enough family and friends to choke a horse."

Despite the bags, Shirley managed to shrug her bony shoulders.

"There you are, then. He's alone and you're alone. I knew I saw something in your stars. I told you as much last week."

Jade sat on the couch, rested the back of her head against a cushion, and closed her eyes. "I told *you* last week that it's dangerous to live your life around all that mumbo jumbo." Even the most casual bargain hunter entering Shirley's shop was bound to be asked for an astrological sign.

"I'll let that pass."

Through slitted eyelids, Jade saw Shirley perch on a chair.

"What's his sign?"

Jade groaned.

"Never mind. I'll find out for myself. He isn't a Scorpio, is he?"

"How would I know? And why would I care?"

"Darkly sexual, they are. Still types with hidden appetites. Lustful and hot-blooded but with a cool outside that covers it all up for the innocents that walk into their hands all unknowing."

Jade opened her eyes.

Shirley squinted in deep concentration and pursed her lips again. "One minute you'll be thinking of soft music and flowers and gentle romance, the next you'll be swept into a vortex of wild passion."

"Vortex of wild passion?"

"Yes. You'll become his sex slave and be completely changed. Black satin and red silk ropes and feathers and melted margarine."

Jade sat forward. "Melted margarine?"

"Yes. You know. All that food stuff's very big now. Massage it all over, they do. To make their skin slip together, I suppose." She shivered. "Imagine that. Being massaged with melted margarine by a sexy behavioral psychologist. Ooh."

"Shirley," Jade said softly. "Why on earth would anyone use margarine?"

"Aha. You do know what I'm talking about. Nobody uses butter anymore. Animal fat's not good for you—clogs the arteries."

Jade laughed. She slipped sideways on the couch and propped

her head on one hand. "Yes, indeed. Well, I'm not expecting to become Dr. Frazer's sex slave." Did she regret that? She grinned afresh. Thank God she still had a sense of humor. "I really should think about making something to eat. So, if you've got whatever you were thinking about off your mind . . ."

"I don't like that phony cream stuff you can buy."

"Neither do I . . . Phony cream?"

"Well, they do say that's something these sex addicts use for—"

"Okay, Shirley." Jade got up. "Bless you for worrying about me, but there's no need. I can assure you that if Dr. Frazer's looking for romantic involvement, he'll have his pick of the litter around here—or anywhere else. He won't look in my direction."

"You're beautiful, Jade." Shirley sounded like a defensive parent. "If he hasn't noticed, I'll find a way to make sure he does."

Jade threw up her hands. "I will take care of my own love life. Thank you, Shirley. Give my best to Sam."

"Yes, well, I will." Shirley struggled to her feet and walked onto the landing. "Oh, my. Will you look at what I'm doing. I'd forget my head if it wasn't screwed on."

Praying for patience, Jade watched Shirley maneuver a turn in the narrow space outside the door and cart the bags back into the living room.

"I don't mind saying how surprised I was."

Jade stepped back, trod on Dog, and almost slid to the floor. "What is it, Shirley? Quickly, before you forget again."

"My, touchy tonight, aren't we?" The two bags were dumped on the yellow chest. "These are for you to give to your mum."

"My mother?" Jade narrowed her eyes. "I don't understand."

"She was in earlier and picked out these things. Then she was too tired to take them with her."

Her mother had always been too tired to do most things, Jade thought, and immediately banished the thought as disrespectful. "My mother came here and bought things?" Art Perron's wife, as her mother always referred to herself, didn't "hold" with the "secondhand junk" Shirley sold, any more than she "held" with Jade living in the flat over the shop rather than at home.

"Not for herself." Shirley smiled. She might affect vagueness, but she'd already let Jade know that her mother's attitude showed. "They're for the boy."

Jade shook her head slowly.

"Ian," Shirley said, sounding irritable. "You know. Ian Spring."

"Why is she buying clothes for him?" Particularly the kind of old and out-of-date things stocked at New to You.

"Because her sister nagged . . . He needs some more things. Evidently your Aunt Muriel asked your mum to see what she could find."

Shirley wandered out again. When she turned back to pull the door shut, she said, "Find out if he's a Scorpio."

Chapter Seven

Ian Spring sat in the recesses of an overstuffed chair upholstered in dusky pink brocade. His hands were spread on his thighs and he kept his eyes lowered.

"Hello, Ian," Jade said, closing the door from the hall to the sitting room in her parents' house. "I'm glad to see you." In fact, she wasn't. She had things to discuss with her mother and he couldn't be present.

"Hi," Ian said, his voice so low Jade hardly heard what he said. He puffed up his cheeks and stared at the ceiling.

Jade glanced at her mother, who hadn't noticed her daughter's arrival. Ian needed a champion. Aunt Muriel meant well, but she didn't know what to do with a young teenage boy and he was suffering as a result. Jade felt his eyes on her and looked in his direction. Instantly he looked away.

The theme music from *Coronation Street* faded. Dressed in a mauve chenille bathrobe and matching backless slippers, May Perron sighed, as she always sighed when her favorite television program was over, and raised her evening glass of Guinness to pale lips. A film of Ponds cold cream shone on her unlined face. Unlike her older sister, Muriel, May had made no attempt to cover the gray in her once bright red hair, but her eyes were the same dark blue as Jade's and vestiges of the pretty woman she'd been still lingered.

"I don't know what he sees in her," May said wistfully, gazing at the television screen. "Too good for a woman like that, he is."

Jade knew better than to ask for an explanation. To May Perron, *Coronation Street* had been realer than her life since before Jade was born. Discussions of plot lines had been known to take hours.

"Mum, I came over to ask you about something," Jade said when her mother showed signs of surfacing from her post-drama reverie. Leaving the bags of clothing behind, Jade had set out for her parents' house the moment she heard the shop door close behind Shirley.

"It's about time you remembered I'm here," May said in wounded tones. "It wouldn't hurt you to spend a bit more time with your mother. Before you know where you are, I'll be gone and then you'll wish you hadn't ignored me like you do."

"I expect you're right, Mum." Jade smiled at Ian. "How's school, then? Have you made any good friends, yet?"

"School's okay."

"A worry, he is," May said. "Our poor, dear Muriel. A saint in her own time, that's what she is."

"Perhaps Ian would enjoy poking around in the work shed. Dad's got lots—"

"Mr. Perron doesn't like strangers interfering with his things."

Jade swallowed. Her mother invariably referred to her husband as "Mr. Perron" but to Ian the comment must seem even more hostile than she'd intended.

The boy slumped lower in his chair and looked at his hands.

"Muriel's got her ramblers' meeting tonight." May sniffed and eyed Ian. "I'm just doing what anyone would do for a sister's boy. My health isn't up to it, mind, but I'm managing."

"He doesn't need . . ." Jade snapped her mouth shut, got up in a rush, and hurried across the room. *A thirteen-year-old doesn't need a baby-sitter*, she longed to say. Another moment and she'd fall into one of the pointless, one-sided arguments her mother usually won through default by silence. "I'll just pop out and see Dad."

She found her father in the greenhouse at the top of the steeply sloped garden behind the house. Tapping a pane, she leaned through the door. "Hello, Dad."

Art Perron turned from a bench crowded with potted starts and waved Jade inside. "Something gone wrong?"

"No. No, nothing like that."

"Are you sure?" Her father might be sidelined by a gammy heart but he would never stop watching Perron and Son like the anxious, first-time owner of a car in a school car park.

"Absolutely sure. Bert's ahead of schedule on the town hall project. Gavin and Will started over in Polruan yesterday—painting the church. And Stuart's almost finished with Mrs. Graham's plastering."

"Hm." Art rotated his arthritic shoulders and arched a stooped back. "And what about you? Ferryneath, isn't it?"

Jade grinned. "Trust you, Dad. Still on top of everything."

"Got to be. No job for a woman. I still think—"

"Drop it, Dad," Jade said, but without rancor. "You know I like what I'm doing, and you also know you'd never find anyone as able as I am to run Perron's."

Art sniffed. "You'll do well to take care of things, missy. The business will be yours and your brother's when I'm gone."

"Between you and Mum, I'm glad I came over tonight," Jade said. "The pair of you. Both talking about how I'm going to feel when you die. You're both going to live for years and years yet. That's an order. Understand?"

"Hm." But a pleased smile creased Art's thin face. His pale blue eyes sparkled. Still six foot tall, despite the stiff forward thrust of his neck and narrow head, he took pride in a full head of thick, iron gray hair. He wiped his big hands on a rag and scrutinized Jade.

"You never come over here on a week night. Did you fancy some sweet williams, maybe? Best in Fowey, they are. I'll cut you some."

"That'll be nice." Even if she'd probably have to resort to using milk bottles as vases. "I didn't come for that, though. Dad, we've got a problem."

Art stopped, his hands clasping the rag in front of him. "I knew it! I should trust my instincts. You never come to see us during the week. I—"

"Dad, it's Ian."

"If Peter had come into the business the way I always planned, none of this—" He pulled his bushy brows together and slowly tossed the rag on a bench. "Ian? You mean Ada's boy?"

"Yes. Ian Spring."

"What about him? He's settling in all right, isn't he?"

"No. I don't think he is." Jade went to her father's side and slipped an arm through his. She poked at the fabric of the old painter's overalls he wore. "You were always fair, Dad. And you were always good with kids." She didn't add, especially boys—especially your favorite kid, my brother, Peter.

"Haven't had anything to do with children. Not for years."

"Don't give me that, you old sham. You're a softie for kiddies, and you know it."

"I hope I'll get to be a softie for some grandchildren of my own one day."

That, Jade decided, was a subject she didn't intend to revisit tonight, if at all. "Ian needs some help, Dad."

"Damn fool Muriel," Art muttered and snatched up a pair of pruning shears. "Damn fool woman's a menace. Thinks I should want to give up every flower in my garden for her church arrangement nonsense. She can think what she likes. I'm not giving her a stalk of anything."

"Aunt Muriel's probably trying to do her best for Ian, but she isn't young, Dad, and she's never had to do anything for a child before."

Art paused in the act of decapitating a sickly-looking geranium. "Ada left the boy to Muriel. That's the way it was arranged. No choice. He'll have to make the best of it."

"We're his family, too," Jade said patiently. "You're his uncle, and Mum's his aunt and I'm his cousin. He's lost his father and his mother and he's only thirteen. Dad, it isn't right for him to be made to feel like a nuisance."

"Feel like a nuisance?" Throwing down the shears, Art reached for the shapeless tweed hat he favored whenever outdoors. "That fool Muriel had better not make the lad feel a nuisance. I'll go over there and sort her out right now."

"No, no." Jade stood between her father and the door. "Ian's in the house with Mum. Aunt Muriel's off at her ramblers' meeting. Look, I usually avoid saying these things, but Mum defers to you. She does and says whatever she thinks you want because that's the way she believes it ought to be."

"Do you find anything wrong with that, missy?"

Jade sighed. "No, Dad. Not if it pleases you and Mum." She had long ago designated her father as a peerless chauvinist.

"If you hadn't felt you had to wear the trousers in the family, you and Doug—"

"Dad," Jade said in a mildly warning tone. "Let's stick to the reason I'm here. Mum went to Shirley Hill's shop today and bought a lot of old clothes."

Art looked blank.

"She bought them for Ian. Because Aunt Muriel asked her to."

"Why would Muriel . . . Your mother doesn't hold with secondhand things."

"I know," Jade said patiently. "And that's exactly what I'm talking about. Evidently Mum and Aunt Muriel decided secondhand clothes are good enough for Ian even though they've never been good enough for any other member of the family. Don't you see? He's been orphaned and sent away from his home to a country halfway around the world—all in the space of a few months—

and now the only family he's got is treating him like a poor relation."

"Hm." Art crammed the tweed bucket hat down to his large ears. "Hm."

"Mum was talking in front of him," Jade said, exasperated. "As if he wasn't even there. Saying Aunt Muriel's a saint to put up with having him. That sort of thing. And he isn't being allowed to behave like a boy should. I wouldn't come behind Mum's back to talk to you about something if this was a normal situation, but it isn't. And I don't know what to do to help." She spread her hands.

"D'you fancy a cuppa?" Art passed Jade and loped down the crazy paved path.

"That would be very nice." She followed, smiling to herself. The set of her father's brows suggested he would at least have something to say on the subject of Ian.

Art stopped and glanced back. "Abandoned by whoever his real mother was, too," he said, his eyebrows positively jutting. "You forgot to mention that. Don't tell me a little'un can't be scarred by what happens the minute he's born."

In her parents' immaculate kitchen, where the aroma of baking bread floated on warm air, Jade's father poured two cups of tea from a pot nestled inside a crocheted cozy atop the stove. He gave one cup to Jade, stirred four teaspoonfuls of sugar into his own, and continued wordlessly on to the living room.

Jade's mother turned her head toward her husband without removing her eyes from the television screen. "Snooker's on, Mr. Perron," she said.

"Hm."

"Get out of Mr. Perron's chair," she told Ian. "Mr. Perron's favorite, that is."

"I'm not staying," Art said, going to stand beside the boy. "Do they have humbugs in the States, then?"

Ian's brown eyes took on an even more worried glitter. "You mean phonies?"

"Thought not." Art stuffed a hand in his pocket and brought out a rumpled, white paper bag. "Humbugs are sweets. My favorites. Want one?"

Ian started to shake his head, then stood up instead and felt cautiously inside the bag until he managed to dislodge a sticky, black-and-white-striped sweet from the clump they'd formed. "Thanks," he said, turning it this way and that before edging it into his mouth.

"Good, right?"

With a pointed lump pushing out first one, then the other thin cheek, Ian nodded.

"Ever seen one of these?" From his other pocket, Art produced a dark wooden peg. "You probably have, but I'll bet you never saw someone actually make one. That's what I do for special carpentry projects. A hobby of mine. Working on a model of the *Frances of Fowey*, I am. Come on out to the shed and see."

Ian took the peg Art offered and examined it while allowing himself to be steered toward the kitchen.

"John Rashleigh's she was. Admiral Frobisher discovered Baffin Land aboard her in 1587." Man and boy disappeared and Jade heard her father add, "Went out against the Spanish Armada, too," before the door to the garden slammed shut.

"Well!" May said. "What's come over Mr. Perron? Really, it's too much. All of us having to go out of our way for a boy who isn't even related."

Jade sat in the chair Ian had vacated and cradled her teacup in both hands. "Mum, you're being too hard on Ian. You don't know him yet. Give him a chance and remember we're all he's got now."

"You don't know the half of it." May unearthed the remote control from the folds of her bathrobe, flipped off the television, and gave Jade her full attention. "That child is worrying Muriel to death. He's been seen talking to strangers."

Jade tipped her head inquiringly. "What exactly does that mean?"

"It means just exactly what I said. He's been seen talking to strange men. Now any sensible child knows better than that. He could get taken off."

The possible terrors of being "taken off" had been drummed into Jade and her older brother, Peter, from earliest memories. "I'm sure Aunt Muriel will warn him about that."

"But that's still not the half of it. He's been asking to go to one of these strangers' houses, mind you. What do you think of that?"

"I don't understand."

"No, I don't suppose you do. He reckons there's this man who's offered to give him music lessons. *Guitar*, mind you. Imagine a boy thinking he should be mucking about with guitars or whatever they are when he should be outside running about."

"As far as I can see, he isn't being encouraged to run about, or do anything else a normal thirteen-year-old should do," Jade said, almost under her breath.

"What did you say? Don't mutter to me, my girl."

"I'm thirty-two, Mum. No girl anymore. Has Ian played the guitar before?"

"I suppose so. So Muriel says, anyway. Lot of noise, I'll warrant."

Jade thought otherwise. "What's wrong with playing the guitar? I should think it would be a nice pastime for anyone."

"He wants *lessons!*" May's eyes stretched wide open. "*Imagine.* Does he think money grows on trees? Our Ada had a bit set aside to take care of the boy, but not enough for frills."

"Surely there's enough for a few extras."

"Oh, no. Our Muriel won't touch that money."

Jade slowly set her cup on a table beside the chair. "I don't understand. Aunt Muriel won't touch the money Aunt Ada left for Ian? You mean she won't use any of it for him?"

"That's exactly what I mean. Muriel's going to keep it for him so's he'll have something when he's old enough to take care of himself. She won't touch a penny. I'm not saying I completely agree, mind, but she's determined to do that for Ada even if it does mean Muriel has to scrimp a bit herself till he can go out on his own."

"Dear Auntie Muriel," Jade murmured. "She never was such a bad stick."

"What a way to talk about your aunt," May said.

"How much can guitar lessons cost?" Jade asked, ignoring her mother's admonition.

"I'm sure I don't know."

"Well, I'm going to find out. If there's someone who could teach him and it's not too expensive, I'll pay for it myself. We all need to do our bit to help Ian feel wanted." She avoided her mother's eyes. "Have you heard of anyone giving guitar lessons in Fowey or Polruan? It would be nice if he didn't have to go too far."

"No. I'm sure I haven't." May fiddled with a loose thread on the arm of her chair. "That man he met who said he'd give him lessons might be all right. But you never know, do you? A man approaching a boy like that?"

"No you don't," Jade was forced to agree. "I'll go out and see how he's getting on with Dad. Then I'll have to get home. I want to make an early start tomorrow."

Total silence met Jade when she walked into her father's work shed. On one side of a central bench, Art bent to sand a miniature plank of wood with careful and patient strokes. Ian faced Art across the bench performing the identical task with another plank.

"Good hands, he's got," Art said without glancing up. "Taking to it like a duck takes to water."

"You need good hands to play a guitar," she said, and saw the boy stiffen. "Did you know Ian plays the guitar, Dad?"

"No." Art's voice held no interest. "He says the kids at the school are nice but he doesn't fit in. They're curious about him, he says. Because he's a foreigner. But he can't fit in because he doesn't know anything about the things that interest them."

"He will. Ian, my mother's been telling me about how you want to take guitar lessons. Did you take them before?"

"Yes. Since I was eight."

"Would you like me to find someone to teach you again?" She almost held her breath. He was fragile somehow, ready to break apart if pushed too hard.

"I've found someone."

Jade stopped herself from lecturing on the evils of talking to strangers. That could come later. "Don't you think we should contact someone official? Someone who knows who's got proper credentials and so on? I could call the music teacher at the school."

"I'd like him to teach me." Ian sounded stubborn. A white line formed around his compressed lips.

"Someone you met once?" Jade asked. "A casual acquaintance? Let me—"

"I've met him lots of times . . . Several, anyway. He's nice and we know a lot of the same pieces of music. He isn't stuffy like some teachers are. We could get together and jam sometimes, too. He said so."

Jade's father had stopped sanding. He looked from Ian to Jade and shook his head slightly.

"People can say things just for something to say," she told the boy. "They often don't mean them."

"He does." Animation brought color to Ian's face. "He's resting up from his job. It's the kind that makes people tired so he's not doing it for a while. For all summer. He comes by the school in the afternoon when I'm getting out."

A tightness closed in the region of Jade's heart. "We'd better talk about this." And someone had better find out who and what this man really was. She shuddered.

"It'd be cool if I could go and visit him." Ian spoke rapidly and the flush of excitement deepened on his cheeks. "Look, he gave me this and said to have Aunt Muriel call if I can go see him."

With a hollow sickness pooling in her stomach, Jade took the piece of paper Ian gave her. "Do you think the music teacher at the school might even give lessons herself?"

Ian scuffed sawdust on the shed floor. "He understands the same things I do."

"I'm not sure—"

"Take a look at the paper," Art interrupted. "At least see where he lives. We can always check him out."

Jade nodded. "I suppose you're right. It's just that . . . Well, you know what I'm thinking." She unfolded the note and read—and read again—and again. Her skin grew tight and cold.

"Well," her father said. "Who is it? Where does he live?"

Very carefully, Jade refolded the paper. She tapped it against her chin. "Dr. Byron Frazer. Ferryneath Cottage, Bodinnick."

Chapter Eight

She was watching him again.

Byron pretended deep concentration on the papers scattered before him across the kitchen table.

But he could *feel* Jade staring at him.

He spread a hand across his brow, took off his glasses, and dangled them between a finger and thumb.

What the hell was the matter with her?

A gust of warm breeze through the open door swept in the heavy, sweet scent of honeysuckle from bushes that mounded the stone wall between the cobbled yard and an alley leading to a cottage set back from the road.

Byron settle his hand on the table and looked up in the same instant: directly into Jade Perron's cobalt blue eyes. "How's it going?" he asked.

She started, seemed to remember the can of paint she'd presumably been stirring, and swallowed loudly enough for him to hear. "Fine," she said. Overly energetic agitation of the paint with a wooden stick ensued. Jade bowed her face over the can, which stood in the sink.

He shoved his glasses back on and opened a book.

The sluggish scraping sounds slowed, and then stopped.

Byron scanned a sentence, scanned it again—and again. To thwart a temptation to aim a sly peek at Jade, he held the book up in front of his face. She'd been the queen of frost since Wednesday. Tonight they were supposed to have a drink together and he hated to confess, even to himself, how much he looked forward to that.

She was probably trying to find a way to say she didn't intend to go.

Damn, but it shouldn't matter so much. It shouldn't matter at all. Maybe it wouldn't if he didn't feel so out of his depth and worried. Ian needed him. Every time he saw the boy, Byron searched for some sign that Ian was settling down and learning to like his surroundings. It wasn't happening.

If he took on the raising of a child, his own life would never be the same.

The words on the page ran together. From the moment he'd decided to come to Cornwall, he'd known he was opening a door he'd never intended to open again.

Ian was the child Lori had wanted so much. Smarting behind his eyes made him blink rapidly. If for no other reason than the responsibility he felt for making sure Lori's boy was happy, he no longer had a choice in what he had to do. *How* he did it was still a mystery. The doctor hadn't dealt with this particular crisis before, not in a patient, and definitely not personally. He didn't know what advice to give himself . . .

A rhythmic tapping drew his attention to the floor beside his chair. Dog—who called a dog, Dog?—sat in a contorted heap scratching an ear. When she saw him looking at her, she stopped, hind leg poised in midair, her bulbous black eyes staring him down.

"Black olives," Byron said to himself.

"What?"

He switched his attention to Jade, who gripped her dripping

paint stirrer like a post hole digger—or a dagger big enough to require a two-handed thrust.

It was Byron's turn to swallow. "Dog," he said and tried, unacceptably, for a casual chuckle. "Her eyes remind me of black olives."

"She's got nice eyes. They're gentle."

"Very gentle." *Very gentle black olives.* Another strike against him. "I thought we'd go up to the Ferry Inn for a drink. Is that okay with you?"

"Oh."

Was that "oh, yes" or "oh, no"? "If you'd rather, we can find somewhere else." *But don't say you've changed your mind.*

"That'll be fine."

Fine appeared to be the word of the day. "Harry Hancock next door said it's a popular place."

"I've never been there before." She still looked less than enthusiastic. "It's expensive." An immediate and very appealing blush washed her face.

Byron pretended not to notice her comment. "Did you know Harry came from Birmingham?" The elderly man who lived in the cottage at the end of the alley had made a point of finding excuses to talk.

"I've never met him."

"He used to drive locomotives." He wanted to talk about other things, like what she enjoyed doing when she wasn't working and what kind of books she read and what music she favored.

Jade made a neutral noise and began hauling the paint can from the sink.

Byron leaped up, almost overbalancing his chair, and went to help. "That's too heavy for you." He covered her hands on the handle.

"I'm used to lifting heavy things."

He thought he felt her tremble.

Up close, he noticed there were black flecks in the deep blue of her eyes and a hint of intense violet around each iris. "You could hurt your back," he said, his mouth unaccountably dry.

Beneath his hands, hers were small and cool. Her full lips parted a fraction. "I know how to lift properly," she said, and her attention flickered to his mouth and down to the region of the open neck of his shirt.

When she took a breath, her breasts rose beneath the shapeless white overalls that were the only mode of dress he'd seen her wear so far. She was compact, but very feminine.

"Humor me," he finally thought to say. "I'm an old-fashioned man."

Byron tightened his grip over hers and they lifted together.

"Is this going upstairs?"

"Yes."

Her skin was so pale as to be almost translucent. Thick, black lashes created soft shadows about her eyes. Byron remembered to breathe. She was stunning in a fragile way that could be considered ludicrous in a woman with her occupation. But the steady thud, thud of his heart and the abrupt pulsing in other regions of his body had less to do with how she looked than how she made him feel.

He was aroused. He was fully, almost painfully aroused, and at the same time a weakness in his legs brought back memories of adolescent uncertainty about the next step to take with a particular woman.

"I'll carry it up for you." The paint can had become a very necessary shield. If she noticed the effect she was having on him, she'd probably run screaming from the cottage.

"I'm not ready to go up yet."

Or would she?

"Where shall I put it?" Preferably in his lap. He was seeing in her, reading in her, what he wanted to see and read.

Jade sucked her bottom lip between teeth that overlapped the tiniest bit in the front. Byron zipped through a minifantasy of run-

ning his tongue along the sharp edge of those teeth—the instant
before he plunged into her mouth. While he plunged into her
mouth, his hands would be full of her breasts and he would be
pressing deep into her body.

"Put it back into the sink for now."

He locked his thighs. "Are you sure? I might as well take it where
you're going to use it." And he could not relinquish his screen, not
at this moment.

The choice wasn't to be his. "Just leave it." Her small hands
tightened under his and she guided the can to rest on its newspaper
once more.

Instantly, Byron swung around, reached the table in a single
stride, and dropped back into the chair. Only one other woman had
ever had the power to shred his self-control—and she hadn't accomplished the process in a matter of days, or even hours, as Jade
Perron had.

Jade hadn't accomplished this—he'd allowed himself to create
the situation. He hated himself for comparing Lori to Jade. They
were different. Period. And Ian should be his only concern. Ian was
his . . . He was very concerned about Ian but any attempt to hurry
things too much would probably be disastrous.

There was a great deal going on behind Jade Perron's blue
eyes—a great deal more than calculating how long to stir a can of
paint.

"You didn't say how the leak test went," he said.

"Nothing to panic about."

No stick for stirring paint had ever been so well cleaned. He'd
swear they were equally aware of each other. This sensation of almost physical connection unnerved him. "How's it all going anyway?"

She looked questioning. "Fine."

Oh, great. Now he was repeating himself like an idiot. "I guess I
already asked you that, didn't I? Sorry." With a forced laugh, he
made himself pick up the book again and start reading. "*Adults who*

were the object of pedophilic abuse are a separate issue," he read yet again.

All too soon, Celeste's patience would snap again and she'd be on the phone, grilling him and refusing to go away without answers. By then he wanted a good story about his plans for the new book—a book Celeste hadn't even known he intended to write.

He grew still.

His fingers tightened on the book.

Damn it anyway. She was watching him again.

"You're really interested in all that stuff, aren't you?"

Slowly, he lowered the book. "Psychology? Yes. It's my life." It had become the only part of his life that seemed real.

"Mm. That book you're reading. It's on pedo . . . How do you say that?"

"Pedophilia."

Jade crossed her arms tightly beneath her breasts. "Something to do with children."

Byron cleared his throat. "My specialty is the family. I do a lot of inner child work. Coming to terms with needs that weren't met for people when they were children and the effect that has in later life. Adult children of addicts—alcohol, sex, violence, rage, and all the other, less obvious addictions we suffer from."

"Can not having needs met in early life cause something like pedophilia? How would you explain exactly what that is, anyway?"

The intense expression in her eyes troubled him. "In simplest terms, pedophilia is a sexual perversion in which children are the preferred sexual object." He felt surprisingly uncomfortable.

Jade shuddered. "That's awful."

"It's a disease. Like any other disease."

"I think it's disgusting."

He wouldn't give her a lecture on treating deviations rather than banishing those who suffered from them. "It's a problem."

She crossed her arms even tighter and came closer. The neck of her overalls was unbuttoned to a point where her breasts pressed together and a dark line of shadow formed. He shifted in his chair.

"Is it true that some people—not you of course—but some people go into fields like . . . Well, do they choose things to solve their own problems?"

Byron affected careful consideration. She couldn't know that the question was one of the oldest in the book. "Like mixed-up psychologists?"

She put a finger on top of one of his sheets of notes and pushed it gently back and forth. "Maybe. Do you think a person can cure himself of some serious psychological deviation?"

He had no idea where she was heading. "It's possible."

"But not usual?"

"Sometimes conditions are dormant for long periods. That frequently ends up causing the biggest problem because the subject builds a normal reputation. Whatever 'normal' is. And when the deviation eventually starts to kick in, the subject is often intelligent enough to camouflage his or her anomaly pretty well."

"But they won't be able to forever?" She pulled up a chair and sat close to Byron. Too close. "Sooner or later they're going to start acting out their fantasies."

He raised his eyebrows sharply. "Fantasies? What makes you zero in on fantasies?"

"Oh, nothing. It was just a word." She leaned toward him, watching his face so closely he wanted to look away. "What happens when they can't suppress the, er, whatever it is anymore?"

"There aren't any absolutes. Sometimes the behaviors come on gradually. Sometimes there's a rush. The trick is to recognize what's happening and head off disaster."

"Oh, yes. I'm sure no pedophilic person wants to take off children."

"Take off?"

Jade became a mass of agitated movement. "Take off. You know.

Lure away by offering them things. Single out a boy who looks lonely and promise him whatever he wants most and then get him to go somewhere. That kind of thing."

To the contrary, Byron knew that in many instances pedophiles had no compunction about pursuing their urges. He wasn't about to upset Jade with that piece of information. "We can certainly hope that may be the case," he told her. "You really like children, don't you?"

"Well . . . I do like them, yes. Byron, there's something I'd like to discuss with you."

The tone of her voice made his scalp feel too small. "Discuss away." Why did he sense he wasn't going to enjoy this?

"I don't want you to think I'm not sympathetic, because I am, but I can't risk keeping my mouth shut and regretting it later. Not that my regret is the important issue."

"I'm used to talking openly on just about any subject. If I can help put your mind at ease about something, I want to."

"It's about, well—"

"Morning." Harry Hancock leaned his stocky body in at the kitchen door. "Thought you might enjoy a piece of my bread pudding. I'm not interrupting anything, am I?"

Chapter Nine

Byron passed the bathroom in the upstairs hall. Dog sat outside the door waiting for her mistress. The dog looked at Byron and drew her lips away from her teeth in what Jade referred to as a smile. Byron wasn't sure he and Dog were on smiling terms.

When she'd finished work, Jade had asked, hesitantly, if she could "wash and brush up" before they had their drink. Then she'd produced a plastic grocery sack from the room where she'd been working. Even though it was larger, she had declined his offer to use the bathroom off his bedroom. And she hadn't met his eyes when she'd said, "That isn't necessary." He hovered at the top of the stairs and smiled. Perhaps he wasn't the only one around here who was feeling some sexual stirrings.

The lock clicked off on the bathroom door.

Byron slipped silently downstairs and into the sitting room. Without putting on the light, he sat on the couch where he could see Jade pass by in the hall and enter the kitchen that lay straight ahead in his line of sight.

He felt his own pulse, strong and heavy—and excited.

This wasn't just an almost forgotten feeling, it was a first in the intensity department.

Her footsteps came softly down the stairs and she walked past the sitting room door—and stood still, looking toward the kitchen.

With her back to him, she looked down and her movements suggested she was checking buttons on her blouse.

Byron leaned forward and rested his elbows on his knees. The pulsing in his veins became a throb. Whatever he'd expected, it hadn't been quite the curvaceous figure in a yellow blouse, simple, tapered black slacks, and flat black shoes who hovered, spotlighted, mere yards from him.

Jade Perron couldn't be classified as a butterfly emerged from a chrysalis. That she was intriguing, he already knew. But an intriguing face with the promise of more had emerged as a totally feminine and elegant presence who had managed to shake this worldly male to the soles of his Ferragamo loafers.

Keeping her arms at her sides, she walked on and disappeared into the kitchen. Dog moved like a shadow in her wake.

Byron got up. *Damn it.* He hadn't come here to get involved with a woman, but he had a notion that might be about to happen. All day Ian had been heavy on his mind. The time had come to make a final decision in that area, and Byron thought he might be ready to do just that. But for tonight, Jade of the freckled white skin and blue eyes, of the thick black hair with a mind of its own, the minuscule waist—and fascinating breasts—yeah, she was the main item on the agenda tonight. He wanted to know more about her, to understand more about her.

Anchoring his hands in the pockets of his slacks with what he hoped was a nonchalant air, he strolled in to confront her. "Hi. I thought maybe we'd be daring and have a drink here before we go out. Ready to be wowed by Byron the bartender?"

Sitting on top of a step stool, with one obviously shapely leg crossed over the other, she turned her face up to his and said, "Why not? I've clocked out. Now I feel reckless."

In that instant, all his years of experience in the noble art of smoothly negotiating the dating dance wobbled dangerously. "What will you have?"

"Whatever you're having."

She'd brushed her hair until it shone like blue-black satin, and drawn it back on one side with a plain ebony comb. He'd never liked red lipstick. On Jade, the unexpected effect acted like a magnet. He wanted to feel that full, soft, carmine-tinted mouth beneath his own. "Do you like wine?" he asked.

"That's fine."

No way would he allow her to retreat into that line of response. He said, "Red or white," and almost laughed at himself for giving her the perfect opportunity to say, "Either."

Instead, she said, "You choose." And she swung a foot, allowing the heel of her shoe to dangle.

Her ankles were narrow. Everything about her felt like something he was noticing for the first time in a woman—as if he'd never noticed anything in particular about a woman before.

He drew in a breath and retreated to grab a bottle of red wine from a rack on the counter . . . and to regroup. They were going to have a drink, exchange a few pleasantries, and then she'd go home.

"You chose red," she said when he handed her a glass.

"Seems appropriate." Like the color of her lips. "What shall we drink to?"

She looked directly into his eyes. "I'm not much good at toasts."

"Try." And let him keep right on looking at her—until he could figure out a way to touch what he was looking at. Geez, he was thinking like the kind of man he'd never wanted to be—an on-the-make-at-any-cost man.

"How about, here's to hope, and honesty and generosity and kindness and"—she wrinkled her nose thoughtfully—"and you finish."

"Finish?" He grimaced. "You're a tough act to follow. I'll just throw in friendship. How's that?"

She held up her glass and waited for him to touch it with his own. "That's just about perfect." Crystal tapped her white teeth and she sipped.

Watching her covertly, Byron took a deep swallow of his own drink. The blouse was made of silk and settled lightly on her breasts. She balanced the wineglass on her knee and turned it by the stem. The blouse was thin. She wore a pale, lacy bra that didn't reach much higher than her nipples. Soft flesh flared above the lace.

"You're staring."

He jumped, actually *jumped*. "Not staring. Thinking and gazing. There's a difference." At least his ability to think on his feet hadn't deserted him.

"What are you thinking?"

"That I'm not sure drinking in a pub with a lot of people is what I want to do." Good God! He rarely spoke without thinking first, but he'd just done exactly that. "But I can be a bit reclusive, so don't take any notice of me. I'll enjoy myself the minute we get there."

"I'd rather not go either."

He paused, the glass halfway to his mouth.

"I've never been very fond of noisy places." She shrugged—the most charming shrug he ever remembered seeing. "It's fun to think about going somewhere. But when the time comes to leave, I always feel a bit sick. Isn't that silly?" She tilted her head self-consciously and flipped her hair back from her neck, a slender, pale neck that carried on down to an equally pale, smooth expanse of skin exposed between the lapels of her blouse.

Byron's brain clicked sluggishly back into gear. "I don't find anything about you silly." *Whoa, boy. The water could quickly get deeper than you're prepared to dive in to.* "How do you feel about being all dressed up with nowhere to go?"

"I already am somewhere." She turned the delightful shade of pink he'd already decided he could find addictive. "I mean, it's nice being able to relax and do nothing . . . in nice surroundings . . . with someone . . ."

Byron laughed. "Someone nice?"

"I was going to say 'different.' But nice, too."

The way she blushed shouldn't please him this much. He said, "Why don't we have something to eat? It's that time."

After a pause, she said, "Why don't I fix something?"

"You're sure you don't want to go out?"

"Absolutely sure now." She slid to stand, with the result that for a moment her slacks pulled tight around her thighs.

As far as he could tell, she had perfect legs and he'd like nothing more than to run his hands up their length, all the way up their length.

Moments later, Jade's head was buried in the refrigerator, which meant that her small, but wonderfully rounded bottom was presented for inspection.

A shudder passed all the way to his toes. This was getting out of hand. There'd never been a doubt in his mind that he was a sexual animal, but his reaction to Jade went way beyond the expected.

"We could use this as an excuse to clean out your refrigerator," she said from its recesses. "You've got bits and pieces of just about everything."

Byron moved behind her. "Sounds great. Hand out the booty and I'll put it on the table."

She started to pass containers and packages to him, then said, "That's about it," stood, and closed the door.

"Hardly a gourmet repast," Byron said.

Jade turned. She stood almost toe to toe with him, her chin tipped up. "It'll fill us up."

He made no attempt to move away.

Neither did Jade.

Unable to stop himself, Byron pushed the fingers of one hand into her hair and used his thumb to outline a high, rounded cheekbone.

Jade passed her tongue over her lips, and the light in her eyes became a glitter that turned them black. "I'll put everything on a tray," she said in a voice that broke. "Shall we eat here? Or in the sitting room, where we can watch it get dark over the harbor?"

"And the lights go on across the water," Byron said, shifting his thumb to her bottom lip and brushing lightly back and forth. "The water shifts under the reflections. It seems endless and bottomless and so soft." And it reminded him of the lady who stood before him.

"So it'll be the sitting room?"

"Uh-huh." Reluctantly, he removed his hand and helped put cheese and meat and an odd assortment of fruit onto plates.

By the time they'd arranged their eclectic feast on the low table in the sitting room, the charged atmosphere between them had relaxed. Byron didn't know if he was relieved. Scratch that. He was almost damned sure he *wasn't* relieved.

"The light in here makes it hard to see the harbor," Jade said, carrying a plate and her glass of wine to a padded seat in the window.

Byron flipped the switch that turned off the overhead light and killed the room's two lamps. "Now I suppose we won't be able to see to eat."

Jade giggled. He never remembered hearing her giggle before. "I could get food into my mouth if you sewed it shut. Ask my mother."

"That's it," he blurted out. "That's what's so different about you."

When he reached her side, carrying a glass and plate of his own, he saw the sheen of her eyes as she looked up at him. "What's different? I'm very ordinary. A working woman with a business to run."

"But you don't take yourself seriously. And you're perfectly comfortable with who you are. Do you know how rare that is? I can't remember the last time I met a woman who didn't seem to be considering the impression she made."

"Who has time? You aren't worrying about the impression you make on me either, are you?"

"No." Not entirely true.

"So we're even."

His next thought was less pleasing. It was very doubtful that Jade Perron had any idea who he was in professional terms. If she did, she'd probably go into the posting, designed-to-attract routine to which he was so accustomed. She absolutely did not know why he was in Cornwall. The idea brought him discomfort. He hadn't told her any lies, but neither had he given her even a hint of the truth about himself.

She carefully balanced her food and wine and pulled her feet beneath her on the seat. Darkness had finally become almost complete, and the harbor waters rose and fell beneath bands of wavering lights from buildings overhanging the river on the Fowey side.

"Have you lived here all your life?" he asked her. Suddenly it seemed very important to know much more about Jade.

"Yes. And my father and mother before me and their parents before them and on and on back for generations."

"And you love it."

"I don't think about it a lot, but yes, I'm fond of Fowey."

"You said you live over a secondhand shop."

"On Lostwithiel Street. New to You, it's called. It belongs to Shirley Hill. Her husband is Sam Hill, who runs one of the water taxi services."

"Do they live in the same building?"

"Next door. Sam's family's been here a long time, too. He owns several pieces of real estate in town."

"Do you have a—er—flat mate? Is that what you call it here?" And would she please manage not to notice that he was prying?

"Flat mate's the right thing. No, I live alone—except for Dog." The animal had remained in the kitchen, asleep in a corner. "We make a great team. I give all the orders. She follows most of them and never answers back. Which makes me the boss."

"And being the boss is important to you."

"It becomes important to people who have lived with tyrants who . . ." Her voice trailed off.

"You've lived with a tyrant?"

"That's finished. It was a long time ago."

In other words: *Back off.*

"How about you?" she asked. "Back in Tiburon? Do you have someone?"

Byron's heart missed a beat. He drank more wine and refilled his glass. He made a production of matching chunks of cheese to crackers.

"Is that yes? I only asked because you asked me first."

He took a slice of pear from his plate and offered it to her. "Do you like these? I don't." When she'd accepted the fruit, he continued, "I tend to think about what I'm going to say for too long. Probably one more occupational idiosyncrasy. I live alone. Don't even have a dog. I'm not married." Saying it aloud gave him the sensation of being punched in the stomach. He probably ought to say he had been married, but he didn't want to explain what had happened to Lori—or think about it yet again.

Jade drank thoughtfully. "You surprise me. I'd have thought by your . . . Well, most men of your . . . I never was very good at nosing around without sounding rude."

"I'm thirty-four." And it was time for a change of subject. "This morning, when Harry Hancock came by, you were about to ask me something. You never got around to finishing."

Selecting a square of Cheddar cheese, Jade put it in her mouth and munched for several seconds. "Mm. I don't remember what it was now. Harry's a nice man. Kind."

"And wise," Byron told her while an absolute conviction formed that she definitely had not forgotten whatever it was she'd wanted to say. "After you went back to work, he said you were beautiful."

Jade shook her head and turned her face to the window. "That's nice. I am surprised you haven't been married."

Evasion could only drag him into a tighter and tighter spot. "I have been married."

"To a woman?"

He almost dropped his glass. "I beg your pardon?"

"Oh, dear. No, that's not what I meant." She shifted and put her plate on the windowsill. "What happened? I mean . . . Oh, dear."

Yet again he had the unpleasant sensation that something quite different from what she presented was on Jade's mind. "My wife died. I was twenty-one. She was twenty." Why, when he never, ever discussed Lori, had he felt forced to bare the truth to a woman who was little more than a stranger?

"That's awful," Jade whispered. "How sad. God rest her soul. I'm very sorry, Byron. What happened?"

No. Now he must tread very carefully. "She had an aneurysm. Two, actually. After the first there seemed some hope, but then the second one happened and it was all over." For a while—for months— he'd thought his life was over too.

Jade found his hand in the gloom and pressed his fingers. "Sometimes I think allowing yourself to love is too dangerous."

"Why?" He wasn't ready to ask about the past she had very clearly shared with someone, some man.

"Because when things go wrong, or break apart, at least one of you is left in pain. The pain makes you feel you want to die. Then the pain goes, but it takes your trust with it and I'm not sure you ever get that back completely."

Silence filled in around them. Byron had the uncanny sensation she could see into his soul—and that, just maybe, he had a glimpse into hers. He could come to like Jade's soul a great deal.

"I suppose that kind of personal disaster could affect a person in all sorts of strange ways," she said at last. "Did it . . . did it affect you in strange ways, do you think?"

He thought about that. "I think it made me wary of going into the expected types of relationships again." An understatement.

"Mm. I know that's true." She scooted a little closer. "What made you come so far away from home?"

Once again an edginess crept into his brain. "It seemed like a good idea. Sometimes we all need a complete break with what's going on, and a chance to assess our lives."

"I see. But was there a specific reason for coming?"

She definitely had something on her mind, but this time she wouldn't find out what she wanted to know. He'd try not to tell an outright lie, but he couldn't risk mentioning Ian. "What do you mean," he said, "a specific reason?"

"Ooh, I don't know." Her next breath was uneven. "Like . . . Like some kind of trouble you wanted to get away from, maybe?"

Byron reached down and set both his glass and plate on the floor. His stomach had executed a perfect backflip. "Trouble?" he asked carefully. "What sort of trouble?"

"Well . . . *trouble*. You know, something that made you feel like going a long way away and starting afresh, I suppose."

He regarded her narrowly in the darkness, an idea forming that caused a mixture of confusion, and deep anger. "Do you think I'm a fugitive from the law, for God's sake?"

"No! No, of course not. Whatever would give you an idea like that? I'm so bad at expressing myself." She raised her wrist to her nose and peered at her watch. "My word, if I don't hurry, I'll miss the last ferry. They stop so early. I don't want to have to call for the water taxi."

Byron felt disoriented. "You didn't bring your van?"

"No. Because we were having dinner, I decided to come over as a passenger."

"But you haven't finished your dinner—such as it is. Stay. I'll drive you around."

"Oh, no. I've got to get on or I won't be worth anything in the morning. I want to get started early on the ceiling in that bedroom. Things seem to be taking me longer than I expected."

He forced himself not to say that he'd been hoping he could find a way to keep her here all summer.

In a flurry, she transported their barely touched repast to the kitchen, rushed upstairs to gather the bag she'd left in the bathroom, and made to leave.

"Hey," Byron said. "Hold on. We've got ten minutes yet and the ferry stops practically at the edge of the garden. Give me the bag and I'll walk you down."

Side by side, they walked downhill past the front of Ferryneath to the landing. In the distance, on the other side of the water, Byron could see that the ferry had yet to cast off and chug in their direction.

"Can we do this again?" he asked. There was much more about Ms. Perron that would probably be very engrossing to discover.

"You want to?" Surprise loaded her words.

He wanted to turn her into his arms, to kiss her until they were both breathless.

The timing was wrong.

"I want to. I think I want to get to know you, Jade. Maybe very well. Does that sound like something that would interest you?"

She turned toward him and looked up into his face. With a single knuckle, she tapped his chest repeatedly. "You confuse me. Yes, it would interest me. It might even interest me a lot. But there are things we'd have to get straight first."

"Such as?"

"I'm not in the market for a casual lover."

Just like that? Byron recovered fast. "Casual lovers have never been my thing."

"There's something more important than that."

"Fire away."

"I—" Abruptly, she swung away and stood with her back to him.

"You what?" Her moods swept back and forth like a crazed pendulum. His tendency had been to avoid bringing his profession into his private relationships, but this lady was beginning to rattle him. "Jade, what is it? You've made several comments that could be classified as strange. Would it be too much to ask you to tell me what's really on your mind?"

"I don't like this. I don't like it one bit."

The ferry barge's engine blossomed to a full rumble that echoed over the water. "Okay," Byron said, fueled by a sense of urgency. "Would you please tell me what it is? I can take it, I assure you."

Stooping, she hauled Dog into her arms and turned to Byron once more. Even in the darkness, he could see anxiety in her eyes. "I've got to ask you why you've been following Ian Spring around."

Everything inside him plummeted. He pivoted on a heel, shoved his hands in his pockets, and looked at her over his shoulder. "Hell. This is a small town and no doubt it has a small-town mentality— in other words, you all live in one another's pockets. But how in God's name do you know I've been talking to Ian?"

"You've been waiting for him outside school and talking to him."

The ferry's engine became a rapidly approaching roar. "I'm not denying that. But you owe it to me to explain how you know."

"I don't owe you anything. You offered to give him guitar lessons and he wants to come."

He laughed without mirth. "This takes the cake. Okay. Yes. Guilty as charged. I asked Ian to come to the cottage and jam. I play the guitar, too. And I'll give him a hand with technique as much as I can. If he's allowed to come."

"Answer my question, Byron. Why?"

For one insane instant he considered doing just that. The urge passed. "I like the boy. We met in the churchyard and discovered we were both Americans. I thought he was lonely and I was right. Put it down to my occupation. I've spent a lot of time analyzing people." If his excuse sounded as phony to her as it did to him, he could expect a lot more questioning. He breathed into a fist, willing the clamoring in his mind to quit. He said, "Do you believe me?"

Jade stared straight into his eyes. "Maybe."

"Maybe? Okay, I guess that's something. Now. How about you telling me where you get your intelligence on Ian and me?" He passed his tongue over dry lips. "And what gives you the right to interfere anyway?"

"His mother was Ada Spring," Jade said quietly.

Byron let his hands fall to his sides. "I'll let you finish before I ask how you know that." And however long she took to finish would be too long.

"Cornish people believe in sticking by family. We don't let anything get in the way of that. I won't pretend I don't enjoy your attention, Byron. I'll even admit that—to quote a certain friend of mine's terminology—you turn me on."

He found his mouth open and closed it. "The feeling's mutual." But he wasn't accustomed to quite such a blunt, matter-of-fact approach.

How did she know about Ada Spring, dammit, how did she know?

"Ada Spring married an American and went to live in the States. They couldn't have children, so they adopted Ian. Only now they're both dead and he was sent here to Cornwall to live with Muriel Cadwen. Ada Spring was her sister."

The possible instigator of this came to light. Ian must have mentioned Byron to his aunt, and Muriel set about spreading gossip about his intentions toward the boy.

"That's why I've got a responsibility toward Ian. Muriel Cadwen is my aunt. She's my mother's sister. Ada Spring was also my mother's sister."

Byron splayed a hand over his face. He couldn't think of a thing to say.

"The fact is that if you've decided to make things harder for my Aunt Muriel by unsettling Ian, I'll find a way to stop you.

"Ian Spring is my cousin."

Chapter Ten

The cottage seemed to be holding its breath.

Jade rose to tiptoe and climbed the stairs with exaggerated steps. Byron was usually up and already at work when she arrived in the early morning. Today there was no sign of him, which probably meant he'd gone out somewhere. He had a Land Rover and parked it farther up the lane, in an old stable yard where they rented spaces. She could have checked before coming into the cottage. But just in case he was still sleeping, she'd try to be as quiet as possible.

She hesitated. After the questions she'd asked him last night, and the suggestions she'd made, he could have decided to leave. The breathlessness she felt had nothing to do with climbing a few stairs. *Don't let him be gone.*

If he was, it would be because he had something to escape from— like being discovered as a child molester.

The next steps Jade took were even slower than those that had gone before. She hadn't had enough sleep and she'd been up since three. First she'd wondered if she should come at all, then she'd waited for the phone to ring—for a message telling her she should not go to Ferryneath until further notice.

The door to his bedroom stood open a few inches, and dim light beyond suggested the curtains were still closed.

Wincing at the creak of a floorboard, she crept on past to the second bedroom and took off the old parka she'd donned against an unexpectedly cold fog that had rolled in during the night.

The time she'd spent talking to Byron was all a confused and vaguely embarrassing jumble now. If she didn't have an obligation to get on with the job, she probably wouldn't have come this morning.

The walls in this room had been stripped of old paper and she'd almost finished rough-plastering the ceiling between beams the owners had agreed to leave exposed—thanks to the good word Byron had put in for her idea.

She rolled up her sleeves and bent to pry the lid from a can of clear stain.

A scraping noise snapped her attention to Dog, who was tugging her favorite hammer from the upper tray of Jade's toolbox.

"Ssh," she warned. "Leave it!"

The lid on the can of stain popped off.

Dog, one eye on Jade, gave the hammer another yank and brought the head clattering to the bare floor. The handle remained gripped in bared teeth.

"Naughty!" Jade lowered her voice. "Naughty girl. You drop it."

Dog obliged.

Jade jumped at the ensuing racket and sucked air in through her teeth.

She waited, listening for sounds of movement from the room next door. None came.

Beyond the uncurtained windows, fog billowed so thick, the river was obscured. From the south, in the direction of St. Austell Bay, came the sonorous cry of foghorns.

A miserable morning, Jade decided. A morning when it would be nice to pull the covers over one's head and remain in bed—like the fortunate Dr. Frazer was probably doing right now.

Dr. Frazer—tall, hair ruffled, powerful arms and legs thrown wide, face undoubtedly handsomely boyish in sleep—stretched out on the bed beyond the wall she faced . . . Thoughts such as these did not make for serene working conditions.

A scraping sound forced her attention precipitously back to Dog who, dragging the wretched hammer, disappeared rapidly into the upstairs hallway.

Jade set down the screwdriver she'd used to pry the lid off the stain can, and scurried after the animal.

Too late.

She arrived just in time to see a long, scrawny, almost hairless tail disappear into Byron Frazer's bedroom. The hammer, apparently less interesting than whatever had grabbed Dog's attention, lay on the floor outside.

"Dog," Jade hissed, bending low and creeping forward until she stood close to the six-inch opening into Byron's room. "Dog, get out here."

Rustling followed and the distinctive sound of Dog's yawn. Then nothing.

"Dog!" She covered her face and tried to think what to do. Byron had never shown any particular fondness for her pet. If he awakened to find her in his room, he might insist that Jade leave her behind in future. "Dog, *come* here." Dog was misunderstood by others. Nobody but Jade knew what a gentle, faithful friend she was.

Hovering anxiously, Jade put a forefinger on the door and pushed, waited, and pushed again, widening the space until she could risk putting enough of her head inside to peer into the gloom beyond.

The bed stood against the wall between two windows; "looking as if a tornado had struck" didn't cover the twisted mess of quilt and sheets heaped on top and trailing to the floor.

Byron hadn't gone anywhere.

Dog, grinning as only Dog could grin, sat nestled in the space between Byron's splayed feet. The evil animal might have short legs, but they always got her where she wanted to go.

As Jade watched, her mutt's long, pink tongue appeared and toured in a leisurely lick from the man's heel, over his instep, to his big toe.

And one of those long, powerful legs Jade had been visualizing jackknifed up.

She covered her mouth and started to withdraw, but the fresh assault on the bed's covers ceased as abruptly as it had begun.

"*Come here*," Jade mouthed to Dog, making extravagant hand signals. "*Now!*"

Still grinning, her tongue lolling out of her mouth, Dog stood, turned around and around and around, then flopped down and closed her eyes.

Grimly determined, Jade bowed lower and advanced like the Grinch about to lift a little Who's candy cane on Christmas Eve.

Dog opened one eye, and scootched until she curled into the dark hollow beside Byron's other leg.

Common sense suggested it was a fine time to retreat and wait for the feathers to hit the fan. A lifelong tendency to try for the impossible if there was the slightest chance of triumph sent Jade treading softly onward until she was beside Byron.

"Dog," she whispered.

Her answer was the sliding progress of a bump that shimmied along the outline of the man's leg—*under* the covers.

Jade planted her hands on her hips.

And she looked at the man. She looked at him with her eyes wide open, and what felt like a fist in her throat.

He was spectacular.

He was breathtaking.

He was the sexiest thing she'd set eyes on . . . ever.

And how right her little fantasy had been. Very tall, one powerful arm folded beneath his head, strongly muscled legs flung wide, dark curly hair tousled . . . face handsomely boyish and relaxed in sleep . . . all just about as she'd visualized.

Something drew her even closer. Something in her, and something in him.

The night's growth of beard was dark on his angular jaw. And his lashes flickered with the movement of his closed eyes. Why hadn't she noticed how thick those lashes were?

He shifted and the bedding underwent another attack. Everything slid until only his hips, anchoring a swathe of sheet, kept the entire mess from landing on the floor.

Byron's right arm swung toward Jade and his hand came to rest, palm up, scant inches from her hip.

Drawing in a deep breath that wedged in her throat, she allowed her gaze to travel from Byron's face in a downward direction.

His shoulders were wide and well muscled, and tanned.

His chest was beautifully defined, the pectorals smooth and each rib covered with toned flesh—and tanned. Dark, curly hair flared wide, then gradually tapered to a line past his navel, and flared again . . . all the way to the twisted band of white sheet.

She'd seen his bare torso and legs before, but not like this, not while he lay before her.

His thighs were solid and well shaped, and his calves, and fine, dark hair lay smoothly on the skin—tanned skin.

His . . . Jade almost let out a small cry. Her hand went to her throat. At this moment, Byron Frazer was one hard man and he had plenty of raw material ready to prove exactly how hard.

"Do you know what they call people who do what you're doing?"

At the rasp of Byron's voice, Jade jumped violently.

His hand closed on her wrist, stopping her from rushing out of the room.

He drew her even closer to the bed until her thighs pressed against the mattress. "They call them voyeurs," he said.

"Dog," she croaked, and coughed. "Dog came in here and I tried to get her out."

In the silvered light of early morning, the man's eyes took on the quality of still, deep water—clear green all the way to some shifting place no one might see.

"I was working in the other room," Jade said. His grip on her wrist didn't waver. "Dog took off and . . ." He wasn't listening.

Her pesky mutt chose that moment to scramble from the bed and scuttle out of the room.

Byron's concentration remained right where it had been—on Jade. "You're a very sensual woman. But you know that, don't you?"

She expanded her chest, but no air filled her lungs.

"Don't you?" He shook her arm slightly.

She moistened her dry lips. "I should go."

"Do you want to?"

Jade made herself look away. "I've still got several weeks of work to do here, Byron. Maybe we should forget last night ever happened . . . and this morning."

"And that's what you want?" he persisted.

"No." Her small voice sounded distant, as if it belonged to someone else.

"I didn't think so. Neither do I. And I think this is as good a time as any to get rid of a few doubts you've had about me."

"Doubts?" Still she didn't trust herself to look at him.

"Poor Jade. You really did intend to do battle with me over Ian, didn't you?"

A dull heat crept up her neck. "You can't blame me for being concerned about what I was told. When grown men approach little boys outside schools, certain conclusions are inevitable."

"I told you the truth. I met Ian. He's a lonely kid and I wanted to help him. That's part of what I do for a living. Help people who are hurting. Do you believe me?"

"Yes." She meant it.

He fell silent. His fingers gentled on her wrist. She could have pulled away. She didn't want to.

Byron began to rub his thumb back and forth over the soft skin on the inside of her wrist. With his fingers, he played feathery touches into her palm.

Neither of them moved.

"Kiss me, Jade."

She closed her eyes. Her knees weakened and she fought against the desire to kneel beside him.

A little tug jerked her forward. "Please. I've been dreaming about your mouth. I've dreamed about feeling your lips part on mine, and about tasting you. I've wanted to push my tongue between your teeth and have you do the same to me."

She looked into his eyes. She had to. The green was more emerald now, intense and glittering.

"I've dreamed about you awake and asleep."

"I'm nobody," she whispered. "A woman who does a job with her hands and goes home to an empty little flat—to no one. I've failed in a relationship, Byron. I promised myself I wouldn't get close enough to anyone to feel a repeat of the kind of hurt that brought me." She couldn't handle this so she might as well get out without even getting in.

He raised his chin and smiled, deepening the dimpled grooves beside his mouth and crinkling the lines at the corners of his eyes. "And you can feel we might have a relationship that would make you vulnerable again?"

She said, "Yes," while she hated the admission.

"Good. It's healthy to be able to get involved again."

"Is it?"

"Kiss me." His white teeth pressed into his bottom lip and he pulled her steadily down until she must either give in or withdraw and turn away from him. "Do to me what I've dreamed of, Jade. And let me do the same for you."

His other hand went around her neck and he lifted his head from the pillow. There was the briefest instant, a tiny beat in time before he urged their mouths together.

Softly, so softly, his lips grazed over Jade's. Back and forth, back and forth, and somewhere in the gentle caressing of skin on skin, the tip of his tongue slipped between her teeth, and withdrew again.

Jade's eyes closed. Only Byron's hands stopped her from falling onto the bed with him. He kissed her with his lips, his tongue, tracing the tender, moist skin just inside her mouth until it tingled, teasing her tongue to join his, then pulling away yet again, leaving her lips swollen and wanting.

In a single movement, he knelt on the bed and wrapped his arms around Jade's waist. "This is too fast."

She nodded, fighting for breath. "I know."

"Sometimes things happen that we couldn't have planned if we'd wanted to. Do you believe that?"

"Yes." Her body felt raw.

"This scares you."

"I'm not impulsive, Byron. It scares me."

"Which makes you very wise. Would you believe me if I said it scares me, too?"

She thought a moment, all the while staring back at him. "I believe you."

"That kiss wasn't enough. Not for me."

Her heart slammed in her chest.

"I need much more, Jade."

She glanced down. The sheet had entirely given up its task. "You want . . ." She laughed shortly. "What a stupid thing I almost said."

"That I want sex? I do, Jade. But with you. Only with you."

"Nothing like this has ever happened to me before."

"And you're thinking it's happened to me?" His hands began a rough, shaky massage up and down her back. "Maybe you even think it's happened often. It hasn't. Not ever. I live a quiet life. There's no one else, Jade. There hasn't been for a very long time." And he cupped her bottom, urged her so near, she braced her hands on his shoulders.

"We're grown-ups," he murmured. "We don't owe explanations to anyone."

"No."

"And it's a cool, foggy day out there." Very slowly, he first spanned her waist, then ran his hands up her arms to her shoulders. "In here it's warm and safe and private—and we can be and do whatever we want for as long as we want. Tell me what you want."

All she could do was swallow hard and watch his face.

Byron kept his eyes on hers and unbuttoned the top button on her overalls.

Jade's hand instantly covered his and she shook her head.

"Okay." He smiled. "Okay, sweetheart. At least stay with me until I get myself back together."

She bowed her head and removed her hand from his. "I don't want you to stop."

He didn't.

The button slipped from its hole, and the next, and the next, until he could spread open the top of the overalls.

"My God," he murmured. "You're going to make me explode."

With the very tips of his fingers, he passed along the strip of narrow satin ribbon where her breasts swelled over the cups of a brief, peach-colored bra.

Jade watched his tanned fingers linger where the wisp of satin didn't cover the arcs of her dusky nipples. He leaned to kiss her there, lightly, moving his head languorously from side to side. She inhaled and closed her eyes against a longing for him to do much more.

Byron slid the overalls from her shoulders and down her arms, waiting until she pulled her hands free before framing her face and taking his time over another long kiss.

The muscles in his arms flexed beneath her fingers. Her hair fell forward to tumble over his shoulders.

Slowly, he ended the kiss and pressed his lips to her brow, her closed eyes, her neck.

"You smell like roses," he murmured. "I noticed that last night."

"I want to forget last night."

"I don't want to forget anything about the time I spend with you."

The time. She recognized the implied limit. Whatever happened between them would be bounded by the length of his stay in Cornwall.

Then he would be gone . . .

"Jade?" His voice held a question.

She looked into his face. "Yes."

"I can feel you drawing away. I don't want this to be something you're going to regret."

Finally unable to control the shaking in her legs, Jade leaned against the side of the bed. "I'm never going to regret it," she told him and knew she was probably lying.

The backs of his fingers passed from her collarbones down to the incredibly sensitized edges of her nipples . . . and dipped beneath the plunging bra.

Jade watched his face, the rigid set of his jaw, the intense concentration in his eyes. Byron watched her body's response.

He unhooked the fastening between her breasts and brushed aside the flimsy garment. Her nipples hardened.

Byron stroked her shoulders. And while his eyes flickered over her, he covered her breasts, held them, pressed them together, and finally, lavished each one with long, dragging kisses that drew her nipples far into his mouth.

Heat and aching flashed from his lips, his tongue, his teeth, to bury themselves deep inside her.

Byron's mouth never left her, not while he stripped her naked, not when he clamped her between his legs, holding her against his rock-hard erection with the relentless force of a vise.

Time and sanity crowded together.

They did not speak.

Byron tipped Jade backward onto the bed and bent over her thighs. With his tongue he found his way through dark hair to pulsing flesh, and sent her into hot darkness where the only sounds were her cry and his murmurs of satisfaction.

When she pushed him away and rolled to stand on the floor again, he knelt once more and tried to pull her back onto the bed. Jade went to her knees. She slid her hands up his thighs. When she cradled him, caressed him again and again, she heard his harsh breathing, then a wild cry of ecstasy—and of surrender.

And when Byron swept her up and deposited her in the middle of his big, tumbled bed, only Jade's muffled whimper and Byron's groan accompanied his entry into her.

In the rush of motion, the sounds they made mingled. Jade arched her hips from the bed, and Byron did what neither of them could have stopped—or would have stopped.

With the last, releasing thrust, he fell, panting, on top of her. His hot, damp skin slipped over hers. He found her hands and stretched her arms above her head, laced their fingers together and rested his face in her neck.

Even as they lay there, breathless and exhausted, Byron's knee moved rhythmically up and down the inside of Jade's thigh.

She wriggled, trying to get more comfortable.

"Don't do that," he said against her shoulder. "Not unless you're ready to repeat what we obviously do so well together."

Jade bit down hard on her bottom lip and held still. She was a quiet woman, a reserved, controlled woman. Never before had she given in to raw sexual need.

"Are you awake?" Byron said when she'd been silent a long time.

"Yes," she said quietly.

He raised his head to see her face. "Are you okay?"

She nodded.

Byron eased aside, rolled to his back, and drew her on top of him. "Tell me what you're thinking."

"I thought knowing what people think was your business."

"Ah." With one large, long-fingered hand, he cradled her face into the hollow of his shoulder. "This is going to be a problem."

"What is?" He was big and lithe and solid—and for this moment he made her feel he could hold away the world.

"Your perception of me versus what I am. You said you were just an ordinary woman, love. I'm just an ordinary man. And what I'm feeling for you is very special. Can that be enough for you for now?"

She didn't understand what he was asking. "What just happened between us doesn't mean you owe me anything. We both took, Byron." God, what had she done? How would she face him each time she came to work from now on?

"And we both gave. Rest, Jade. Don't think. And let me hold you."

She made her body relax. After several moments, she put an arm around his waist and nestled until she was comfortable.

"You feel so good," Byron murmured. He grabbed the quilt and hauled it over them. "I don't know about you, but it's fine with me if the world stops right here."

"Mm."

"Does that mean you wouldn't mind either?"

"It means . . . Byron, I've never done anything impetuous before—not like this."

"I believe you." He combed her hair with his fingers. "Maybe you'd consider doing it again sometimes?"

She stiffened and tried to pull away. Byron held her fast. "This was . . . I don't want to say this was a mistake," she told him. "But it wasn't rational."

"You didn't enjoy it?"

She squeezed her eyes shut. "You're never going to know how much I enjoyed it. But it can't happen again. Not if my life is going to stay in one piece."

"I don't understand."

"Of course you don't. You're here for a vacation—and to write or whatever you're doing. Then you'll return to California. You won't be thinking about a woman you . . . had sex with in a Cornish village. And that's the way it should be. Maybe I can do the same thing in my own way."

"Why shouldn't you?"

She felt slightly sick. "I can. And I will. But not if I come here each day and find you waiting to take me to bed." He wasn't denying that she classified as a casual encounter.

"I didn't have any plans to take advantage of you, Jade."

"I've got to go." Sitting up, she swung her legs over the side of the bed, and remembered she was naked. "Please look the other way."

"Why?" He sounded amazed.

"Because I'm embarrassed, that's why. I'm not used to walking around in front of a man like this."

"I know you're not."

She faced him. "*How* do you know? What makes you think you're the only man who'd be interested in me?"

His hand shot out so fast she had no time to evade his fingers. "Jade Perron. No man could look at you and not want you. And no man could look at you, then get to know you even a little, and not want you again and again. I'm in the latter category."

Her arm was firmly clasped and he began to pull her toward him. "Thank you," she said. "I think. But that's exactly what I'm afraid of. I've got a job to do here. And I've got to get it finished in a reasonable length of time."

"How long is reasonable?" His gaze centered on her mouth and his lips parted as he leaned closer. "One month? Two? Six?"

"Let me go, Byron. This is serious."

"It most certainly is." He kissed her, gently pulled her bottom lip between his teeth. And while he grazed and nibbled the already tender skin, he used his free hand to smooth a path over her hip and waist, up her ribs, and finally to her breast. Her nipple sprang instantly to rigid sensitivity and Byron chuckled against her mouth. "You are a very sexy lady."

"Enough!"

Springing away, Jade shot from the bed and rushed around to retrieve her clothes.

Byron watched her every move. "Could I recommend a nice, hot shower before you dig into your plastering or painting or whatever? You may find you've used a few muscles that were rusty. Hot water would take the ache away."

With her fragile underwear in one hand, she glowered at him. "You're so sure of yourself, aren't you? What makes you think any of my muscles would be sore just because . . . Well, just . . . Well . . ."

"Well, just because I know, that's why. And I'm into civilized behavior. So, like the gentleman I am, I'm going to go downstairs and whip up some coffee and juice and eggs and toast and whatever else I can find while you take that shower in peace."

He got out of bed and Jade quickly overcame her natural inclination to look away. Smiling at her, he moved with confident grace to pull a pair of jeans from a closet. These he stepped into. To Jade he tossed one of his shirts.

"What's this for?"

"For you. Why not be comfortable while you eat? Pretend we're on an extended, romantic weekend. Lovers doing the things lovers do."

"We're not—"

"I know that. Why not do it anyway? Then I'll leave you alone and you can go back to work." He was already heading out the door. "And if it's what you want, we'll forget this morning ever happened."

Within twenty minutes, showered, wearing her silk underwear beneath Byron's crisp, long cotton shirt, Jade padded barefoot into the kitchen.

"Dog!" she said, scandalized. "*What* are you doing?" Dog appeared to be eating the best cut of prime rib from a Wedgewood dish.

"Uh, uh, uh," Byron admonished, slathering butter on toast that looked more than slightly overdone. "No talking to my champion that way. My friend, Dog, deserves the best of everything. She has demonstrated the depth of her concern for my well-being and I intend to pay her back."

Jade had to smile. She passed Byron and removed the pot from the coffee maker. He'd put two mugs on the table and she filled them, sniffing appreciatively as she did so.

"The eggs didn't work out," Byron said. "I think I'm out of practice."

Jade replaced the coffeepot. "Television personalities probably don't get much opportunity to cook their own eggs."

He became still. "So I have been noticed—other than as a potential child molester."

"I'm sorry about that. But I don't . . . I didn't know you and I was worried about Ian."

"Your cousin," he said in an oddly constrained voice. "Somehow it's hard for me to imagine that. Will he be able to come and visit?"

"Why do you want him to?" With cream and sugar, she returned to the table.

"Like you, I'm fond of kids and he seems special. Does there have to be more reason than that?"

"You don't have any kids of your own?"

The toast he'd been carrying almost fell from the plate. He caught it just in time. "I told you I'm a widower."

"Widowers sometimes have children."

He put the plate on the table. "Intimacy really scares you. You want it—I can see that in you, feel it in you. But something happened to make you wary. Somebody must have hurt you. Who hurt you, Jade? Who made you afraid to risk getting involved with another man?"

"My husband."

He stopped, his head bowed. "Mr. Perron?"

"Mr. Perron is my father. I already told you that. I was married to a man called Doug Lyman. It didn't pan out."

She could have sworn he sighed. "Do you want to talk about that?"

"No."

"Uh-huh. That was pretty definite. Was he the son in Perron and Son? As in son-in-law?"

"No. The son is my brother, Peter."

"I see. So Peter works in the business, too."

"No. Can we drop this subject?"

Byron looked back at her. "Which one? Doug Lyman, or your brother?"

"Both. I'll talk to Aunt Muriel and see if she'll agree to let me bring Ian over."

"You will?" He straightened and smiled. "That would be great."

"What will you charge for the lessons?"

Byron frowned. "Lessons?"

"The guitar lessons. I'm going to pay for them."

A swatch of red spread over each of his cheekbones. "You won't be paying me for anything. No one will. What I do for Ian, I'll do because he's my . . . Sometimes it's good just to do something because it makes you feel good."

"But we can't—"

He grabbed her, silencing what she'd intended to say, and swung her in front of him. Bending her backward, Byron kissed her, and kissed her until she clawed his shoulders and wrenched her face away.

"You are so beautiful." He looked at her and there was no gentleness in that look. "I want you, Jade."

"No." She shook her head. "We can't do this."

"We already did. Now I want to do it again."

Her head told her that if she didn't stop him, the next weeks would be impossible.

"Give me this, Jade. Please." The green of his eyes turned dark and intense. His lips parted and he anchored her with an arm behind her back. "Will you?"

She said nothing. But neither did she make any attempt to stop him.

Shirt buttons flew and scattered on the floor. Byron sat on the edge of the kitchen table and hiked her up to sit astride his hips. He kissed her until she moaned, and worked the cups of her bra beneath her breasts until he could roll her still-tender nipples between fingers and thumbs.

"Kiss me," he ordered. A pulse at his temple throbbed visibly.

Jade kissed him, putting all the force of her own need into the taking of his mouth.

For a moment, he set her on the floor once more and she heard his zipper part. He didn't bother to remove his jeans, or her panties.

What Byron Frazer wanted, and what Jade Perron needed, was easily accomplished. He thrust her down upon him, filled her, took and gave back.

In the warm kitchen, closed in by gray fog that closed out the day, Jade wrapped her legs around Byron's waist.

It was too late to go back.

Chapter Eleven

"Shirley told me I could come up," Doug Lyman told Jade. "Why wouldn't she?"

This was absolutely the last thing she could face today. "Why *would* she? We both know I've asked you not to come here."

Blond, brown-eyed, with the same appealingly innocent air he'd had when he and Jade had been in school together, Doug spread his calloused, fisherman's hands and raised big shoulders inside one of the navy blue Guernsey sweaters she'd once found solid and comforting.

"I didn't come to argue, Jay. We've known each other a long time and—"

"Don't." She shook her head and returned to stabbing the wire-like stems of a fresh delivery of sweet Williams into a vase with a too-narrow neck.

"Come on, Jay." Doug held a black belt in wheedling. "Why keep on carrying a grudge? It's Sunday morning. The sun's shining—"

"And I suppose you just came from church and one of Reverend Alvaston's rousing sermons on brotherly love."

"*Brotherly* love wasn't what I had in mind."

Jade shot upright.

Doug actually looked abashed. "Sorry. I shouldn't have said that. You make it hard for a man to keep his mind off . . . well, we both know how I feel about you."

If she were to spend the rest of her life analyzing Doug Lyman—and she didn't intend to spend even a moment on the project if she could help it—but if she did, Jade would never comprehend the man's incredible nerve.

"Anyway," he continued. "It's such a great day I thought, why not try again? You're worth it, Jade. I'd come crawling as many times as it took if we could put the past behind us, you know that."

Jade glanced at the door—foolishly left open earlier when she carried in the vacuum stored in a cupboard at the top of the stairs. Doug had simply climbed those stairs and walked in, smiling and trying to do what he'd once done so successfully: convince her that, for him, she was the only woman who could ever truly be important.

"Where's Rose?"

Doug's smile wavered. "Downstairs with Shirley."

"Oh." Jade crossed her arms and sat on the edge of a chair. "So that's how you did it."

"You always were so suspicious. Can't you try—"

"No. I can't try anything where you're concerned. You know Shirley putters around in the shop on Sundays. And you know Shirley's a sucker for children. Particularly very sweet little children, like Rose. So you used your own daughter as a diversionary tactic. You knew Shirley wouldn't turn Rose away—"

"Jade—"

"You sure as hell knew she'd turn *you* away."

"I need you."

She felt suddenly, deeply sick. "Don't let yourself do this, Doug. You need *someone*, you don't need me. Once I hated you enough to wish for a moment like this. Now I don't hate you, I don't feel any-thing for you—except embarrassment that you'd make such a fool of yourself."

"When did you learn to be such a bitch?"

"Get out." She stood up and her knee collided with the yellow chest forcefully enough to rattle her collection of lacquered boxes. "Go now. Be good to Rose, Doug, and be grateful God gave you someone so special who'll love you regardless of what you are. I love her, too. She's important to me because she's Rose, and because you've made sure she's important to me. I want to be here for her when I can, but I'd be happy never to see your face again."

"I said I need you, dammit." He approached but Jade felt no threat. Doug might be a basic louse but he was a gentle, basic louse. He said, "This last year has been hell. I bought the new boat and I don't have to tell you the runs have been down—way down. You know how tight money is right now. I can't get the kind of loan I need to tide me over."

Slowly and heavily, her shoulders relaxed. He would always man-age to shock her. "You came to ask me to lend you money?"

"No!" He reached for her, but Jade drew back. "I'm here to ask you to . . . Give me another chance, Jay. I need you, and Rose needs you. You've just admitted it. We both need a family and you're the only one who can give us that."

"This is unbelievable!"

"Don't shout. Shirley might hear. And Rose."

"I'm not shouting. We're finished. We were finished years ago when you decided to have an affair." She wouldn't mention names. Names made it all too real again.

"A partnership is what I'm suggesting," Doug said. "Yes, I want more than a business relationship with you, and I think that'll come in time. But Art never appreciated you like he should. I'm going to give you the opportunity to become part of something that'll really be yours."

Jade studied him, uncomprehending.

"I'm going to have my own canning business one day. Lyman's will be a name that's known all over the country for canned fish. All I need is the capital—enough to get me caught up—and I'll never look back. Diversification is what counts. I've got the ideas, Jade, and you've got the money."

"You're talking about a small fortune," she said slowly.

"Don't tell me you haven't salted away a small fortune in the past few years," he said, his lips thinning.

"Since you got out of my life and stopped taking every penny that was mine for your own? Is that what you mean?"

"A wife's possessions are her husband's." His voice rose a notch. "What was yours belonged to me by right. I married you."

"My God." She could scarcely concentrate. "*You* married me? Thank you so very much. A wife's possessions are her husband's? Doug, we're out of the bloody Middle Ages, in case you haven't noticed. Go away and leave me alone. The answer is *no*. It will always be *no!*"

"It's always been good enough for your mother to let your father wear the trousers." He came a step closer. "And you've worked since you were eighteen for a man who made a partner of your brother—*when your brother doesn't even work in the business and you do*. I'm offering you a chance to *share*, Jade. I'll look after you and your name will be the one over the door."

"My name," she said softly. "You mean Perron? Jade Perron?"

He stared. "Don't be daft. You know I'm asking you to marry me again. Lyman's the name. Lyman would *be* the name. Doug Lyman. If we're married, it'll be your name, too, won't it?"

NEW TO YOU.

Byron stood on the opposite side of the narrow street and read, and reread, the red script sign over the shop with double display windows and a central door also painted red. A card wedged in the corner of one window announced that the shop was closed.

Another door stood to the left of the shop, and another to the right. Small metal crates containing empty milk bottles glinted dully in the afternoon sun.

With his hands in the pockets of his jeans, Byron crossed the road and approached the door on the left side of New to You. A name had been written on a minute piece of card and inserted into a brass-rimmed slot below the bell. Patting his jacket in search of glasses, he peered and read: *Trevay.* By the time he reached the other door, he'd located and donned the glasses. *Hill.* He considered. Yes, Jade had said she rented her flat from a woman named Hill.

Damn it all, anyway! Ian was his reason for being here and he was going to spend some time with him. He was almost sure Jade would find a way to bring him together with the boy. Even if the decision about Ian's future was Byron's to make—which it legally was not—he couldn't make that decision without weighing all the potential outcomes. It could be that helping Ian to be happier where he was would be right. It could be that stepping over a very dangerous line and telling him who he was would be more confusion than an already uprooted thirteen-year-old could take.

An image of his own father came to mind. Byron shut the man out. He was not part of who his son had become. It would be great not to remember anything about a childhood filled with people who left you. Always leaving. All the ones he'd loved, or wanted to love, always leaving him.

A victim by default, and never able to fight back because he couldn't fight someone, or for someone who wasn't around anymore.

His own history was being repeated in Ian's life, but it didn't have to keep on being repeated.

Byron turned his back on the shop and pushed the glasses, which fuzzed his distance vision, hard against the bridge of his nose. Yesterday had been heaven. And it had been hell. He'd argued for a day off, pointed out that it was Saturday. Jade had flatly told him that she couldn't afford the luxury of lazy Saturdays. They'd both attempted to work. Finally, when it had become obvious that neither of them would get anything done as long as they remained in the same space, Byron had left. When he returned—by the nine o'clock and last ferry—she'd gone.

They had to talk.

What exactly did he hope to say, and to accomplish?

Yesterday should be classified as a mistake, but who could classify such a . . . Not a mistake, just a potential disaster, a wonderful potential disaster that *had* to be handled with extreme care.

He had hurt Jade.

Byron slipped off his glasses, folded them, and turned back to the shop. His life was dedicated to mending people, not hurting them. And Jade was one of the last people he could bear to wound.

The shop door was whipped open to reveal a dun-colored woman: dun-colored braids, pale dun-colored skin, dun-colored clothes of some cotton stuff, the loose skirts of which brushed the tops of dun-colored feet in brown sandals.

"Morning." She smiled and he realized her eyes were a very pleasant shade of golden brown. "No. Afternoon. Sorry about that."

"Hi. I'm looking for—"

"You're Byron Frazer."

Even in the States, the average citizen on the street didn't recognize him. "Yes."

"Behavioral psychologist. American. Personality on the telly."

"I do appear on television."

"You don't like to be called a TV personality?"

"It always suggests a talk-show host—or maybe an evangelist. That's not really the image I hope to project."

"I suppose that's important in your line of work? Image?"

He probably should ask who she was. "Trust is probably the issue more than image."

She seemed to consider that. "Doesn't fit," she said in a preoccupied tone.

"I beg your pardon."

"I don't very often make mistakes. Of course, I hadn't met you. Have you suffered a great deal from the jealousy of others?"

Byron experienced a rare and total blank.

"A leader," the woman said. "Yes, of course. And easily upset and excitable. Very concerned with the opinions others form of you."

He collected himself. "This is all very interesting. Are you, by any chance, Miss Hill?"

"Mrs. Hill." Her eyes cleared. "Shirley to my friends, and you qualify. I expect you're looking for Jade."

He experienced an odd discomfort which quickly perished. In this town, everyone knew everyone else. He'd already discovered that his presence had been noted. No doubt it was also common knowledge that Jade Perron was working at Ferryneath.

"Did you want to see Jade?" Shirley thrust her chin forward inquiringly.

"Well—yes." Jade had left him in no doubt that she would not appreciate any suggestion of a personal relationship between them. "I want to talk to her about the cottage. Is she in, perhaps?"

Shirley sighed hugely. "Oh, yes. Very rarely anywhere else unless she's working. It's about time that girl had herself some fun, Dr. Frazer."

"Byron."

"Byron. Jade's very beautiful, you know."

He barely stopped himself from effusive agreement. "An attractive woman, yes."

Shirley Hill's brown eyes became sharp. "Yes, well. Go on through the shop and into the storeroom at the back. You'll find Jade upstairs."

"Thank you." He waited for her to stand aside, then passed into the shop's dim interior. "Interesting business. Different stock all the time, I suppose."

Shirley closed the door again. "Everything in this shop has a story to tell," she said seriously. "Some of them have many."

Byron murmured concurrence and moved on purposefully to the back of the showroom.

"Was this an impulse?" Shirley said.

"An impulse?" He'd entered a windowless room crammed with boxes of every shape and size.

"Picking up and leaving the States? Coming here? Did you get a sudden urge to get away from your surroundings and examine your soul in a distant land?"

He opened his mouth to say no. "Ah . . . Yes, in a way. Yes, I suppose you could say that." A lucky guess on her part, but he couldn't deny that she'd come close to the truth. "Thank you for letting me in." She didn't exhibit signs of substance abuse—at least none that he'd noted.

Partway up the stairs, Byron paused. From above came the sound of a man's rumbling voice. He leaned against the wall and felt foolish. There had been an instant, vaguely jealous and decidedly possessive flare in response to those masculine tones.

He had no right to feel possessive of Jade Perron.

But he did.

Jade had a father and a brother and probably other relatives and friends who didn't qualify as romantic interests. Hell! He knew better than anyone that she hadn't been close—not *close* close to a man in a long time.

How did he know?

He just did. And anyway, she'd said as much.

Would she be embarrassed by his arrival?

A contrary burst of determination propelled Byron upward. He intended to spend a lot more time with Jade. She could try to resist him, but he could be one very determined man. No, he didn't know where it would lead and, yes, he acknowledged it might be a long time before they . . . If he didn't cool it, she'd probably find a way to avoid him altogether and that wasn't what he wanted. He wanted to at least find out what he wanted.

And he wanted her to trust him enough to bring Ian to Ferry-neath. For now he refused to address the potential problems presented by her relationship by adoption to Ian Spring, or by whatever her reaction might be to discovering what had brought Byron to England in the first place.

At the top of the stairs was a short hallway. A door with two pebbled-glass panels stood ajar at the other end. His tennis shoes making no sound, Byron walked on.

"You spoil her, Jade," the male voice said. "Five-year-old girls don't need a pound to spend on sweets."

Reminding himself that Shirley Hill had told him to go ahead and see Jade, Byron tapped a glass panel.

"Come in, Shirley," Jade said.

Byron pushed open the door. "Not Shirley, I'm afraid. Hi, Jade. Is it okay if I come in?" Even as he spoke, he advanced into a room the color of the sunshine outside.

Jade wore a red scarf over her hair. The tails of a red-and-white-checked shirt were tied in front—exposing several inches of smooth, bare midriff above tight, oft-washed jeans. Her feet were bare and a vacuum parked near a rattan chair covered with yellow cushions suggested Sunday was housework day.

She looked absolutely wonderful.

He'd like to pull her into his arms right now . . . and that was only the beginning of what he'd like.

She also looked as if someone had just dropped ice down her back.

Byron smiled engagingly and turned his attention to the room's other occupants. A tall, broad-shouldered man with blond hair stood there. He held Rose's hand. Rose looked at Byron and raised her shoulders to her ears. She grinned, showing a gap in her teeth, and glowed as if seeing him was a special treat. Then she looked from Jade to the man, and pure, innocent delight lit her eyes. In the palm of her free hand she displayed a shiny pound coin.

The child eyed her prize and then checked for Byron's reaction. He made suitably round and approving eyes, and said, "Hi, there, Rose. Lucky you."

The man promptly pulled the child closer and settled a protective hand on her mop of curly black hair. His expression sent only one message. He hated Byron on sight.

"Hi. I'm Byron Frazer." He shot out a hand, which the man eventually held and instantly released. "I came to have a few words with Jade."

"What about?" The tone matched the glare.

Some men could smile and acknowledge the potential for hate at the same time. Byron smiled. "It's personal." He kept his voice soft, his engaging grin in place.

"Jade doesn't have any secrets—"

"Doug!" She appeared to have just remembered she was alive. "Doug, thanks for bringing Rose by. Good luck with . . . Well, good luck."

"I'm Doug Lyman," the man said.

The ex-husband. "Good to meet you." Even honest men sometimes lied in the name of civilized behavior.

"You're over at Ferryneath."

He barely smothered a groan. "So much for peace and anonymity in a quaint Cornish town. I'm staying at Ferryneath, yes."

"That was something else I wanted to talk to you about," Lyman said to Jade. "Word has it you're working over there on your own."

"I almost always work alone." She played with the lapel of her shirt.

"You need to look out for things like that," Lyman said. "Working alone in a house with a man. I don't like it."

Byron watched Jade's face turn even paler than usual. She inclined her head toward Rose. "This isn't the time, Doug. Please be careful on the stairs."

"What's he here for?" Lyman spoke as if Byron were deaf . . . or dead. "People are already talking."

He heard a snapping sound and saw a flower stem fracture between Jade's fingers. Coming had been a bad idea.

Jade walked behind Doug Lyman and opened the door wide. "You watch how you go, Rose. Daddys can be clumsy sometimes."

Lyman stared at Byron. For the first time in his life he knew he was confronted by a man who had picked him out as a threat to his relationship with a woman.

Divorced or not, Doug Lyman still regarded Jade as his.

"Can we go to buy sweeties, Daddys?" the child asked.

Jade stooped quickly and hugged Rose. "Don't you spend all that on sweeties at once, snippet. You'll get a tummyache."

Lyman collected himself and turned his attention to his daughter. "Daddy will take care of his girl, won't he, pet? We'll go and buy some of those Smarties© you like. How would you like it if we put the change in your pig? Then we can pop up the sweet shop lots of times."

Rose nodded. "Can we have chips with our dinner?"

"Chips with dinner, it is." Without another word, Lyman led the girl from the room and down the stairs.

When the sound of their footsteps had entirely faded, Jade flopped onto the couch, rested her head back, and closed her eyes.

"Mr. Lyman wasn't pleased to see me," Byron said. The tense set of her face loaded him with guilt. "Does that matter?"

"You shouldn't have come here."

He spread his feet. "I asked if it mattered that your ex-husband disliked seeing another man visit you."

Her eyes opened. "What does or doesn't matter to me," she said in an even voice that didn't fool him into a second of comfort, "is none of your business. Anything about me is none of your business. It's none of anyone's business but mine."

"True," he said. "Sorry. Rose is such a little sweetheart."

"She is." Jade's expression became closed.

Byron thought about the child, about her dark curly hair and pale skin, and screwed up his eyes. "Five, you said."

"No, I didn't say. You must have overheard."

Jade had been divorced more than five years. "She has her father's eyes." The timing of her divorce didn't have to mean a thing. "Mm."

But where did the black curls and pale skin come from? Byron discarded his line of thought. Jade wasn't the only woman with that coloring.

"Does Lyman's wife approve of him behaving like a possessive husband with you?"

Her stare made him wish he'd kept his mouth shut.

"Doug doesn't have a wife."

He could just come out and ask if Rose was her daughter. No, he couldn't. And whether she was or wasn't had nothing to do with Byron's involvement with Jade.

"I'm going to arrange for someone else to finish Ferryneath," Jade said.

His heart did something decidedly nasty—and so did his stomach. "Why?"

Jade pushed to the edge of the couch and stood up. She advanced upon him until they stood close enough for Byron to see the fascinating violet halos around the pupils of her eyes.

"I'm not playing any more games with you, Byron."

"Have we been playing games? Is that what we did?"

"You heard what I said. No games. What you're doing now is definitely a form of game playing. You ask me why I'm getting someone else to work at Ferryneath and I'm supposed to say you know why. Then you'll say 'Trust me,' or something equally original, and I'll be supposed to solemnly ask if you think you can trust yourself—or maybe I'm supposed to say I'm not sure I can trust *myself*. And so the game goes on until you get what you want."

"Do you trust yourself?"

"Yes." She dragged the scarf from her hair. "Of course I do."

"Then what's the problem? I didn't rape you, Jade."

"Oh." Her throat moved convulsively. "I . . . What a horrible thing to say. You were the one who started what happened."

"I never forced you."

She pressed the scarf to her mouth and shook her head.

Byron knew a moment's utter self-disgust. "But I did start it, Jade. You're right. Please don't . . . Don't feel badly about what we did. That's why I came, to tell you I wouldn't change a thing about being with you, except knowing that you were going to have a hard time with it afterwards."

"I don't want to talk about this."

He knew he mustn't try to touch her. "Okay. We won't, only please don't cut off something that might bring us both a lot of happiness."

"Happiness?" Her eyes glistened with tears. "I enjoyed being with you. I'm not going to pretend I didn't. But I'm not the kind of woman who goes to bed with a man she hardly knows. I shouldn't have done that."

She didn't have to tell him how much she'd enjoyed him, and herself *with* him. "We didn't just go to bed, as you put it," he reminded her. "Sweetheart, you and I made spectacular love in more places than bed."

Jade covered her ears. *"Don't* say that."

He did reach for her then, and she whirled away.

"Okay. For a man who makes his living saying the right things, or trying to say the right things, I'm making a hash of this. I came to tell you I don't regret making love yesterday, but I do regret that as a result of what I caused, you feel in an untenable position." And now he sounded like a legal argument. "You have my word that I won't put a finger on you again if you don't invite me to do so, Jade. Please carry on with the job you've started. If you suddenly insist on turning it over to someone else, you may do exactly what you don't want to do."

"Which is?" She raised her chin in a defiant gesture that made Byron feel better.

"You could cause more rumors of the kind your husband mentioned."

"*Ex*-husband," she said with enough vehemence to bring Byron a real surge of good cheer. "And I don't give a damn what people say about me."

"I doubt that. Anyway, there's nothing to fear from good old, well-behaved Byron anymore. The other reason I came was to ask if you could arrange with Miss Cadwen for Ian to come over after school tomorrow. He called me and sounded pretty down." And Byron had barely contained himself from rushing over to Muriel Cadwen's house to claim his son. Then sanity had returned and he acknowledged he had no right to do any such thing . . . yet.

"It won't work," Jade said.

"Yes it will. The boy needs to be around a man who understands the things that interest him." Even without the obligation Byron felt, he was very qualified to know what the lack of caring male influence could do to a boy.

"I wasn't talking about Ian. It won't work for you and me to try pretending yesterday never happened."

"I don't have any intention of pretending it didn't happen." He would not lie to Jade. "Wonderful things don't happen often enough and I'm not about to toss one aside. But I've got plenty of willpower. It's something I've had to have in my life. Like I already

135

told you, we won't make love again until you let me know it's what you want."

"Until?"

"Okay, unless. Is that better? Is it okay?" He bowed, bringing his face a little closer. "I'm a trustworthy man. If you don't believe me, you can get plenty of references."

"You make it sound as if it's only a matter of time before . . . You talk as if we will be lovers again when I come to my senses."

He grinned. "Something like that. But I also admit I've been known to be wrong. At least, I probably was once."

She let him coax a smile from her. "I don't think I should work at the cottage again."

"I do."

"I don't."

"My sexual magnetism is so strong you won't be able to resist me? Understandable."

She cocked her head. Her hair was tied in a ponytail, leaving her vulnerably slender neck very exposed. Byron's eyes fell to the dip behind her left collarbone, where the shirt lapel lay open to a trace of bra strap—red bra strap. He swallowed.

"Can we give it another try? With you working at Ferryneath, I mean?" Byron used his best, reasonable tone.

"I'm not sure. What if the try fails?"

A stimulating thought. "We won't let it. Please, Jade. I'm going to feel so responsible if you have to change plans you made a year ago."

She slipped the splayed fingers of one hand inside the neck of her blouse.

Byron followed the gesture and remembered her breasts, naked in the silver light of a foggy morning, dusky, uptilted nipples springing hard from such silken, white skin.

"I think you should go and speak to Aunt Muriel yourself."

Byron blinked and met her eyes. "Why would I do that?"

"Because she's Ian's legal guardian and she's the one to make decisions about him."

"Jade." *He must not touch her.* "I'll be happy to go to Miss Cadwen if you'll come with me."

She crouched to stroke Dog, who had slept throughout on a braided rug before the empty fireplace. "You don't need me, or anyone, Byron. You're a very self-assured man."

He could correct her. He could say that he was a very self-assured man on the outside and to some extent on the inside—but only to some extent. "Will you come anyway?"

For a moment he thought she'd refuse. But she dropped to sit cross-legged beside Dog and sent Byron a wry look. "You are very persuasive, Byron Frazer. No wonder you're such a success as a psychologist. All right. I'll come with you to Aunt Muriel's."

"Tomorrow?"

"Well—"

"Ian really sounded needy."

"Aunt Muriel is a kind woman." There was more than a hint of defensiveness in Jade's voice. "She's doing the best she can. There has to be a time of adjustment—for both of them."

"Of course. You're absolutely right. But tomorrow will work for you? We can go over on the ferry together and bring him back." He didn't miss the pursing of her lips. "I'll probably be out a good deal of the day—while you're working—but I'll get back in time to come over to Fowey. Then I'll be busy with Ian and you can get on with things again."

"I ought to refuse."

"But you won't."

"I . . . won't." Jade bounced to her feet. "I'll see how it goes, Byron. But I meant it about . . . Well, I meant what I said."

"So did I." And he remembered what he'd said, and what he hadn't exactly said. He didn't want to leave her now, but she showed no sign of encouraging him to stay. "I'd better let you get back to whatever you were doing, then?"

"Yes. Is Shirley still in the shop?"

Byron shook his head. "I don't know."

"I'll see you out and lock the door."

He followed her downstairs, searching for some way to prolong the visit.

Shirley Hill's face, popping into the storeroom, squelched any hope of inspiration. "There you are," she said. "Sorry about Doug, Jade. Rose is such a little darling and—"

"And we both love kiddies," Jade told her. "Don't be sorry. Doug isn't a problem."

Something in the exchange brought Byron satisfaction. Doug Lyman wasn't a popular visitor in these parts.

"Are you going out?" Hope shimmered in Shirley's eyes and in her trilled words. "Readymoney Cove is lovely on a day like this."

"The dust in my flat isn't lovely on a day like this," Jade said. "And I'm sure Dr. Frazer has things he needs to attend to."

The dismissal was there. He wouldn't push again today. Jade saw him to the door and stood there, her arms wrapped around her bare middle, as he stepped onto the sidewalk.

"Enjoy your dusting," he told her.

"I will."

"I'll see you tomorrow, then?" he risked asking.

"Yes."

He looked at her and couldn't manage a smile. "Goodbye, Jade."

"Yes."

Shirley's face appeared yet again, this time from behind Jade's head. "Byron," she said, sounding breathless. "When's your birthday?"

He glanced at Jade, who gave no hint as to how he should react. "November second. Why?"

Shirley let out a shriek of delighted laughter. "I was right in the first place. Toodles, Byron." Dismissing him, she began to pull Jade back into the shop. "This is perfect. What did I tell you? Ooh, exactly right. Dark. Deep. Black and red. They thrive on passion. But you've got to watch out for anger, mind you. The temper can be a challenge. Willful, very willful. That often needs taking under control."

The last word that Byron heard before the door shut was ". . . Scorpio."

Chapter Twelve

Like two honor guards, china dalmatians flanked an oak case clock on the high mantel in Aunt Muriel's parlor.

The only sound in the room, the clock's ticking grew louder and louder, or so it seemed to Jade.

She watched the brass second hand flick rhythmically on its way around the steel face.

Aunt Muriel sighed loudly, and from the corner of her eye, Jade saw her aunt uncross her sensible brown brogues and recross them in the opposite direction.

Outside, the temperature had climbed close to seventy degrees, but a dispirited fire stroked flames over the blackened firebox.

Byron coughed. He sat beside Jade on an overstuffed couch covered with dark green crushed velvet splotched with brown peonies.

At Jade's suggestion they'd arrived early at the terrace house in Fowey. Her idea had been to deal with any awkwardness between Aunt Muriel and Byron before Ian got home. So much for careful plans.

"Nice clock," Byron said.

Jade stuffed down the laugh that rose in her throat.

"Thank you," Aunt Muriel said. "They gave it to me when I retired . . . from the library."

Silence slithered in to settle between the ticking once more.

"Will you have more tea?" Aunt Muriel asked.

"No, thank you," Byron and Jade responded in unison, and laughed uncomfortably.

"Your hanging baskets are great," Byron said.

"In front?" Aunt Muriel, kept her eyes on folded hands in her lap.

"Yes," Byron said. "The begonias are . . . they're really something. You must have a green thumb. And your roses are wonderful. Very therapeutic, gardening. Many of my patients take it up."

Jade caught her bottom lip between her teeth and stole a glance at Aunt Muriel, who didn't "hold" with people telling their "personal trials" to strangers. To Aunt Muriel, all members of the psychiatric community were classified as strangers.

"It certainly is a comfort to me," Aunt Muriel said, shocking Jade with the first deviation from expected behavior she ever remembered in this woman. "I expect you deal with a lot of troubled souls. Sort of like a minister, aren't you?"

Jade's mouth twitched. This time she looked at Byron. "Is that how your patients view you, Byron? As a spiritual leader?"

He did not appear amused. "Your aunt's choice of words was quite appropriate. My job is to minister to people—to families— who feel they've gotten a bit lost. Or to people who've found parts of themselves they thought they'd lost and who don't like what they've been forced to look at. What time will Ian be home, Miss Cadwen?"

She raised her arched red brows even closer to her hairline and checked the clock. "He's usually here by three-thirty at the latest." There was another sigh. "But you can never tell. He hasn't had a lot of guidance, Dr. Frazer. Ada, my dear departed sister, was a gentle woman. Soft, some might say, but I always thought of Ada as having a deep strength. Anyway, she was widowed a few years back and I can only think she let the boy run wild. He just doesn't understand the things a nice English boy understands by the time he's thirteen."

"He does know we're coming?" Byron said.

Aunt Muriel leaned over the arm of her chair and rummaged for something Jade couldn't see.

"I don't hold with getting children excited," she said, surfacing with a large skein of peachy orange wool, a pair of knitting needles, and part of a garment. "Best not let them spend too much time thinking about things, if you know what I mean."

"You didn't tell him we were coming."

"No." Aunt Muriel consulted a dog-eared knitting pattern for several seconds before driving a needle ferociously through a loop and springing into rapid action.

In the ensuing seconds, the nerve-destroying squidge, squidge of nylon-covered metal obliterated the clock's ticking.

Jade glanced around at the high sideboard with its long, embroidered white runner, at the chairs that matched the sofa upon which she and Byron sat, at an ancient player piano in a recess beside the fireplace, and finally, at a drop-leaf table buttressing one wall. Showcased on the table was a pink glass bowl filled with plastic fruit.

Over all hung the aroma of old dust anchored to wooden surfaces with lavender wax.

Byron shifted forward on the couch. "I do want you to understand that I believe it may do Ian some good to spend time with a fellow American."

The needles stilled. "Ian's English now, or he will be just as soon as we can arrange to have him naturalized."

White formed along Byron's clenching knuckles, startling Jade. "Ian's decided he wants to take British citizenship?" Byron asked.

Something in his tone grabbed Jade's attention. She watched him covertly, noting a small twitch in the muscle beside his mouth and the tension in his compressed lips.

"Some things have to be decided for children until they're old enough to decide for themselves. When Ian's twenty-one, he can do as he pleases. Of course, by then he'll be proud to have embraced his mother's country."

"What about his father's country?" Byron's mild delivery didn't deceive Jade. There was something here that troubled him deeply.

"He doesn't have a father anymore," Muriel said, yanking out yarn from the skein like a fireman about to attack a major blaze.

"No, and I'm sorry both the Springs died." Byron raked his fingers up and down his thighs. "I don't have a father or mother anymore either. That doesn't mean I cease to be an American."

Jade caught Byron's eye and shook her head slightly. Antagonizing Aunt Muriel wasn't the way to help Ian.

"This is his country now." Aunt Muriel sounded stubborn. "He'll grow up here and go into a trade here and this is where he'll want to owe his allegiance."

"You sound very committed to the boy," Byron said.

"One does what one's duty demands."

"Even if the duty is onerous?"

Aunt Muriel clicked away with freshened fury. "Ian's a good enough boy. And he was my sister's. She loved him and it's my responsibility to love him, too."

Jade's eyes stung. Byron Frazer wouldn't understand, but this woman, with her clumsy, ungracious turn of phrase, had the gentlest heart Jade had ever encountered. Through all Jade's growing years, it had been Aunt Muriel to whom she had turned and Aunt Muriel who somehow managed to fill May Perron's slot without ever criticizing the sister she loved.

"Do American boys do a lot of this guitar playing, then?"

"Playing an instrument's a valuable accomplishment for any boy or girl—or man or woman—regardless of where they come from."

"Mm." Aunt Muriel fished beside her chair once more and pulled aloft a skein of brown yarn. "I always liked my pianola, I must say." She laughed with an unexpectedly young abandon that had the power to make others laugh. "The pianola was my mother's. She gave it to me because she said a girl with ten thumbs might do quite well on the pianola. Ten thumbs and a tin ear."

"You don't like music?"

"I *love* it." Bright blue eyes cast a reproachful glance in Byron's direction. "I can't paint, but that doesn't mean I don't enjoy beautiful pictures. And I can't act, but I'd travel miles to see a good play."

"Point taken." Byron looked at Jade. "Jade has said she'll be responsible for making sure Ian gets home each time he comes. All he'll have to do is get on the ferry. I'll meet him at the other side."

"Why would you go to so much trouble for a boy you don't know?"

Jade, still looking at Byron, saw his eyes fix and become distant. "Let's just say I've always had a nose for need." He gave a short laugh. "And maybe I've got an overdeveloped sense of responsibility, too."

"You're not responsible for Ian. I am."

"Ian's still trying to adjust," Jade said. "It'll make it easier on you if he's got something he likes doing to divert him, Auntie. It's going to mean I can get to know him a bit better, too. He's a member of the family, after all."

"Yes, he is," Aunt Muriel said with a determined pushing back of her shoulders. "One of our own. And we look after our own, don't we, Jade?"

"We certainly do."

"But you think this guitar business will be all right?" Aunt Muriel said. She was much more disturbed than she wanted anyone to know.

"Absolutely," Jade told her. "Byron's very good with young people."

Jade drew in a breath and let it out slowly. How did she know how good Byron was or wasn't with children? She didn't. And she could scarcely believe she was pleading his case.

Why did he want to spend time with Ian?

Were there people who just responded to perceived need?

"All right, then," Aunt Muriel said. "If it's all right with you, Jade, then it's all right with me. Ian can go."

"It'll be good for him," Jade heard herself say before the enormity of the situation made itself felt.

She was sitting here, inches from the only man who had made her feel totally female in as long as she could remember, if it had ever happened before at all. Byron had the power to breathe life into her—emotionally and sexually—yet she knew she must keep her distance from him. At the same time she felt at some deep level that he was a kind, good man who wanted to help Ian and who would be a positive influence on him.

Crazy.

"Do you think he'll like this?" Tentativeness had crept into Aunt Muriel's voice. She displayed what was evidently the front of a V-necked sweater. "The colors are nice, don't you think, Dr. Frazer?"

"Oh—very nice," Byron said.

The sweater was a monstrosity, a large version of a child's garment which, even then, would be more appropriate for a girl.

"I thought the little trees in the border were boyish." She fingered a row of small, billowy brown trees that ran along the neck and the hem of the sweater front. "He doesn't have a single hand-knitted jumper. Can you imagine that? I always thought it showed people cared—hand-knitted things. I don't want you to think I blame Ada, I don't. She must have had her hands full, poor love."

Byron and Jade murmured simultaneously.

The front door slammed.

"There he is now," Muriel said and Jade didn't miss the anticipation in the woman's face and movements. "He'll need to have some tea before he goes."

145

"He can eat with me," Byron said.

Footsteps went slowly past the parlor door.

"Yoo, hoo!" Aunt Muriel called. "In the parlor, Ian!"

After a pause, the footsteps returned and Ian came into the room.

"Take off your shoes," Aunt Muriel ordered, frowning at Ian's perfectly clean, highly polished black shoes.

He did as he'd been told, but not before he returned Jade's smile and cast a cautiously pleased look at Byron.

"Your cousin Jade, and Dr. Frazer, have been kind enough to take an interest in you. What do you say?"

Ian finished pulling off his shoes and screwed up his eyes. "Thank you?" he said uncertainly.

"I should think so. Come here a minute. I want to hold this up to you."

A bright red flush stole up the boy's neck and over his cheeks. He went obediently to stand before Aunt Muriel.

She tugged him down on his knees and pinned the sweater front to the shoulders of his T-shirt. "Oh, look at that. It's going to be perfect. Oh, I'll see if I can get it done by Sunday so you can wear it to church. Wait till Effie Harding sees it. She'll be wanting to borrow the pattern to do up for her son's boy."

Jade got up in a rush. "Look at the time. I've got to get back to work." And she had to get away from this painfully embarrassing scene.

"Run along with you, then," Aunt Muriel said, unpinning Ian. "Don't forget your instrument."

"No, Aunt," Ian said, backing away.

"Tie those shoes properly before you go out. I don't want you falling over and breaking something."

"No, Aunt."

Aunt Muriel got up and followed the boy into the hallway with its ivory on ivory flocked paper above shiny brown-painted wainscotting. "And mind your manners. Be sure to say thank you to Dr. Frazer and your cousin Jade."

"I will."

When his shoes were firmly double-knotted and he stood by the door with Byron and Jade, Aunt Muriel approached, tutting, and produced a jacket made of shiny purple nylon with white sleeves and VIKINGS written across the front in white. "Put this dreadful thing on," she said, holding it out. "As soon as I can manage it, we'll have to get you something more suitable. You look like one of those awful gang members in one of those American films."

Wordlessly, Ian took the jacket and shrugged it on.

"That hair needs a good cutting. Effie's girl does hair cutting at home. Effie says it costs less than half what they charge in the real shops. I wouldn't know about these things. I've done my own for years." She plumped her tight curls with the palm of a hand. "I suppose I could cut a boy's hair, too."

"Don't you worry, Auntie," Jade said, her stomach turning at the trapped look in Ian's brown eyes. "I'll make sure he gets a haircut. You've got enough to do."

"I'm not complaining about that," Aunt Muriel said. "One does one's duty."

Byron smiled at Aunt Muriel. "You certainly do, Miss Cadwen. More than your duty. You're a very kind woman." He sounded kind, gentle, and Jade's eyes stung yet again.

Aunt Muriel flapped a hand in dismissal, but her pleasure showed.

At last, with Ian ahead, guitar case in hand, Jade fell in beside Byron to walk down the front garden path.

Muriel waved from the doorway. "Watch how you go, mind. And remember what I said about not making a nuisance of yourself."

"I'll bring him back when I come," Jade said, hastening her pace. "Don't worry about him."

"I can't help worrying. Boys and trouble go together. You should hear Effie Harding's stories about her William when he was a youngster. Worries you to death to think about it."

"Ian will be fine, Miss Cadwen," Byron said, his voice far too level.

"Don't stand at the edge on that wretched ferry, mind. There was a boy did that some years back. Fell. Hit his head on the deck on the way and drowned before anyone could get to him."

"He won't stand too close to the edge, Miss Cadwen."

"It'll be cold when you come back. Do up that coat, mind. We don't want you catching a cold."

Behind Ian and in front of Byron, Jade walked toward the corner of the street.

Ian stared straight ahead.

"Ian," Jade said. "Are you all right?"

He turned his face halfway toward her and away again, but not before she saw the trembling of his mouth and the tears that filmed his eyes. "She's a nice lady," he said very quietly.

Chapter Thirteen

"**G**o for it!" Byron stopped playing and watched Ian. The boy smiled up from his bowed posture over his guitar, his face old and young at the same time. He sang about a gambler and laughed as his voice cracked. "Dang! It goes up. It goes down. Can't do anything about it."

"Sounds perfect Country and Western form, to me," Byron said loudly.

There was no music Ian didn't like to play. In the two hours that had fled since they'd arrived at the cottage, they'd swung into popular pieces and fallen just as easily into Bach and Vivaldi. Whereas Byron played with self-taught adequacy and the results of a lot of help from a friend, Ian was inspired with the confidence that came from a combination of talent and training.

Ian narrowed his eyes and began a rapid run. With his head inclined to his guitar, it was the old, knowledgeable face that took precedence over the young.

"What is that?" Byron asked.

"Falla. Spanish Dance." Faster and faster his fingers moved. "Mr. Benetti taught me to love this."

Mr. Benetti, Byron had already decided, must have quickly seen the wonderful raw material he had in his pupil. And the Springs had done the very best they could for their boy.

The short piece ended with a flourish. "You like it?"

"I like it." Byron picked a few notes. "I can't teach you anything, Ian. You know that, don't you?"

"Playing is learning. Being here gives me a chance to play. And you understand."

It wasn't necessary to ask what it was that Byron understood.

"Come and play whenever you can. Perhaps you can teach me." And perhaps they could learn together—and the subjects would be more varied than Ian could possibly imagine at this moment.

"Nah. You're good," Ian said.

Unabashed, Byron said, "More enthusiastic than good," and they both laughed.

He was digging a hole with smooth sides. And it was getting deeper and deeper. *Just take a look. Make sure he's all right, then duck out.* Ian was all right, wasn't he? He was starting to adjust?

Was Byron all right himself?

"Fogelberg?" Ian asked, pausing and beating out a staccato rhythm on the sounding board of his old guitar.

"Uh-huh."

"Yeah," Ian said. "D'you know his stuff?"

"Some of it."

" 'Leader of the Band'?" The boy's long, capable fingers stroked a chord. "D'you know it?"

Why that? "I know it." Every word, and every word still made him jealous of the man who wrote the song.

Ian led the way and Byron followed, until he could fade out without Ian noticing. The child/man's voice climbed and fell, unselfconscious now that he'd forgotten Byron.

They had a lot in common, the boy and the man; both denied the opportunity to imitate a man whose blood ran in their veins and whom they could trust never to desert them.

The boy played on, all the anxiety rubbed from his face—a face so like Lori's.

Byron propped his guitar on one knee. If he'd been able to see into the future back then, just before Ian was born, how different might his life have been now?

Lori . . .

"I feel like an elephant!" Lori said, rolling her brown eyes.

"An elephant in very early pregnancy." Byron chuckled and handed her a glass of milk. "Elephants are pregnant for nine years."

"Baloney!"

"Two years?"

"I don't know, but it isn't nine years."

Byron sat on the fake leather ottoman she'd pushed away from her feet, and scooted between her knees. "Does it matter? You look beautiful, Lori. Pregnancy suits you."

The smile faded from her face. "You're so good to me."

"I love you."

He waited, waited for the words. "I know you do," she said. "I'll always thank you for that."

And that was as good as it ever got now. But he could ask the question, take a risk on her answer.

No, he couldn't. He'd settle for the sweet-sad words they exchanged before they slept: "There's nothing I won't do for you."

The old apartment was stiflingly hot. He ought to be able to do better than this for her. She deserved it. She'd had so little, but she never complained.

"Do you wonder what she'll look like?" he asked.

"She?" Lori shifted, pushing her hips forward to make more room for her swollen belly. "Any daughter of mine would have the self-respect to make sure she entered the world gracefully—not like a whale. This is a whale. A boy if ever I met one."

Byron settled his hands over the shifting humps and bumps of the baby. "I hope it is a girl." He felt an elbow, or a knee—a bottom. "She's running out of room in there."

"Why do you hope it's a girl?"

"Because she'll look like you and I'll like that."

"Oh, Byron." Letting herself slip awkwardly back to lie against the couch, Lori looked at the ceiling. *"You've been wonderful. And I know this hasn't been an easy time."*

"I love you." Why couldn't he stop telling her?

"I know. But I've made things difficult for you."

"We've made things difficult for us. We went into this together, remember?"

Lori reached for his hand. *"Will you promise me something?"*

"No."

"Byron—"

"We've been over all this before, Lori. Nothing's going to change. And nothing's going to go wrong."

She sighed. *"You won't face reality, will you?"*

Byron kept on smiling. *"What do you think she'll like to do after she's born?"*

"He'll be just like any other little boy, I guess. Trucks and Lego—and music, of course. You'll make sure of that. Two of you on the guitar."

Byron saw a picture, himself a few years older, and a boy—who looked exactly like Lori—seated beside him. They were playing guitars and the boy laughed a lot. And soon the boy was older and he still laughed, only now he played the guitar better than his father.

"We'll do things together," he said, feeling almost guilty that his dream had excluded Lori. *"The three of us—"*

"Byron, I can't go on pretending. We've got to face the truth."

"No! No, we don't. Only the truth as I—as we choose to write it. Everything will be fine."

"I shouldn't have brought this on you. You, of all people."

He forced himself to laugh and moved to sit beside her. *"Things happen. You didn't do it on your own, sweetheart."*

"You've had to fight so hard for everything you've got. You've earned the right to what you want. Promise me, Byron. Promise me that whatever happens, you won't let . . . We can't let our consciences rule us."

"Will you be quiet?" He gathered her clumsily into his arms and smoothed her soft, fair hair. *"None of this has to be said, Lori. We're going to be fine."* If he had a soul, it must be what ached and pressed so heavily on his heart.

"If something happens. And if you do change your mind about . . . about wanting to . . . Byron, I won't ever blame you. Say you believe me."

"I don't want to talk about this."

"Byron"—she sounded desperate—"I don't think it's going to be long."

He sat up straight and stared at her. *"Something's happening? It isn't time."*

She smiled. *"Don't be so textbook male-not-in-control. Please, I . . ."* Her body clenched. He felt it, felt her swept by a force neither of them could control. *"Do not sacrifice yourself. No one would expect it of you, or blame you for deciding to put yourself first. Say it. Say you'll opt out the minute you don't think you can handle it."*

He'd never made the promise. In the hours that followed, when Lori went into labor and delivered Ian, he'd steadfastly insisted he could cope with whatever came.

And then, in the end, when the worst imaginable disaster had occurred, he'd taken the coward's way out and fled. Byron Frazer had succumbed to self-pity and panic and turned his back on the only remaining person in the world who needed him: Ian Frazer, aged two days and a motherless child.

At the foot of the stairs, Jade stopped. She remembered Dog and the hammer she carried just in time to remove the potential noise hazard from the animal's teeth.

"Hush," she whispered, pushing Dog's scrawny rump to the floor. "Sit and stay."

Since returning from Fowey, she'd been putting the finishing touches on the plasterwork between the bedroom beams. And while she'd worked, she'd listened, mesmerized, to the music that soared upward from the sitting room.

The latest piece drew to a close.

"How did you know you wanted to play?" Byron asked. "First wanted to play, that is."

"I don't know. I always did, that's all."

For several seconds, only the sound of odd notes played with a pick broke the silence.

"My dad used to say I probably came into the world singing and playing something or other."

Jade could tell that one guitar had dropped out.

"I was adopted."

After a short silence Byron asked, "Was that okay?" and added, "I mean, do you feel okay about that?"

"I guess so."

"You're not sure? Those are feelings you need to look at, Ian. Are you angry your . . . Do you wonder about your real parents?"

"Some. My mom always said she was pretty real herself. Then she'd laugh. I think it bothered my mom more than it did me because she was always afraid I felt . . . I don't know . . . like I was missing something."

"And did you?"

The psychologist at work, Jade thought. He really did care about people. She squeezed her eyes shut. What was she going to do about the snare into which she was being pulled . . . or pushing herself?

"My folks were real good to me. I miss them." Ian's voice sounded tight, as if he was deliberately holding it in place. "But I do wonder who they were—my other parents, I mean. Dad wouldn't talk about them. But Mom used to say they gave me away because they couldn't give me what I needed. And she said that made them brave because it's the hardest thing in the world to give up your child.

"I guess I'd like to know why it was too hard for them to have me with them. Then it'd all be okay."

"It would probably help."

"Yeah," Ian said. "Maybe they were poor. Or sick or something. Or maybe they already had too many kids."

"Maybe," Byron said. "But it wasn't because they didn't love you . . . You do believe they did what they did for your sake, don't you?"

"I guess."

The music began again. And it was Byron's voice that sang the words in a gravelly bass that was wonderful to Jade's ears because it was his.

She held the back of a hand to her mouth. Whatever happened, there would never be a honeysuckle springtime or a moonlit night in early June that didn't play the memory of Byron's voice—singing or laughing—and show her again his image.

Dog, who hadn't progressed past basic obedience class, forgot the instruction to stay and trotted into the sitting room before Jade could stop her.

Jade followed and stood just inside the door feeling like an interloper.

"Hi, Jade," Ian said. "She's a neat dog." Dog had gone to sit at his knee and stare, unblinking, into his face.

"She's good company."

Byron looked back at her from his perch on a ladder-back chair. "How's the work going?"

"Good." She'd come to say it was time to get Ian home, but couldn't persuade herself to bring the happiness she saw on the boy's face to a close. "Just taking a break. Come here, Dog. Sorry, she thinks everyone's as glad to see her as I am."

"I had a dog," Ian said, scratching between Dog's ears. "He kind of wandered into the yard one day and just stayed. A big old puppy with short hair and a long tail. Kind of like a black lab. Goofy-looking, my dad said he was. So that's what I called him—Goofy. Mom and Dad said I could keep him. They were like that." He bent far enough over Dog to hide his face.

Jade looked to Byron and caught his eye—and felt his empathy for the boy all the way to her soul.

She smiled.

He didn't.

"Ian," Byron said. "Why don't you take Dog outside and throw a stick for her?"

"Is that okay?" Ian kept his head bowed.

"Um, yes," Jade said. "Only she probably won't go. She doesn't like to be where she can't see me."

Ian got up, his face vaguely pink. He set down his guitar and clicked his fingers at Dog—who immediately pranced along beside him as if she'd known him from the moment of her birth. She didn't even glance at Jade on the way past.

"Huh." She put her fists on her hips. "So much for single-minded allegiance. Look at that."

Boy and animal disappeared and then the door to the side yard slammed.

Byron rose and stood his guitar beside Ian's. "Isn't he a great kid?"

"Yes." The awkwardness began to seep in. "I'd better get back to it."

"I thought you were taking a break."

She looked at her plaster-spattered hands. "I'll just get a glass of water from the kitchen."

"You don't have to run away from me, Jade."

"I'm not." Her words hung between them, hard and too loud—and too defensive. "I'm not."

"Aren't you? You managed to stay out of my way all day. I didn't hear you arrive and I didn't see you until it was time to go to Fowey."

"We already decided it was best if we didn't get in each other's way."

"You could never get in my way," he said softly.

Jade's heart missed too many beats. "We made a deal," she said, feeling light-headed. "I don't want to present ultimatums, but I told you I can't work here if . . . You know what I told you. And you agreed."

"Maybe I'm rescinding the agreement."

She looked directly into his eyes. "You're not being fair."

"And I think you may be making the biggest mistake of our combined lives."

"Which is?"

"Putting road blocks in the way of what could be really great between us."

"A really great summer affair? Is that what you're talking about? I don't think that's such a good idea."

He strolled across the room until he stood in front of Jade. "I said I'd stay out of your way if that's what you want."

Jade crossed her arms.

"*Is* that what you want?"

"I want peace." But she didn't want to as much as consider not seeing Byron.

"You aren't answering the question."

"I've answered it as well as I can."

He touched her jaw, very carefully, and brought his thumb to rest on the point of her chin. "I think I'm going to take that as a hopeful sign. You didn't tell me to get lost, Jade. Very hopeful."

Jade made no attempt to draw away. Vibrating, almost tangibly, was their shared knowledge of what had already passed between them.

"Do you regret what happened?"

She didn't have to ask what he meant.

"Jade?"

"I don't want to talk about it."

"Because it embarrasses you?"

She did jerk away then. "I'm not good at this sort of thing. Clever sparring. I'm a simple woman, Byron. From a simple world. Not your type at all."

His hand, closing on her upper arm, surprised Jade. Byron pulled her very close, so close she craned her neck to see his face.

"You aren't in a position to know what *my type* is," he said. "I make my own rules and live by them. That means I *choose* the people I want around me."

His intensity shivered between them. "Sometimes we can't have what we choose," she told him.

"And sometimes *we* are smart if we don't waste opportunities that aren't likely to pass our way twice." When he narrowed his eyes, their deep green became a quality more than a color, a quality with the power to cut.

In the seconds that followed, he looked from her eyes to her mouth and she felt her willpower begin to unravel.

"Ian will be back shortly," she reminded him.

He averted his head and she heard him breathe deeply. "Yes, Ian. There's something I want to ask you."

"All I know about Ian is what you probably already know. He—"

"Not about Ian. About Rose."

"Ah, Rose. You didn't choose the best time to show up on my doorstep."

"Would there be a best time?"

She hesitated. "I'm not sure."

He smiled. "Good. I think that's another score for the guy in the white hat."

"I think you'd look better in a black hat. More in character." And distinctly appealing.

"Rose." His fingers slackened on her arm and he stroked from shoulder to elbow and back.

"Rose, what?"

"She's pretty. A sweet little kid."

It was Jade's turn to narrow her eyes. "Yes she is. And lovable. Everyone loves Rose."

"Including you?"

"Yes, including me." His touch on her arm distracted Jade. "What are you asking me?"

"Is she yours?"

At first she could only stare at him. "Mine? You mean is she *my* daughter?"

"Yes. The coloring's similar. And she's five. Did having her result in your divorce? Didn't you want to be responsible for her all the time?"

"Rose?" Jade said slowly. "What rotten things to say about a person."

"That she might be the mother of a lovely child?"

"No!" She wiped suddenly sweating palms on her overalls. "That you think I'm the kind of woman who could give up a baby."

Jade saw the pupils of his eyes dilate. She felt him grow utterly still.

"No," she said. "No, Rose is not my daughter."

"What kind of . . . What kind of person do you think gives up a baby?"

"I don't know." Turning from him, she looked through the windows at the river traffic. "It's just not what normal people do, that's all."

"Look at me, Jade."

She continued to watch a green-hulled ketch slip toward the English Channel. He'd not only made a horrible assumption about her, he also wanted to make her believe he didn't think badly of her. Because he was a man who got "what he chose." And he'd chosen her, would have her at any cost—until it was time for him to go home.

"Jade?"

Reluctantly, she faced him. "You don't have any right to pry into my life. And if you do pry, you certainly shouldn't come up with theories that couldn't be true of me in a million years."

"Because you're above being human?"

"Human? You think it's human to give up your own baby?"

"I did."

She'd misheard him. "You what? What did you do?"

"I gave up my own baby."

"You . . ." He didn't make sense. "You gave up your own baby? I don't know what you're talking about."

He pushed his fingers into the hair at his temples and closed his eyes. "I was twenty-one and still in school. I got left with a baby I couldn't"—he shook his head and his face contorted—"I didn't have what it took to bring him up on my own."

Every thought that came her way refused to be nailed down.

"I didn't have it in me to do **what** Doug Lyman did—bring up a child on my own."

"Bringing up Rose is the only thing he's ever done without thinking of himself first. He was a lot older than twenty-one when he had an affair with Rose's mother. She left him alone with the baby. He didn't have any choice."

His laughter was more wrenching than if he'd cried. "He had the same choice I had."

"Oh, Byron—"

"You should respect the man for what he's done, and—given your beliefs—you should hate me. But I'm going to put it right."

She walked almost blindly to the settee and sat down. "Was it your wife's child?"

"*He* was my wife's child."

"Did she die because of having the baby?"

"Yes. Because of blood clots. It happened twice. Once during labor. The second immediately afterward. The second one killed her. She'd been ill for months and the doctors were worried about her. Lori was sure she wasn't going to make it."

"I'm sorry. Silly words, but they're all we've got."

He wasn't seeing her anymore. Byron Frazer was far away in a place she'd never seen, a place he wished he'd never been.

"I've decided what I've got to do," he said. "It won't be easy, but it's right."

Jade dug her fingertips into the seat of the settee. She wanted to help him but didn't know how.

"I'm going to give Ian the home he needs. With me, he'll get the chances he deserves. They're his by right, anyway."

"You're talking in circles. What are you saying?" She worked her way along the couch until she sat within feet of where Byron stood. His eyes were closed again. "Byron, will you please explain?"

"Yes. I'm going to get custody of Ian and bring him to live with me."

He'd lost his mind. "You can't just decide you've taken a liking to a child and then rush off and demand to own him."

"Not own him. I don't want to own him. I want to look after him."

"They won't let you," Jade said, stressing each word as she might to a particularly obtuse child. "You have absolutely no claim to Ian Spring."

"Oh, yes I do." He opened his eyes and leveled them on Jade. "I've got the best claim in the world. He was born Matthew Frazer. Gift of God. He was born my son."

Chapter Fourteen

Nothing but a glimpse of the sea, then meadows, hedgerows, and sheep—and more and more meadows.

Byron had trekked from New to You in Lostwithiel Street, all the way to Readymoney Cove south of Fowey town itself. "You'll find her," Shirley Hill had said of Jade. "I knew I saw something in her stars this morning. I knew someone tall, dark, and passionate would come for her. Aha, I said, Mr. Scorpio. I didn't try to tell her. Not that she'd take any notice of me if I did."

After two gruelling days in London, his nerves were frayed. Only the thought of seeing Jade had kept him from pulling off the motorway and finding an anonymous room where he could sleep and forget.

She should have been at Ferryneath. Instead, the door had been locked and if Harry Hancock, Byron's bluff neighbor, hadn't strolled down the alley to remark on having seen "that pretty young Perron woman working away outside," there'd have been no way to know she'd been there at all.

"If she's not at Readymoney," Shirley had said as she waved him off at her shop door, "you'll have to carry on. Go behind the cottages on the far side of the cove. There's only one road. It'll take you into Allday's Fields."

Well, what he was looking at had to be Allday's Fields. Meadows rose from a rim above the sea to climb in mounds that grew higher, the farther inland they stretched.

"Allday's," Byron muttered. "Appropriate. Tromp over them all day and you wouldn't get anywhere. They go on forever." And Jade might or might not be up there.

He saw her.

Striding downhill along a path bordered by trees swathed in bright, trembling new leaves, her small figure, black hair flying, was unmistakable. Dog's presence at her heels would have overcome any doubt.

Byron hoisted himself to sit atop a wall formed of gray-white flakes of stone piled one on top of another with no mortar between.

A sinking sun drew a thin net of white cloud in its wake. Evening hovered, awaiting its turn upon the land. The breeze carried a burden of sharp salt scent from the sea and the first bite of cooling hours to come.

Jade disappeared around a bend and Byron grew anxious she might strike out in a different direction. But then she reappeared, close enough this time for him to see the flapping ends of a red scarf that tied her hair at her nape.

She hadn't sighted him.

Byron braced his weight on his hands. Just seeing her, watching her jog nimbly over rocks in the path, swing her arms to balance, soothed him more than it should. Two weeks ago he hadn't known Jade Perron existed. Today he needed to see her more than any other human being.

A gust of wind sent dust eddies into the air. Even as he waited, dusk began to slink more confidently to take the sun's place.

Jade's hands were behind her head, tugging the scarf into a tighter knot, when she saw him.

He waved.

She came more slowly.

"Hi!" He wanted to jump from the wall, to run and sweep her into his arms.

Jade's unsmiling face riveted him to where he was.

Several yards distant, she stopped. "I suppose you thought you were cool."

"Cool?" Tipping his head, he looked at her quizzically. "Cool?"

"I told you I was a simple woman. My language is probably behind the times, too. Cool says it as far as I'm concerned. You thought it was perfectly acceptable to take off after dropping the kind of bombshell you dropped on me, and then stay gone for two days."

"I left a note."

"You did that. Yes."

"I said I'd be back by tonight."

She came toward him, one reluctant step after another. "When we talked on Monday night, you promised me you wouldn't do anything about . . . You know. You said you'd give it a whole lot more thought before you upset a bunch of other lives just to satisfy some guilty whim of your own."

If she'd intended to wound, she'd succeeded. "This is no whim," he said quietly. "This is the biggest—the second biggest decision I've ever had to make."

"What was the first?"

"To give Ian up for adoption." His mouth dried out and he turned his head to gaze unseeingly at the Channel. "I talked to him for a while on Monday—about his being adopted. Some of the things he said made me know what dying must feel like."

"About his mother saying his real parents were brave?"

He closed his eyes. "You were listening."

"I was outside the door. I couldn't help hearing."

"Can you imagine how I felt?"

Her expelled breath was audible. "You already said it. Like dying.

Byron, you said you'd give me more of an explanation. That's why we dropped the subject the other night."

"I couldn't risk talking about it in front of Ian. Not until . . . God, how am I going to tell him?"

"Don't tell him."

He snapped back to look at her. "What?"

"Don't tell him. Thirteen years ago you decided you wanted out of his life. He was adopted by two people who loved him as much as any parents could—"

"Not as much as . . . Not as much as I would have."

She pushed her hands into the pockets of white jeans. "I don't agree with you. From everything I've been told—added to what Ian's said himself since he's been here—my aunt and her husband were wonderful parents. You heard what he said. He's curious about his natural parents. That's to be expected. But the people he'll always think of as his mother and father are dead.

"Leave it like that, Byron. Don't start something you can't finish. Don't spoil what will eventually become a good situation for him here."

He jumped down and stood with his back to her. Straggler sheep crowded to the other side of the wall, butting heads, and bleating. "You don't hesitate to drive in the knife, do you, Jade?" he said.

Her touch on his back was light, fleeting and then gone. "That's not fair," she said.

"But it's fair for you to call it like you see it with me?"

She came to stand beside him. "Leave me out of this. Except as a possible voice of reason. Where have you been?"

"I don't owe you an account of my movements."

"No. But you'll tell me, won't you?" she said.

The scent of roses—her perfume—drifted to him. He looked sideways at her and felt the changes that were shifting in his life. So many changes, so fast.

Jade met his eyes. "It's got something to do with Ian, hasn't it?

Did you go away to think about everything and decide I was right? Leaving well enough alone would be a kindness, Byron. *If* you've got a right to do anything else."

For several seconds he hardly knew what she'd suggested. "Jade? Look at me, please."

She stepped closer to the wall.

"I said *look* at me."

"No. That's something else that's a good idea. For me not to look at you."

Even through his growing anger he felt a spark of triumph. "Because I've begun to mean something to you?"

"Forget it. And forget Ian."

"I can't forget Ian." *And I can't forget you.* The question would be whether or not he'd have to try. "I do have a right to claim Ian. He was mine and he will be again."

"What about your parents? And Lori's parents. Didn't they try to stop you?"

"No. That's all you have to know. I didn't have a rich family waiting in the wings to help out. My own father was already dead." First dead drunk—for most of the years Byron could remember—then dead because he *was* a drunk. "My mother wasn't coping with what she already had to deal with." Herself. She'd never been able to care for herself, let alone the four children she probably loved when she remembered she had them.

"And you became a behavioral psychologist specializing in the family? Interesting."

She did know how to hurt. "Textbook, lady. You summed me up right after we met. Every psychiatrist and psychologist goes into the specialty so they can spend their working years trying to make sense of their own problems."

"Is that what you're doing?"

"Maybe." Muscles in his spine clenched till they ached. "That isn't the issue here. Ian is."

"Yes, he is. Will you at least tell me where you've been?" Turning her head, she looked at him over her shoulder. "All the note said was that you'd be back tonight."

Strands of her black hair had worked free of the scarf to whip across her face. Her shoulders, hunched inside a white cotton V-necked sweater, gave her an even more fragile appearance than usual.

With difficulty, he returned his attention to the horizon. "I went to London. To talk to a lawyer—solicitor, as you call them."

"Oh, my God," she said, almost in a whisper, and turned to him. "Oh, Byron, don't do this. Please, don't do it."

"Don't try to give a boy what he needs?"

"Don't start something you can't stop even when you wish you could. And if you do this, you will wish you could stop it."

For the second time he was being told he should give Ian up for the boy's own good. "It seemed the right decision at the time," he said, seeing again that small, impersonal interview room. "I couldn't give him anything. They convinced me that if I gave him up, whoever took him would love him enough to make up for the loss. He'd have a stable home with two parents who were committed to raising him."

"And he had that," Jade said. She grasped the lapels of his sport-jacket. "And now his extended family is making a good start at making sure he has it again."

"With a retired spinster who thinks knitting him ugly sweaters that'll embarrass the hell out of him is an act of love?"

"Now who's being cruel?"

"I've retained a lawyer. That's fact." He tried not to look at her and failed.

"Byron"—Jade flattened her hands on his chest—"I still can't believe this. A long rest and a chance to write a book had nothing to do with you coming here. You lied to me from the beginning."

"Yes. But I am getting some work done." To his own amazement. "I don't like thinking about lying to you."

"How did you find him?"

"I've kept tabs on him all his life. An investigator did the necessary footwork after Ada Spring died. I came over here to make sure he was all right."

"And he *is* all right."

"No, he's not, Jade. We both know that. He's hanging on by his fingernails and slipping a bit farther every day. A less well-balanced kid would have run away from this mess by now."

His black wool turtleneck was rough beneath her fingers. "You don't have any idea what you'll be getting into if you try this, do you?"

"Try it?" He covered her hands. "You haven't been listening to me. I'm going to *do* it."

"I don't think so. You don't know these people—my people. Go after one of us and we close ranks. We stand shoulder to shoulder."

"*We?*" He chafed her hands. "You, and what you call your people, against me? I'm the enemy?"

When she would have pulled away, he held her fast.

"No, Byron. You're not the enemy. I . . ." She turned her face up to the breeze and searched for the right words. "I'm worried about Aunt Muriel. I know you see her as a silly, narrow-minded woman, but I care about her. She's good and she deserves to be considered."

"I'm sure she does. And she will be if that's possible without sacrificing Ian."

This time he made no attempt to stop her from pulling away. "You've made up your mind what's best for Ian and you aren't even prepared to consider you might be wrong." She began to hurry on toward Readymoney Cove.

Byron fell in beside her, kept up at an easy stride while Jade almost ran. "You're letting emotion be your guide. Face it: Muriel Cadwen isn't a fit person to bring Ian up."

"Oh!" Jade halted and turned on him. "Fit? A few days ago

you confronted me with the suggestion that Rose Lyman might be my child. You *accused* me as if I needed to be shown how bad I was."

"No, no, I didn't suggest that."

"You *did*. Double standards aren't going to help your cause around here. You don't have any right to be judgmental. You're the one who gave up a child, Byron. Not me, and not my aunt."

Her eyes shone with her anger. She was the one person he needed, and she was so beyond his reach at this moment.

"Let's calm down, Jade."

"I will not calm down." Speeding away from him, she set off at a trot, accompanied by Dog.

"Jade." Byron caught up, slipped his hand under her arm, and pulled her to a standstill. "Ian isn't happy, damn it. And he doesn't have the things he needs—the things I can give him."

"Money!" She tossed her head and the red scarf slipped from her hair. "With people like you it's always money and the power it can buy. Aunt Muriel has enough money."

"Not enough to bring up Ian properly"—he stooped to pick up her scarf and stuffed it in his pocket—"or not as far as I can see. She made some comment—a completely inappropriate comment— about his Vikings jacket."

"She's an elderly Englishwoman, Byron. She doesn't understand kids' fashions, especially American kids' fashions."

"And she never will. But that's not the main point. She remarked that when she could manage it, she'd buy Ian another coat. How much does a coat for a boy cost, for God's sake?"

Jade marched back and forth in front of him, her hair tossed this way and that by the rising wind. "You don't know what you're talk-ing about. You don't know where Aunt Muriel's coming from. Ian's mother left money for him, do you know that?"

"No, I don't know that." He felt himself waver. These Cornish people thought differently from the types he was accustomed to, and he must never forget the fact. "What's Muriel using Ian's money for?"

"What do you mean?"

"You said Ada Spring left money for Ian. Muriel's sure as hell not spending it on him, so where's it going?"

Jade raised her chin. She curled the tip of her tongue to her upper lip.

"Not quite so fast with the answers?" he said. "It does give one pause, doesn't it?"

"How dare you," she said in a low voice that cut through him. "You're a psychologist. Why? Your instincts about people stink. Aunt Muriel won't touch a penny of the money Aunt Ada left. That's why there's a question of how much can be spent on Ian and when. A woman living on a pension—bringing a teenage boy up on that pension—has to be a little cautious."

"Won't touch a penny? That's asinine. Ada must have left the money to pay for Ian's needs. Why wouldn't Muriel spend it on him?"

"Because she considers it her duty to safeguard every penny and give it to Ian when he's old enough to be on his own."

Byron breathed in slowly. "I see."

"Do you? Do you see that she's a scrupulously honest woman who only wants to do what's best? Her plan is to give Ian a nice nest egg when he turns twenty-one.

"Now, you'll have to excuse me. It's getting cold. I want to go home."

Byron let her get a few yards ahead before catching up again. "I was wrong about Muriel. I'm sorry."

"Don't waste your apologies on me. Aunt Muriel's the one you've wronged."

"Nothing would be gained by telling her I thought she was ripping off the boy's inheritance."

Her step faltered. "I can't believe you'd actually put that into words. It's despicable."

She ran a few paces and fell into a rapid stride.

Byron didn't have to run to reach her side. He took off his jacket and wrapped it around her shoulders—and prepared to pick it up when she threw it off, which she undoubtedly would.

Jade didn't throw off the jacket. She held the end of a sleeve in each hand and hurried on.

"Muriel wouldn't be able to put Ian through school."

"We don't pay for school here."

"Some people do. And I'm talking about college. He's very intelligent and he deserves to get every advantage possible. That'll mean a university—the best that'll take him and I'll make sure that'll be any school he chooses."

"What does it feel like to know you can manipulate the world?" When she glanced at him, tears stood in her eyes.

"Oh, Jade, I don't know." His pace quickened again to keep up with hers. "I've never had the kind of power that world manipulation would need. But I have gotten to a point where I can afford to help my child."

Dog sloshed through a rut filled with sea water from the last high tide. Droplets sprayed in either direction and Byron jumped out of range—almost. He swept at wet spots on his gray slacks.

Past the pretty cottages that backed Readymoney Cove, they rushed. Byron barely had time to take in shiny front doors and a profusion of climbing roses in lemon yellow and cream and a dozen shades of red and peach and pink.

Finally, after marching along the Esplanade in gathering gloom, Jade turned at Lostwithiel Street and charted a direct course for New to You. At the shop, she worked a key from the pocket of her jeans and opened the door to the showroom.

"*Your* child, you say," she flung at him, breaking her silence. "I don't understand any of this. What proof do we have that he's your child?"

His stomach twisted. "I'm not planning to kidnap Ian. I went to London to engage legal advice. This will be done through the proper channels."

"My Aunt Muriel will be told how inadequate she is through *proper channels.* Lovely. You didn't try to get him back for the first thirteen years of his life. Why now?"

"I've already told you. Because he didn't need me before. He does now."

"You're so cold about this," Jade said, starting to close the door on him.

Byron pushed it open, walked in, backing Jade before him, and shut the door with a backward flip of his hand.

"We've said enough." Her voice wobbled. "You shouldn't be here."

"Why?" He continued to advance upon her. "I like it here."

"Here?" She spread her arms and bumped into a table laden with lumpy heaps of clothing. "In a secondhand store that must offend your taste for finer things?"

"You're making assumptions about me again," he said. "Simple things, yes. I love simple things, beautiful things—like you. What you don't know, lady, is that I came from nothing. I'm intimately acquainted with need and I don't carry a whole lot of fond memories of the experience."

She edged past the table and continued, still walking backward, toward the door leading to the storeroom behind the shop.

"When I was Ian's age, I spent more time with my mother's sister than I did in my own home and I hated it there."

"Ian doesn't hate it with my aunt."

"I think he does. My Aunt Dorothy never missed a chance to say that she was doing her duty to her sister—my mother—by taking me in even though she had a whole brood of her own kids to care for. She was 'doing right' by my mother in her time of trouble."

"I'm sorry," Jade said and he saw her throat jerk. "But that just isn't what's happening to Ian."

"Your aunt has said—several times in my hearing—that she's bound by duty to look after her dead sister's child. She's bound by duty to love him and she's bound by duty to stagger beneath the weight of the worry 'a boy like that' might bring."

Jade had reached the storeroom and fumbled to turn on a light. "I don't believe she'd ever call Ian 'a boy like that.' She's too kind."

"One of her friends said it and Muriel didn't argue. She also didn't argue when the same friend referred to his not being what she termed 'blood' and begged Muriel not to go on trying to look after a child whose background was bound to *show* in the end."

"Someone said that?" She stopped at the foot of the stairs to her apartment. "My aunt wouldn't take any notice anyway."

He'd always subscribed to fair play. "No. I admit she didn't agree with what the woman said. But she didn't fight it very hard, either. Muriel rather enjoys being the center of pity, doesn't she?"

"Good night, Byron."

"I'm not leaving."

"Yes you are." She started up the stairs. "All I ask is that you think this through some more. Please."

"Persuade me."

Jade looked down on him. "What? What are you asking me?"

He climbed slowly behind her. "I'm asking you to persuade me that I ought to wait before letting Muriel and Ian know my intentions."

"How would I do that?"

"I can think of a way." As soon as they left his lips, he regretted the words.

Jade took the rest of the stairs two at a time, and at a run. She went into her flat calling "Goodbye, Byron" in a voice that sounded suspiciously full of tears.

"You've got my coat," he told her, walking in and closing yet another door behind them. "And I'm sorry for the suggestive comment. I'm exhausted, but that doesn't excuse me. Will you forgive me?"

"Men have a way of using sex to deal with anger. Big mistake. Some women may like that sort of thing. I don't."

He deserved her disgust. "Forget I said that. We can work our way through this."

"Why are you doing this? We aren't supposed to be talking about us." She gave a short laugh. "There isn't any *us* to talk about."

"Yes there is." She was right about one thing—this probably wasn't the time—but he couldn't help himself. "Whatever happens with Ian doesn't have to come between us, Jade."

"How can it fail to come between us? Damn it, Byron. We've already decided there isn't anything between us in the first place."

"We haven't decided anything."

"Yes we have, and—" Dog whined and scratched at one of two doors on the left side of the room. "I've got things to do. My dog needs feeding and so do I."

"And so do I," Byron said, following her into a kitchen decorated, predictably, in bright yellow.

Jade remembered she still wore his coat, shrugged it off, and tossed it at him. "I'm tired. All I want to do is get finished here and go to bed."

"Me too."

She glared at him and he couldn't even feel remorse.

"There you go, girl." A metal bowl was quickly filled with dog food and a second with water.

"Good night, Byron. Please lock the shop door when you go out." Leaving the animal crunching noisily, Jade swept past Byron into the sitting room and then through the second door on the left.

"This room looks like you," he told her from the threshold. "Soft and bright and touchable."

"God, what a line."

Byron laughed. "Yeah. Only it wasn't a line." He was staring into the throat of disaster. "Please can I stay with you?"

"No, you can't. And you know why."

The room smelled of roses. Of course it did. "All I want is to hold you." Lying hadn't gotten him anywhere so far. "That's a lie. I want to do a lot more than hold you, but I'm not so dense I don't know you're not in the mood."

"All we have is now," she said, and she sounded far away. "We're the world's least-likely-to-succeed pair. You don't fit with me and I don't fit with you."

The temptation to be flippant blessedly fled. "Do you think we can say goodbye and never look back?"

"I can't. But admit it, what I said is true. We're not a match. You may be happy with a few hot times together—I'm not. So it's in the past. You and I are in the past."

The sadness that hit him was an unexpected blow. His life was never going to be the same. Jade was wound in and around what had happened here in Fowey, and he wanted her with him. But she was right. Her world was here, and his was far away.

"It isn't meant to be. Only I'm not sure how to proceed from here. Why don't you help me."

"Can I sit down." He indicated a wire chair shaped like a manta ray and with a fat black and red cushion on its seat. "You go to bed and I'll sit there. I want to watch over you. Please let me do that."

"Byron, even if Ian didn't loom between us, there isn't anything ahead for you and me and I won't allow myself to give in to wanting you."

All the little signals she gave him tightened the invisible bonds between them. "We want each other. How can . . . It's so damnably cruel that this chance came along—you and me—in the kind of circumstances no one ever expects."

He heard a rustle and watched her fiddle with puffy yellow-and-white-striped draperies at the window.

He kicked of his shoes. His feet ached. "I'm not ready to give up on us. It's what I want." The fact that he hadn't intended to say anything remotely binding didn't seem to matter anymore.

Jade smoothed a drape. She faced him slowly. "You don't mean that."

"How can you remember what happened for us and think I wouldn't want something lasting with you." The words should scare the hell out of him. They didn't.

"I wouldn't have thought you were the type of man to risk causing a woman pain just to get his own way," she said. Feeling her way, keeping her so-blue eyes on him, she dropped to sit on a linen chest under the window. "You want a diversion, Byron. A diversion while you deal with what I now believe really was your reason for coming here. I'm not going to be any man's convenient pastime."

"I'm too old to be looking for a pastime—that kind of pastime."

Those blue eyes speared him. "What does that mean?"

"It means I've gone over the line of just wanting sex with you. I'm not going to say I don't have a tough time not thinking about what you look like naked."

She blushed, but didn't look away.

"I do it all the time. Particularly at night when I'm trying to sleep. That's when I feel you naked, Jade. I feel your skin, the skin on your face and neck, and your arms and back. I feel your long legs stroking the length of mine."

"Byron . . ."

"Okay, okay. I also know the call on this one isn't mine to make. Only don't send me away tonight."

She buried her face in her hands.

"If I could only hold you through the night, I'd be a happy man. We're both hurting, but I trust you, and I think—although I shake things up around here—I think you trust me, too."

"You'll go away again." She leaned to rest her head on her crossed arms, on top of her knees. "And it's going to tear me up. The sooner we put some distance between us, the better. I've got to get over you."

"Men and women can be good friends, too, y'know. They can help each other through difficult things. If you aren't comfortable lying on the bed with me, we'll sleep on the couch."

She kept her face hidden. "You don't get it, do you? I don't trust myself. I don't want to make love again—yes I do, I do. I want it too much and you wouldn't help me make sure it didn't happen."

If he were other than human, he'd manage not to smile with triumph. He was very, very human.

Whatever it took to feel her in his arms again, he'd do it. "We're not going to make love tonight, Jade. I promise I'll make sure we enjoy feeling safe together, but that's all. But I'm not going to lie anymore. I'd like us to have a future."

Her face registered shock. "You'd lie about something like that?"

"I'm not telling anything but the truth." His heart seemed to stop beating. "Do you wish we could be together—after all this?"

"Yes. I probably shouldn't say it, but I can see you when I close my eyes, Byron." She crossed her arms tightly.

"I see you, too." Oh, did he see her? "We both needed comfort and closeness and we needed it with each other. No one else would have been right for me, Jade. Do you believe that?"

She breathed in through her nose, then nodded.

"Good. I'm no more promiscuous than you are. Sex for its own sake has never been a big deal for me—except—well, we were all teenage hormone heaps once." He chuckled and was grateful to see her answering smile. "You don't have to worry tonight. I'm going to be strong enough for both of us."

"You can honestly say you won't try anything?"

"Honestly. And if you try anything, I'll fight you off." He got up, took off his shirt, and stretched out on top of her bed. "Come on. Work your magic. Heal my heart."

Fully dressed, she climbed on the bed beside him and they lay, side by side, staring at a very white ceiling. "Your heart will heal," she said. "You'll get swept back up into your busy schedule."

"I don't believe I'll be able to." He didn't believe he'd ever get through a day without thinking about her.

Jade's heart was heavy. "Go to sleep," she said. "I don't want to talk anymore." And she didn't want to think about how soon he'd be gone, never to return.

She turned on her side and raised her head so he could put an arm around her. This feeling, the comfort and safety of being in his arms, would be a memory forever.

Chapter Fifteen

One moment he was asleep, the next wide awake, staring. "Jade?" His outstretched arm felt warmth where she'd lain, telling him she'd left the bed only moments before. "Jade?"

"I'm here."

Rolling his head toward the window, he saw her. Cast in gray shadow by dawnlight through the open curtains, she knelt on the linen chest, her elbows propped on the windowsill.

"Come here."

"The sun'll be up soon." A silvery nimbus outlined her half-turned face, her neck, and her hunched shoulder.

"I'm not ready for the sun."

"It doesn't care."

The beginning of a curling cold feeling formed in his stomach. "Do you? Do you care if I'm not ready for the sun?"

"What I care about won't make any difference."

He pushed himself up on the bed and shoved pillows into a pile behind his head. "Come back to me, Jade."

"I need to shower and change."

"Why?" He already knew, or thought he could guess.

"Because I am what I appear to be—a working woman."

"Are you trying to make a point? Like I'm *not* what I appear to be?"

Jade sat back on her heels. "You aren't what you tried to pretend you were when you first came here."

"I know. And I've apologized for that. And I will again. I'm sorry it was necessary to be devious at first, but it *was* necessary. I told you that if I'd decided Ian was okay, I would have moved on pretty quickly."

"You did say that. You'd have moved on—probably by now?"

Byron sat up and held his upraised knees. "What am I supposed to say? What would make you happy?"

She laughed, a short, sharp, brittle little laugh.

"Is that supposed to be an answer?" he said.

"Drop it, Doctor. Save the analysis for paying customers. You know what's bugging me. We don't have to talk about it."

Angry, evasive people were nothing new to Byron. "I'm not clair-voyant. Try explaining the details to me."

"Oh, damn." Her sigh whispered across the room. "What is it about you that makes me behave like someone I don't know—someone I've never known?"

This time it was Byron who laughed. "Just call it my raw, sexual magnetism. What can I tell you? I'm irresistible."

"Yeah. That must be it."

"Jade, even if everything had been okay with Ian, I couldn't have walked away from Cornwall after meeting you."

At that, she turned to look at him. "Why?"

"You know why."

"No, I don't—other than the obvious. Maybe that's all there is, the obvious."

"Sex?"

"You aren't arguing, Byron."

She was asking him for more than he could give—yet. "The sex was great. It's the least of what drew me to you. And I am drawn to you, lady." Like the proverbial moth to the proverbial flame, but he couldn't even begin to think of a way around the chasm that divided their lives; if he even wanted to.

"I can't believe I've made such a mistake." Stacking her arms on the sill, she rested her forehead. "Such a huge, irrevocable mistake."

Why couldn't he take her in his arms and say there was no mistake because their futures would become one future and what had passed between them was a great big healthy building block toward that end? "I meant what I said just now—about not being able to leave Cornwall because of you."

"Sure. Only I don't have any way of knowing whether to believe you since you *do* think Ian's in dire danger because he's living with my demon aunt and, therefore, you've decided you have to stay anyway."

"Let's keep the topic focused. It's you and me that's got you staring out into the dawn like a beautiful, sad wraith."

"Hah!" Her head snapped up. "Hah! Don't flatter yourself that I'm over here pining over what we don't have together. I happen to love the dawn."

"Of course you do," he said softly. "Dawn becomes you, Jade." He should have been able to tell her how his heart filled just at the sight of her, but he'd been that route before and he still wasn't ready to commit so much again.

She got up from the chest, a small, but very female form in a white terrycloth robe whose long, black hair curled riotously.

Moments later she'd entered the bathroom and he heard the shower come on.

In the meandering twilight zone of his mind, he sought, first in one direction and then in another, and another, for answers. She thought what had already happened with them wouldn't be enough to keep him here. *How did a man prove to a woman that she'd started out like a grain of sand in the sterile, oysterlike shell his life had become—a minute irritant in the midst of emptiness—and then managed to take on pearly dimensions that offered to fill the hollow man with rich purpose?*

How did a man prove to a woman that she was important, even while he wasn't sure what he could, or would, do about it?

How did a man set about proving, again, what he'd once set out to prove before . . . to another woman?

Early one evening, almost fourteen years ago, the sky over San Francisco's Golden Gate Park had been South Pacific blue and cloudless. Sitting with his back against a tree, he'd waited for Lori and prayed this was the right tree, the tree she'd described to him on the phone an hour earlier.

With the swish of neon-colored nylon, joggers had passed. Cyclists meandered, riding one-handed, and children chased dogs or balls or other children to a chorus of parental warnings. The drone of a lawn mower went on and on and the scent of freshly cut grass hung over all.

And then he'd heard Lori's voice:

"You came."

"Hi." He twisted to see her crouching at his right shoulder. *"Of course I came. Don't I always?"*

Sun shone on her blond hair, turning it almost white. "You're going to wish you hadn't this time, Byron."

He offered her a hand and she took it, let him guide her to sit, hip to hip, facing him. "I told you a long time ago that all you had to say was 'come' and I'd be there—wherever there was. That isn't going to change."

"Yes it is." Her brown eyes filled with tears, tears that overflowed to slip silently down her pale cheeks. "But it's only fair that I tell you."

He felt a tiny death deep inside. "What is it?" His grip on her hand tightened until she flinched. "Lori, what's happened?" Why didn't she know that if anything happened to her he'd be lost?

"I'm going back home. To Indiana."

She didn't know. Before Lori, there'd been no one in his world who made him feel connected. "There isn't any home in Indiana. We're both orphans, remember? That's part of the pact—we don't outdo each other because we don't have anything to outdo with. So what are you talking about?"

Her smile touched him as it always had, all the way to the place he called his soul. "I was happy there when I was a kid," she said. "I don't know. Maybe the place could be home and I'll be able to . . . Byron, I've got to find somewhere to be that'll make me feel safe."

"You don't feel safe?" For weeks he'd known with slowly exploding fear that there was something about Lori that was too bad for him to fix this time.

"I can't do it by myself anymore."

"Do it? Do what? You're not on your own."

"I'm going to be and . . . Byron, please, will I always be able to at least write, or call if I've got the money?"

His fear broke, spilled over him like something cold and sticky. "Lori, for God's sake, will you tell me what's going on here?" He could contain his hands no longer. Grasping her shoulders, he pulled her so close he saw the changing light in her eyes.

"You've got your own life." She drew back her chin, flinched, but made no attempt to pull away. "And you've already given me more than I deserve."

When he wrapped her in his arms, he felt her restraint collapse. "I'm the one who made the mistake," he told her. "I caused you to doubt me." But he'd believed he could make her forgive him for the black moods that had overtaken him for a while.

"I made a stupid mistake," she said, her voice breaking. "A great big destructive mistake. And now I'm going to have to take care of it the best way I know how."

"Lori—"

"I'm going back to Indiana to have my baby."

Baby. Baby. Baby. His brain refused to stop stuttering.

"For a few days I tried to consider . . . I can't do anything else but have the baby. It's going to be tough, but I'll manage. And somehow I think it'll be easier in a small place."

"How?" Dumb question. "When?" he asked simply.

"About three months ago."

Three months? Yeah, of course. "When I . . . When I forgot who my best friend is?"

"Don't try to put any of the blame on yourself."

"It's my fault."

"No! No, never your fault."

He knew better. "I pushed you, Lori."

"I did what I wanted to do. The decision was mine and now I'll deal with the result."

"No you won't." Slowly, he rocked her, turned her face into his neck, felt her hot tears on his skin. "You are sure about this?"

"I'm sure."

"You've got to marry me."

She struggled then, but Byron was stronger, much stronger.

"I don't want pity from you." Lori tried to force her fists between them. "And I won't take it."

"Pity?" He laughed, but there was no mirth in it. "This isn't about pity, Lori. It's about need. I need you. That's it. All of it. And now I need this baby, too. Don't you understand? You're the only human being I ever knew I could rely on. The only person who ever put me first. I can't let you go. I won't."

"You've got school. You're going to do important things. I know you are."

"Does that mean I can't have a wife? . . . A wife and children?"

"Byron, not—"

He pressed a finger to her lips. "Byron, yes. That's what I want to hear you say. Say, yes."

She shook her head and the tears kept right on flowing.

Sighing, he kissed her cheek, kissed away tears that were so salty on his lips. "Say it. Say, yes. I'll always be here for you, Lori. Say you want that."

A small child ran, full tilt, into his knees and plopped to fall on a diaper-padded bottom.

Instantly, a young man appeared to scoop up the boy. "Sorry," he said to Byron. "The basic skills still need work."

"Sure," Byron said, and to Lori, "I'm going to be darn good at basic skills, kid-teaching variety. And basic skills . . ." His throat seemed to jam shut. "I'll make a good husband, if you'll have me."

Her great, luminous eyes looked at him in question.

"Yes," he whispered. "Yes, it's what I want. Forever, Lori. I want you forever, and the baby. Will you take me forever?"

The breeze tossed her fine hair across her brow. Leaning, she framed his face in her cool, slender hands. "Okay. Yes. Forever."

A long-ago California evening faded before a here-and-now Cornish early morning. Byron blinked, realized his eyes stung and pinched the bridge of his nose between finger and thumb.

"She lied! She said forever!"

Funny, he'd forgotten having shouted that in the little interview room where he'd agreed to give away Lori's baby. He wouldn't think anymore about that day from hell. There had been too many other things said that he'd rather forget. Now it was time to make it all right—for Lori's sake, and for Ian's—and for his own.

Jade came from the bathroom, wrapped in the robe, a white towel wound about her hair. Her face was scrubbed and shiny and her clean scent filled the small bedroom.

How did a man convince a woman she was important to him, perhaps more than important, when he wasn't sure about things like forever. "Forever" had nearly broken him once. "Forever" was a word he'd sworn never to offer or accept again, and he wasn't ready to change his mind.

"Jade." He had to touch her. "Come here."

She stopped, the towel half-pulled from her hair. "We'll get past this. I don't pretend to understand what it's all been about. But I'm going to forget all about it. Mistakes are things you have to accept and put behind you."

He scrambled from the bed and reached her in two strides. "Mistake?" The moist warmth of her skin reached out to him. "No mistake. It's never a mistake when something's so special."

Slowly, she dragged the towel completely from her hair. "You mean you never consider . . . making love a mistake if it's good? If it makes you feel good?"

"No. How could I? Do you?"

"What you're saying is that anytime you've been with a woman and it's been good for you, that's made it right, the right thing to do."

"Well . . . I guess."

"So, what you'd like is for the two of us to start making love again—frequently?"

Unable to stop himself, Byron slid a hand beneath her wet hair and urged her closer. "Yes, that's what I'd like. How about you?"

She took a deep breath, drawing his gaze to the loosely crossed robe and the rise of her breasts.

"Jade?" He was hard again.

"I want it. But I'm going to need more time to think about it, Byron."

When he pushed the robe aside from one breast, she didn't try to stop him. And when he dipped his head to take the nipple in his mouth, she finished shedding the robe herself.

With their bodies layered together, Jade ran her arms over his shoulders and locked her hands behind his neck. She reached up, flattening her breasts to his chest, grinding her pelvis into his arousal.

"Oh, Jade," he murmured.

She didn't answer. And she still didn't answer when he grasped her hips and lifted her from the floor. Jade was silent, still silent—

but for the rasp of sobbing breath—as she wrapped her legs around his waist.

"So, good," Byron said, driving deep. "So, damn good."

So good, except for one missing element: Byron traveled the road to dark, hot satisfaction, but it left him empty and knowing exactly why.

Jade's body made the journey with him. The lady herself wasn't anywhere around.

"I'm going to drive up through Bridgend and avoid the ferry for a change," Jade told Byron as they walked north along Rawlings Lane.

"You've got enough supplies at the cottage not to need your van, haven't you?"

"Yes." Even as she still tingled from the loving, a longing filled her like none she'd ever felt before. "But it's a nice morning for a drive." And she needed to get away from him and decide what she was going to do.

"The Land Rover's parked near the ferry. I'll take you."

Obsessed. She was obsessed with him. "No, thank you. I don't intend to take very long about it. I'm already far enough behind."

"Is that a problem?"

The problem was that she had to figure out a way to break herself of the habit he was becoming. "I'll pass on the offer this morning, thanks anyway."

Byron pulled her to a stop.

They'd reached the back of Place, the huge, centuries-old, fortress-like home of the Treffry family. Incongruously cottage-style baskets of fuchsias hung outside a gate in a wall built as if to close out twelve-foot-tall interlopers.

She stared at the fuchsias, then at the stone wall.

"What's the matter with you?" Byron demanded. "Why are you behaving as if I'm poison? We've just—"

"I *know* what we've just done," she said, scarcely able to draw a breath. "I'm not sure how yet, but I'm going to figure out a way to stop myself from doing what I seem to want to do almost every time I'm around you."

He smiled, showing his very white teeth. "I'm glad to hear we both have the same problem. Don't worry. Relax and go with it. You'll get used to the idea."

"Damn you!" She tried to walk around him, only to be cut off. "I'm going to work."

"Fine. First I want you to come with me to your Aunt Muriel's."

She stopped, her mouth open.

"I want to feel I've done things the way they need to be done. Fairly. The woman's trying her best with Ian. I know that, Jade, and I want to work things out in a way where everyone comes out a winner."

"No." He mustn't do what he planned. And he wouldn't if she had her way. "Please give it up, Byron. Believe me. You're making a mistake in this."

"I'm going to see Miss Cadwen now. Will you come with me, or shall I go alone?"

"Why are you doing this? Why are you rushing in—now—this morning of all times?"

"This morning when you and I are as close as a man and woman can be, you mean?"

"No . . . Yes. I don't know what I mean."

"I'm not turning back. Ian needs me and I've left him to cope on his own for too long. It'll never happen again and I want you with me. If Muriel Cadwen sees that you and I are . . . Well, if your family realizes we're very good friends, I won't be such a threat."

Her skin prickled. Fumbling, she found the keys in her pocket and clutched them until her fingers hurt. "You intend to let my family know about? . . . You think you can use me to get what you want?"

His eyes became like green ice. "Is that the way you interpret what I just said?"

"How else could I *interpret* it?"

Byron looked up in the direction of Place's turreted tower. "How many times do we have to learn the same lessons?"

"What does that mean?" she asked, her voice shaking.

"I doubt if you'll ever know. But you've obviously worked out my motives very well. People are bound to be more sympathetic to my claims on Ian when they realize you've accepted me."

"Byron—"

"How can Muriel Cadwen and the rest of *your* people object to Ian being claimed by his cousin's lover?"

Chapter Sixteen

Trouble had a particular sound.

As Jade pushed open the door to the public bar at the Bell and Preacher near Town Quay, she was met by a blast of warm air—air already used too many times—by a heady smell of full-bodied beer and by the unmistakably discordant notes of trouble.

The Preacher, as regulars called it, was one of Fowey's oldest pubs. A darkly half-timbered building had crooked windows, and doorways built for shorter men of earlier ages. The walls bulged outward as if from centuries of supporting a stone roof.

"Here's Jade!" The voice that bellowed to greet her belonged to Albert Frye, landlord of the Bell and Preacher for as long as Jade could remember. "Come on in, girl. What'll it be? Sam here's buying, aren't you, Sam?"

Sam Hill, huge and ruddily handsome, waved a beefy arm encased in regulation navy blue wool. "That I am," he said and proceeded to drain a pint tankard of beer in one open-throated swallow. Shirley sat happily on a stool beside her husband, a glass of her favorite parsnip wine in hand.

"Speak up," Albert boomed. "We've got business to attend to here, but you'll be needing a drink to tide you over first."

"Bitter lemon," Jade said, then raised her voice to shout, "Bitter lemon, please, Albert. Thank you, Sam."

"Ah, you want something stronger than that," Sam roared predictably. "Have a nice little parsnip wine like my Shirley."

Jade smiled at Shirley. "I'll stay with the bitter lemon, thanks."

While Albert flipped the top off a bottle, Jade looked around at the assembled cast she presumed had been summoned by her father to meet here.

Art Perron, complete with the single tot of whiskey he allowed himself nightly, sat on a bench beside the bar. His arms and his feet, were crossed, and a somber expression deepened the lines on his thin face.

"Hello, Dad," Jade said. "Sorry I'm late. I only got back half an hour ago."

"Hm." Her father settled in a little more and cast a glance in the direction of Jade's mother and Muriel Cadwen, who occupied wooden chairs on the opposite side of a table from him. "Got my message, then?"

He'd always had a way of asking the obvious. "Yes. And I came right over." And all the way she'd struggled against rising panic. Had Byron revealed their relationship?

A short, white-haired man in clerical black and a white clerical collar rose from a chair beside Muriel. "Do you have any idea why we all decided to get together this evening?" Reverend Alvaston asked, his mustache jutting with his habit of sucking in his bottom lip between words.

"Care" was the key word here. "I expect you'll fill me in, Reverend." Until she knew for sure exactly what these people knew, she wasn't about to give them information they didn't need to have.

"The public bar's no place for a lady," Muriel said, suddenly and loudly. "Lounge would be far more appropriate."

"Oh, hush, Muriel," May Perron said. "This is special. A special occasion."

"Public bar's for the men," Muriel insisted. The faint red tint to her nose was easily traceable to the almost empty pint glass of Guinness before her.

"Not to worry, Miss Cadwen," Reverend Alvaston said in his sonorous, echoing voice. "I'm sure the good Lord quite approves of your being here on this occasion, since you have a matter of importance to this community to discuss."

Jade set her jaw against a rush of irritation. "What's this all about? I've got a lot to do this evening."

"Pretty late getting home, aren't you?"

She had no need to look behind her to know it was Doug who had spoken. "This is my busiest time of the year," she said neutrally.

"Busy over at Ferryneath, right?" Doug strolled to lounge against the bar near Reverend Alvaston. "Should put you in a position to be of some use in all this."

"Reckon Doug's got a point," Sam Hill said jovially, handing Jade her drink. "Gives you a good chance to keep an eye on the subject. P'raps you should see if you can spend some time with this Frazer chap away from the cottage. Easier to get to the bottom of what he's up to that way."

Jade's gaze shot to Shirley, who immediately concentrated on her parsnip wine. So, Shirley, for whatever reason, had chosen not to mention Byron's visits to Jade's flat. That, at least, was something.

"Jade's not spending any time with that bloke," Doug announced. "I'll see to that. He was dropping in at her place last time I took Rose over for a visit. Isn't that right, Jade? Pushy lot, these Americans. Got to keep them in their place, that's what I say."

She realized she was holding her breath, but couldn't seem to release it.

"At your place?" her mother said sharply. "What was he doing at your place?"

And so the lies would begin. "Dropping off a spare key," she improvised.

"He's one of those men who're always in a hurry," Shirley said, to no one in particular. "Scorpios are like that. Here, there, everywhere, and not stopping anywhere for long. He could hardly wait to get away, you could see that. Why, when he rushed out, I said to myself: Typical Scorpio. Rushing around—"

"He does seem very directed," Jade said, grateful to Shirley but afraid she might reach the point of overkill at any second.

"Directed to victimizing upstanding Englishwomen," Albert Frye announced.

"Only he's not getting away with it," Doug said. He settled a hand on Jade's neck. "He doesn't know how we Cornish people pull together to defend our own when it's necessary, does he?"

A chorused "No" rippled around the group.

Jade shrugged very deliberately away from Doug.

"I think Miss Cadwen should tell us all exactly what's happened," Reverend Alvaston said, rolling up onto his toes and bobbing. "All we know so far is that this Dr. Frazer has made some threat that she feels will reflect poorly on all of us if it's pursued."

"Oh, I couldn't say it aloud," Muriel said. "Not here."

"Certainly you can," the Reverend said encouragingly. "We're all your friends and we want to help you with this; whatever it is."

May Perron handed Muriel her glass. "Have another little drink. It'll give you strength."

Muriel did as she was told.

"There you go, Miss Cadwen," Sam Hill said, clearly enjoying every minute. "Now you tell us exactly what this Dr. Byron Frazer said to you. You want to hear the kind of things they say about him out on the yachts. Fair makes your ears burn, I'll tell you."

"Sam," Shirley said, digging him with an elbow. "Not in mixed company."

"What do they say?" May Perron asked, all brightly avid.

Sam waved his tankard expansively. "Well, you know. He's famous in the States. Lots of money. Used to getting what he wants—that sort of thing."

"And the parties, Sam," Doug said, moving in to stand at Jade's shoulder again. "Tell 'em about the wild parties and the women."

Reverend Alvaston cleared his throat. "I hardly think this is the place for that."

"He's like a lot of those television evangelists," Doug persisted. "Working some sort of hysterical thing on the women so's they—well—so's they give him what he wants and I don't only mean money."

Jade's temper rose, notch by notch and by rapid increments. "Dr. Frazer's a psychologist, not an evangelist."

"Same sort of thing if you ask me," Doug said. "Working on people's minds."

"You don't know what—"

"Now, now," Art Perron said in a voice that drowned Jade's. "We're not interested in hearsay here. Muriel, speak up. *Now.*"

Muriel showed signs of being close to tears. "Dr. Frazer came to see me this morning," she said. And then she did start to cry. Sniffling, she produced an embroidered handkerchief and rubbed her eyes.

"For shame," May said, settling her chin into the collar of her brown woolen coat. "Picking on a helpless woman."

Byron hadn't returned to the cottage all day, and all day Jade had wondered where he was, and watched for him, and wished she could at least talk to him.

The scene in the bar became a distant blur. All Jade could see clearly was Byron's lean, tanned face—his clear green eyes. Through the previous night they had held each other, sometimes sleeping, sometimes awake, but never speaking. She loved him, but couldn't have him—not that she'd ever know if there could have been a chance for them together.

"He told me he's going to take our Ian away from me," Muriel said in a strangled voice. "He said I'm not fit to bring up the boy."

Blood drained from Jade's head. She gulped some of the lemon drink.

"Did you hear that?" May Perron said. "And he made threats. Tell them, Muriel."

"He said the boy belongs to him by right."

Silence fell and Jade realized that, until now, some members of the assembled group hadn't known exactly what Byron's supposed transgression had been.

"Take away Ian?" Doug said. "Why would he say a thing like that?"

Jade felt disoriented.

"My dear woman," Reverend Alvaston murmured to Muriel.

"Tell them, Muriel," May prompted again.

"Dr. Frazer wants me to give Ian to him. He says he can offer him the kind of home he needs."

"But that's monstrous," Reverend Alvaston said. "You mean he's suggesting he *adopt* the boy? Just like that?"

"Well, I suppose . . . No, not exactly."

"Tell them—"

"You keep quiet, May," Art Perron snapped. "Let the woman speak her piece at her own rate."

May subsided, but not without casting her husband a wounded glare and drawing her glass of Guinness to her breast.

"He . . . He says he's Ian's father."

Nothing moved.

In the stunned space that followed, Jade closed her eyes and waited. He *had* to do it. For all that she'd warned him how much trouble he could cause, Byron had gone ahead and done exactly what he'd threatened to do.

"Ian's father?" Doug said finally. "What do you mean? I thought Ian was Ada's boy. Isn't that what you told me, Jade?"

She nodded. Doug stood beside her exactly as if he had a right to be there.

"He said"—Muriel sniffed—"he said he had to give Ian up right after he was born. He reckons he always made sure things were all right with the boy and that he came here after he found out Ada had died so he could make sure Ian was—with—someone—fit!" Her voice squeaked and a hail of sobs shook her body.

"Oh, dear." The Reverend's mustache worked rapidly. "We'll all have to keep very calm, I can see that. This is most peculiar. I've never heard anything quite like it. And in all my years as a man of God, I've heard a great deal, I can tell you."

"I think it's sad," Shirley Hill said clearly. "Oh, poor man. Having to give up his baby. I wonder what happened to his wife."

Jade almost started to tell them. She couldn't, not without giving herself away.

"Poor man, my foot," May said. "Whatever happened, he doesn't have any right to come here and bully our Muriel. Ada was Ian's legal mother and she gave him to our Muriel. She said as how Muriel was the one to have him if anything happened. And it did happen and Ian's Muriel's. We look after our own and that's that." Her chin sank farther into her collar.

"Bastard," Doug muttered.

"Not in front of the ladies," Reverend Alvaston said sharply. "This is a serious matter. Did Dr. Frazer give you any intimation as to how he intends to . . . er . . . Did he say what steps he intends to take in this matter."

"He's got a solicitor in London." Muriel wailed afresh and allowed herself to be pulled into May's arms. "Things are in motion, that's what he said. Eventually there'll be some sort of hearing and there'll be a decision made. A legal decision."

"He gave the boy up," Art said, breaking his silence. "I don't see how he can get around that."

"Dr. Frazer said he couldn't have got around it while Ada was alive. But with Ada being dead, he says he's got grounds to prove he'll be better for Ian than me. And he says he's got the money to bring the boy up the way a boy needs to be brought up. Good schools, the best of advantages, he said, or something like that. He told me it would be easier for everyone if I just gave up because I wouldn't win legally anyway, not once he shows the truth of how— how—*unfit* I am."

If Byron had been within reach, Jade would have loved to shake him. He'd spoken of being fair, then gone to an elderly woman doing her best to do what she saw as her duty, and terrorized her with the one thing guaranteed to rattle her to the roots of what little confidence she had: the suggestion that she was failing in that duty.

"Well," Sam Hill said. "And what are we going to do about it, then?"

Jade glanced at him, deciding that, as nice as Sam might be in most instances, she didn't like him tonight. Tonight Sam Hill was thoroughly enjoying his little part in a drama where a boy's future was at stake.

"We're going to make sure Frazer doesn't get him," Art Perron said, smacking his glass down on the table. "That's what we're going to do."

"Oh, Mr. Perron, I do hope it'll be that simple," Reverend Alvaston said. "When it comes to matters of law, one can never be quite certain of one's ground until all precedents have been examined."

Muriel snuffled and coughed. "What am I going to do? He said he'd pay for me to have a solicitor, too. But I can't let him do that, can I?"

Jade tipped up her face and caught her bottom lip in her teeth. He was trying to be fair. A gentle warmth stole over her and she felt Byron's arms, his sensitive fingers on her skin, as tangibly as if she'd lain beside him. She closed her eyes.

"Don't take on, Jade."

Her eyes snapped open and she turned to Shirley. "What?"

"I said, don't you take on so. Byron Frazer's a good man. He's got a big problem here, too, and he's trying to do what's right. I say we—"

"You'll keep what you might say to yourself, Shirl," Sam said, but indulgently. "It isn't your place to meddle. I say as how Frazer's planning to buy Miss Cadwen a solicitor he can control. Plain as the nose on your face, that is."

When there was a quiet opportunity, Jade would have a few very direct words with Sam Hill.

"We'll deal with the solicitor's fees," Art said.

May nodded and made righteously affirmative noises.

"In the meantime," Art continued, "you keep the lad away from Frazer."

"I will," Muriel said.

"Never get him, he won't," Art added.

"That's right," Doug said. "Not after what he did. Giving away his own child. *If* he is his own child. I'll want proof of that. How could a man give away his own child. I think of my Rose, and . . ." He shuddered eloquently.

It's none of your business, Jade longed to tell him.

Muriel drew herself up. "He asked me to just give Ian away. Like he was a box of chocolates that wasn't the kind I like."

"Shame," May muttered. "Run off, he should be."

Byron loves him, Jade wanted to say. The power of her defensiveness of him shook her.

"I'll tell you what I told him," Muriel said, collecting herself and rising to her feet. "I told Dr. Frazer that *he* gave his child away. I told him Ian's mine now and *I* could never give him away. What would people think if I did a thing like that?"

Art stood up beside his sister-in-law. "You did the right thing, Muriel." A stranger would never guess that he'd always despised his wife's sister and regarded her as a small-minded nuisance.

Red-nosed and piteous, Muriel said, "Why, thank you, Art. You give me strength. You all do. Dr. Byron Frazer will never get Ian. Not after what he did.

"What's more," she added, "he's never going to as much as lay eyes on him again if I get my way."

Jade let herself into the kitchen at Ferryneath. The cottage felt empty, but she'd seen a light through closed curtains in the sitting room. And Byron's dark green Land Rover all but filled the little side yard.

Listening to the beat of her own heart, she automatically rose to her toes and crossed into the hall. By the time the meeting at the Bell and Preacher had broken up, the last Bodinnick ferry had already left. Jade barely gave a thought to waiting until morning to confront Byron. She had to see him tonight.

She'd made the drive through Bridgend for the second time that day—this time along narrow lanes made menacing by the heavy darkness of a night devoid of moonlight.

A narrow strip of light showed at the edge of the sitting room door.

Jade tiptoed nearer. She should have gone around to the front door and rung the bell.

The sound of Byron's voice jolted her. He said, "There's absolutely no chance of that," very distinctly, as if speaking to someone who didn't hear well. "Absolutely no chance. I'm sure there'll be a legal hassle, but I'm up for it."

There was still time to go back outside and ring the bell. Or to change her mind and go home.

"I'm not giving up the idea, Celeste," Byron said. "Perhaps we'd better continue this conversation later, when you've had more time to remember that I make my own decisions."

Jade had heard Byron speak to his agent on several occasions and he always sounded at least slightly annoyed.

"I will get custody of Ian, I tell you . . . What do you mean, I won't do anything stupid, will I?"

Jade pushed the sleeves of her sweater up to her elbows. Somehow, she must make Byron listen, really listen. He had to stop this. Surely his motive for wanting to take Ian was no more than a response to the pricking of his conscience.

"Yes, Celeste, I do know where I belong, and I'll be back there just as soon as I have . . . As soon as I can bring Ian with me."

A huge weight seemed to wedge into Jade's breast. Suddenly light-headed, she leaned her back against the wall. Just like that, he would leave as soon as he could. Somewhere, in a place she'd pretended didn't exist, she'd told herself he cared for her as more than a fill-in lover.

"That's the second time you've said that," Byron said, the volume of his voice growing. "What the hell do you mean by *something stupid?*"

Moments later he made a noise that was almost a growl. "Do you think I'm a fool. Of course I know I'd be arrested if I tried to *kidnap* him. For God's sake, you've been watching too many bad movies . . . No, don't you even think of coming here . . . No! No, you could not be of help to me.

"Good . . . Who called? Raddich? What did he want?"

This time Byron's "uh-huh" punctuated the following and much longer interval.

At last he said, "I'll be damned. Two years ago this was the guy who said he was born an adult and proud of it. My, how success changes the tune. So now he's ready to produce my next series and he suggests we call it: *Finding the Child You Never Were?* Priceless.

"We'll talk to the man. Will you stop nagging? Believe me—this offer won't go away if we don't snap it up tonight."

After another pause, Byron said, "No, Celeste, and no. No I can't tell you when I'll be back and no I absolutely do not want you here. Tell Raddich we'll get back to him later. *I'll* call you and soon. Good night."

Jade jumped at the sound of the receiver smacking into its cradle. She couldn't walk in on him without warning.

In the act of tiptoeing back the way she'd come, soft guitar music stopped her, soft music and Byron's soft voice singing a searing song about a man and a woman, how they were alike and how they were different.

They were from different worlds, she and Byron.

Worlds so far apart they didn't make bridges long enough to reach between.

Jade wanted to be part of Byron's world.

She wanted him to be part of hers.

She wasn't part of what kept him in Cornwall. If she chose to be with him while he was there, the onus for the way she would feel once he was gone was on her head.

Abruptly, he stopped playing and singing.

Stepping carefully, she moved toward the kitchen.

The swishing open of the sitting room door made her flinch. "What the . . . Jade?"

She whirled around. "I'm sorry. I didn't mean to shock you."

"Well, you did shock me. Damn, I'm glad to see you."

"I should have rung the front door bell. I didn't think of it till I'd come through the kitchen." She shrugged. "Habit, I suppose."

"Come here."

She shook her head. "This isn't . . . Byron, I've got to tell you a few things and then I'm going home."

He smiled. In the shadows, his eyes were black. "Come and talk to me, Jade. Come on."

Byron offered her a hand and Jade couldn't stop herself from slipping her fingers into his palm. "I had to drive around. I don't want to be long."

"Mm." He drew her close, tipped his head, and looked down into her face with a preoccupied concentration that brought a heaviness to her insides.

She let him kiss her brow, but when he tried to nuzzle his way to her mouth, Jade planted a hand on his chest and pushed firmly away. "Where were you all day?" Byron still held her free hand but she walked into the sitting room, taking him with her.

"You were angry this morning," he said.

"Yes."

"I decided you needed some space. That's why I didn't come back here. I went shopping in St. Austell."

She stared. "Shopping?" The idea was incongruous.

"Shopping." He pointed to a guitar case resting against one wall. "It's a Martin. I bought it for Ian. He deserves much better than that old piece of junk he's playing."

"Ian isn't a deprived child," Jade said before she could stop herself. "You're reacting, Byron. Reacting before you think. That isn't smart and you're a very smart man."

Rather than amused or affronted, Byron looked interested. "What brought that on?" He released her hand and proceeded to smooth her hair away from her face.

"Life doesn't always give us what we'd like to have." Inspiration was what she needed and right now she was searching for some and coming up empty. "Please give up on trying to get custody of Ian."

"No."

Jade sat on a chair that creaked and sent up puffs of dust. "You won't just be taking on an old lady who's easy to push around. My aunt has a lot of people who'll get behind her."

"That won't help her cause. And I don't push old ladies around. I take it you've spoken to Miss Cadwen since this morning."

"Why did you tell her she was unfit to care for Ian?"

"I—"

"That was low, Byron. Low and cruel and completely unnecessary. And in case you've miscalculated, she's also very intelligent. You won't find her so easy to sweep aside."

"Whoa! If I didn't know better, I'd say you've allowed yourself to be brainwashed by your intelligent aunt. I said I was more fit than she is to bring up a teenage boy. And I said I was sure she was doing her best, but—"

"But her best wasn't good enough?" Jade scrubbed at her face.

"Yes, I know. All of Fowey knows what you said to Aunt Muriel and all of Fowey intends to help her make sure you don't get what you've said you intend to get: Ian."

She opened tired eyes and found Byron kneeling beside her.

"I've missed you today," he said. He shifted and slipped a hand beneath her hair and behind her neck. "All day I kept wishing you were with me."

Whatever happened, she mustn't let him lull her into forgetting the promise she'd made to herself while driving here: she would not be lured into his bed tonight.

"Muriel isn't going to allow you to see Ian anymore."

He drew a thumb along her jaw and brought it to rest on her bottom lip. "Let me worry about that. You and I are a separate issue, Jade. I'm going to kiss you."

She swallowed.

Byron brought his face nearer.

Jade averted her face.

Byron pulled her against him and stroked her back. "Weren't you the one who said I wanted my own way? In everything?" He nuzzled her hair aside and kissed her ear. "Well, you're right. I want everything. I want Ian back, and I want you."

Anything she said would only make this more difficult.

When he drew away, he kept her in his embrace. His breathing was short. "I didn't think I'd see you until tomorrow. Damn, Jade. I didn't know how I was going to wait that long."

"I'm not staying."

"We'll see."

"I only came to make you listen to reason."

"We mustn't waste any time, Jade. There's never enough time for the things that matter."

Never enough time before a man with another home, another life, decided it was time to return there.

Jade wrenched away and stood up. "No, Byron. I meant what I said."

Immediately, he was behind her, wrapping her in his arms again. "Some things aren't possible to fight. You and I are one of them and I'm not going to try."

"No." She struggled and he instantly released her. "I'm not sure what . . . I don't know if you and I are going to carry on having an affair while you're here." Avoiding the truth of what they shared wouldn't change a thing. "But whether we do or not, the issue of Ian has to be dealt with. You've come here expecting everyone to sway before you, as if you were some sort of omnipotent wind moving through a worthless field of grass. And you haven't even considered it necessary to give a proper explanation for your actions."

Byron pushed back his shoulders as if they ached. "I told you I was left with a baby I had no means of caring for properly. What I decided then was right for the time. Ian needed a family and a home and I couldn't give him either. If nothing had changed with the Springs, he'd still be there and I would never have interfered. The Springs are dead and I *have* to interfere. I've explained all this to you."

Crossing her arms to chafe her shoulders, Jade turned sideways, passed Byron, and paced between the fireplace and the couch. "You had *no means* of caring for a baby. What exactly does that mean?"

"I've told you as much as you need to—"

"You haven't told me as much as I need to know or as much as my family and I have a *right* to know. Look at the statistics. Single parenting isn't unusual."

For a long time, Byron didn't move. He stood where he was, staring at Jade as if he were trying to see inside her head. "What are you suggesting?"

"I'm asking you to make me understand the decision you made," she said.

"You're thinking about Doug Lyman," he said in a low voice. "You're too gentle to tell me he's a better man than I am, so I'll say it for you. He didn't put his own needs before Rose's."

Jade couldn't move.

Some emotion passed over his features and left his face a strained mask. "I never planned to do it," he said. "I promised I'd care for him whatever happened. Then I let Lori down. It wasn't what . . . How could I ever have guessed that the worst I'd dreamed of would have been a picnic in comparison with what actually happened. In the end, what I was faced with was unimaginable. I cracked. I went back on my word."

Jade went to him. She had to. "Byron, please, I'm sorry if I've brought up painful things. Please, let it go."

She touched his face and he turned his cheek into her palm.

"No," Byron said very softly. "Peel away all the excuses and you find a man who has taken until tonight to face the truth about himself. Lori told me not to give up my studies. She was the most unselfish woman I ever met. I let what she said become my excuse through all these years.

"When I had to choose between Ian's future, and mine, I chose mine. I'm not much better than"—he dropped his voice—"my rotten father."

Chapter Seventeen

"Geez," Ian said in awed tones. "This is some pool room."

Byron glanced at Jade and saw in her smile a mixture of mirth . . . and pity. From her, even pity was something he could accept.

"Wait up, Ian." He followed the boy along a stretch of faded green oriental carpeting. "It's billiards around here, not pool." The carpet had been woven to fit the outer dimensions of a heavy Victorian game table.

"Yeah, billiards." Ian stood with his hands behind his back, studying one of the black-and-white photographs displayed above richly paneled wainscotting. "This whole house is really something. This is a real old school photo, isn't it? A cricket team, or something?"

Byron moved behind Ian. "That's what it is." Rows of long-dead boys, their cream shirts and flannels appropriately rumpled, grinned confidently out from another age.

"Lanhydrock House is a success, then?" Jade joined them and Byron looked over his shoulder at her. She raised her brows. "You were right, and I was wrong."

He flashed her a grateful smile. "I made a wild guess." She'd thought no thirteen-year-old boy would be interested in trailing around one of England's stately homes. Byron had thought otherwise—in Ian's case. "Thank you," he said quietly. Without her help, there was no way he'd be spending this day with Ian.

"He's a nice boy," she said reflectively when Ian had moved on to continue circling the billiard room. "I hope I'm not doing the wrong thing."

"You aren't," Byron assured her. "I need to spend time with him, Jade."

"That's not the way my family sees it."

"He's too old not to be given a choice."

"A choice?" She frowned at him.

Even he wasn't exactly sure what he meant. "I think—no, I know he should have some say in his future."

Alarm crowded into her eyes. "You won't tell him . . . Byron, you don't intend to tell him everything, do you? Not today?"

"I should have explained exactly what I hoped to accomplish." And he knew he'd deliberately avoided telling her. "You wouldn't have agreed to help me if I had, though, would you?"

"No. And I don't like being used." She crossed her arms. Today she'd tamed her hair into a French braid that emphasized a finely boned face. "You're already taking advantage of me, Byron. I can feel how you're suffering and you know it. Oh, Byron, how could you? This was so wrong of me and I knew it was."

"I know." He glanced anxiously at Ian, who stood, rapt, before another bank of photographs. "I want to do the right thing and I'm having a hell of a time deciding exactly what that is."

"Don't say too much to Ian. Not yet."

"Because you don't think I'll get custody of him?"

She shook her head. "It isn't even an issue yet, Byron."

"It is to me. I'll tread lightly. But I'm going to talk to him. He'll have to be told eventually and I'd rather it was by me than some kid in the schoolyard."

"Maybe he won't find out." Desperation hushed her voice.

"You know better."

"I've told him not to say we met you here today." She rubbed her arms through the sleeves of a red cotton shirt. "I don't like lying. And it is lying to pretend something didn't happen."

"I know. I don't like having Ian avoid the truth either. Or you. But what else can I do?"

"Drop the whole thing."

"No."

"Byron—"

"Will you *think*, rather than leading with your family feelings? Muriel Cadwen should already have told him. She would have if she had any sense."

"That's not fair."

"That, sweetheart, is simple logic."

Stepping around her, he followed Ian. He would not be diverted from what he'd decided he must do, not even by the one human being whose opinion mattered to him around here.

He stopped and turned back.

Jade stood where he'd left her.

They looked steadily at each other. Even at a distance her eyes were intensely blue. She raised her chin and her lips parted on an indrawn breath.

The one human being whose opinion mattered to him around here.

He felt his own pulse beating, heard it in his ears.

Her opinion wasn't all that mattered. *She* mattered. Jade Perron mattered very much to Byron and the great sex they'd shared had hardly a damn thing to do with that.

"Hey," Ian called. "Will you look at these tennis rackets? Square!"

Byron watched Jade exhale. "I can't tell you what to do," she said. "But please be careful. The decision's yours, but remember, Doctor, a lot of harm could be done here today."

"I know," he told her. "I'll have to let my instincts guide me."

The furrow between her brows told him what he already knew. "If I think I've lost my objectivity, I'll back off. Fair?"

She pressed her lips together.

"Fair, Jade?"

"I think you'll try to be objective."

He screwed up his eyes. "What do you think is going on inside his head right now? He has to be watching us and wondering what the hell's up. Jade, you know that boy started questioning this whole setup the second you told him not to say he's seen me today."

She drummed the fingertips of one hand against her mouth. "I shouldn't have had any part of this."

"You were right to help me. When you helped me, you helped Ian and that's *right.*"

Byron saw that Ian hovered in the doorway. "Come on. He must be about ready for lunch." And Byron was ready for a break in the electric tension he'd felt through every second since they'd rendezvoused at the entrance to this centuries-old house.

They caught up with Ian in the Smoking Room. Smiling, Byron strode across thick Turkey carpet to join him, but the boy's relaxed air had vanished. Once again there was about him a pinched apprehension.

"What's up?" Byron asked.

Ian puffed up his cheeks and his eyes slid away. "This is a lot of trouble, isn't it?"

"Trouble?"

"You're trying to be nice to me because I'm from the States, too, right? And you feel sorry for me."

Byron wouldn't let himself look at Jade. "Wrong." He strolled past deep buttoned armchairs to look at a cluster of trophies. "Maybe not completely wrong. Twisted back to front, that's all. I'm drawn to you because we are . . . We have things in common."

"Both being American, you mean?"

What was in the boy's eyes? Simple question—or hope?

A dull ache began to gnaw in Byron's head. He had to glance at

Jade. She stared at him and he saw and understood her silent plea. "I guess that's it," he told Ian. "And the music, too. I only wish I played as well as you do."

"You play great." Ian smiled once more.

Byron felt the opportunity to come clean with Ian slipping away. "We're going to jam again real soon—regularly, too." He intended to see to that, with or without permission from the Cadwen/Perron clan.

"I'll ask Aunt Muriel," Ian said in a rush, and then blushed wildly. "Gee, sorry."

This was only getting worse, more awkward. "Why sorry?"

"For being a pain."

"You aren't—weren't."

Jade slipped an arm around Ian's shoulders. "How about some lunch, cousin? I packed enough food for an army and we're going to need plenty of time to eat because I'm not taking anything home."

Byron thought to say they had yet to see the second story of the house. He changed his mind and followed in Jade's footsteps as she steered Ian determinedly through the ground floor until they all emerged into warm sunlight.

"It's the River Fowey that runs past this estate?" Byron asked, more for something to say than because he wanted to know.

Jade hitched the strap of her purse higher on her shoulder. "Yes. Shall we go near the water to eat?"

"Sure." They walked against a tide of arriving sightseers. Byron sidestepped a laughing group of German students. "D'you like the sound of that, Ian? Eating by the river?"

"Sure."

Byron shot Jade a stare and sensed she was thinking what he intended her to think: he'd been right in the billiard room. Ian was trying to figure out just what was going on.

The chatter of passersby was a welcome diversion from the uncomfortable silence that hung between Byron, Jade, and Ian. From the granite gatehouse with its arches and columns, they walked the length of a grand drive lined with beech trees to find Jade's van in the parking lot.

As Byron had hoped, Ian was impressed with the Land Rover and climbed in eagerly for the drive to the river. Jade rode with them, giving directions to a quiet spot close to the water.

"Now for the menu," Jade said when they were settled on an old blanket with a collection of paper sacks in the middle. "Salmon and cucumber sandwiches. Shrimp paste sandwiches. Lemon bars. Pilchard and tomato sandwiches. And butter and Marmite sandwiches."

"Marmite?" Byron and Ian asked together.

"Tastes like beef. It's good. Sort of beef-flavored spread."

"Oh," Byron said—also with an echo from Ian.

"And we've got pork pies," Jade continued, apparently unruffled by lack of enthusiasm. "And pasties, of course. And pickled eggs. And sausage rolls." She scrabbled into a fresh bag and began unwrapping more packages. "Jam sponge cake. Raspberry jelly rolls. Lemoncurd tarts . . . and some fruit. And there's tea in the thermos, of course."

"Of course," Byron said, knowing without asking that milk would already have been added. "Are we expecting a dozen or so people to join us?"

"I'm very hungry," Jade said and pointed at Ian. "Boys have big appetites, too, don't they? Eat."

Ian hadn't said a word since they got into the Land Rover. He sat, cross-legged, tearing up blades of grass.

"This isn't bad," Byron said of a sausage roll. He hardly tasted the food. Ian's discomfort was palpable.

Jade poured tea—milk-laced tea—into yellow plastic cups. "What kind of sandwich will you have, Ian?" she asked. Byron heard the tightness in her voice.

"Um—that Marmite stuff, I guess." He ate several bites of the sandwich he was given. "It's okay."

"It's my favorite," Jade said. "Look at the dragonfly."

Byron looked. He set down the tea, stretched out, and rested his weight on his elbows. "All over in a day, huh," he said of the flitting, whirring creature. Wings that captured the colors of oil on water beat away the short life.

"If you only had one day to live, this wouldn't be a bad one, though," Jade commented. "Look at all this. Not a cloud in the sky."

From the corner of his eye, Byron saw Ian's hands, still holding the sandwich, drop to rest on his calves and said, "Smells great. Young grass and wildflowers and warm earth. Great." It would all be even greater if the boy wasn't miserable. Even without knowing exactly what Ian was thinking, Byron's intuition convinced him the boy was thinking of home, of other times when his . . . when the Springs were there. Ian was grieving.

Jade closed her eyes and smiled. "Listen to the water."

The river ran rapidly, swishing around rocks on its way toward Fowey and the sea. Reeds at the bank waved softly in the breeze.

Byron couldn't stand the tension anymore. He scrambled to stand up. "Wait here, people. Nobody moves a muscle till I get back."

Without checking for reactions, he jogged to the Land Rover, hauled out what he'd stowed behind the backseat, and hurried to rejoin Jade and Ian.

Sitting down, he pushed the sleek black case in front of Ian. "For you," he said. "I saw this when I was in London."

"Geez." The fingers that touched the case trembled. "Oh, Geez."

Byron had to smile. "Is that all you can say? Geez?"

"Oh, Geez!"

Jade laughed. "You really do like those things, don't you, Ian?"

She didn't really understand what the boy was looking at. Byron leaned closer to Ian. "Open it."

"It's okay?" Ian glanced up.

"Sure. It's yours."

"It's a *Martin*," Ian said when he'd raised the lid. "Oh, wow. A *Martin*."

"Someone who plays the way you do deserves the best."

"I looked at some in a store in Minneapolis—with my mom. She said maybe one day I'd be able to have one." He removed the beautiful guitar and stroked its satiny sounding board. "I bet . . . Boy, I wonder what it would feel like to play something like this."

"Play it," Byron told him. His heart did strange things.

"Nah. You play it."

"It isn't mine, Ian. It's yours." Byron stopped him from replacing the instrument in its case. "I mean it. I bought it for you. Try it. Play something."

Ian shook his head. "I can't. I can't take *this*."

"Yes, you can."

Jade had set down her cup. "Play, Ian. Please."

The boy still hesitated, but wrapped his fingers around the neck.

"Play," Byron softly urged.

With a tightening of his lips, Ian settled the guitar in his lap and bent his ear to the strings while he tuned, hummed, and tuned.

And then he played.

Byron gazed directly at Jade and saw an echo of the awe he felt listening to someone so young, yet so accomplished. Ian curled over as if folding himself into the instrument, and the music. The piece was classical, haunting, and perfect for an English afternoon by a Cornish river with a dragonfly dancing and reeds swaying and water rushing to the sea.

As he watched, Byron saw Jade sway like the reeds. Something near pain smote at him. This was a perfect moment, here, with these two people—and it would be a memory too soon.

Ian's fingers shifted with the economical mastery of long practice. And then the last chord was played and he lifted his right hand.

Seconds passed.

Byron flared his nostrils, drawing in the sweet afternoon air. "What was that? Who wrote it?"

"John Dowland," Ian said in barely more than a whisper. "It's called 'Welcome Home.' "

At the catch in Ian's voice, Byron looked at him sharply.

"It's as old as that old house," Ian said. "Maybe older. Do you know Dowland?"

"No," Byron said.

"He was wild," Ian told him. "Elizabethan. Always owed tons of money and got into trouble."

The stick Byron jabbed into the ground snapped. "You've really studied, haven't you?"

"Yeah. I guess."

"Do you want to play professionally?"

"I don't know."

Regardless of what Ian did or didn't think he wanted to do, he was too special not to be given every opportunity to pursue his interests. "Play something else."

Ian shook his head. He put the guitar away. "I won't be able to keep it."

"Yes, you—"

"How?" Something close to anger flashed in Ian's brown eyes. "If I can't even say I've seen you today, how am I going to take a new guitar home?"

"Your aunt won't know how . . . good it is," Byron finished slowly.

Jade made a small, distressed sound.

Damn. "Forget I said that. I don't want you trying to deceive Miss Cadwen. I'll keep it at the cottage for when you come over."

"That's a good idea," Jade said. She offered Ian a jam sponge but he ignored it.

"We'll figure out a way for you to visit real soon," Byron said with a sense that he'd lost all control of the situation.

Ian placed the guitar case very carefully to one side, drew up his knees, and wrapped his arms around his shins. "I don't get any of this. Why am I supposed to pretend we didn't see you today? What's wrong? Something is, isn't it?"

"Byron—"

"It's okay," Byron told Jade quickly. "I should have listened to you. But it's okay." The great psychologist had botched this job.

"What's going on?" Ian persisted.

"Nothing." Jade got to her knees. "We should probably start back."

"There is something going on," Byron said levelly. "Jade, what I said earlier goes. If we—if *I* don't tell him, some kid's going to blurt it out. It's better this way."

She thudded to sit on her heels. "You shouldn't have started this. Things would have worked out fine."

"I wouldn't change a thing," he told her, resolute. "Ian, I'm not sure how to do this without shocking you. I'll just tell it quickly and pray you'll want to understand."

He pinched the bridge of his nose. *Just tell him?* Hell. "I'm . . . I was your legal father. Your father . . ." Words failed him. His throat dried out.

Ian's face turned paler and the pupils of his eyes dilated.

"Your real mother's name was Lori Frazer," he said rapidly. "My wife. She died a few hours after you were born."

He heard Ian swallow. When he started to speak, his voice squeaked away to nothing.

"I was in college at the time. My father was already dead and I came from a family that couldn't help me anyway. There was no way I could give you a decent home. I couldn't even look after you. Now I know I should have tried to keep you. Other people get through. But I didn't."

A wash of red replaced Ian's pallor. "You're my father?"

Byron nodded. "I'm not sorry I did what I did. You needed a family. A mother and father. The Springs wanted you so much and they were good to you, weren't they?"

"Yes. They were my folks."

"Of course they were. And I would never have made myself known to you if I hadn't found out what happened to them. I came to Cornwall to make sure you were happy. I thought you would be. I didn't plan to stick around. But you need me, Ian."

"You're my dad. My real mom died. Two moms died."

Jade covered her face with her hands.

"Is that okay, Ian?" Byron asked. He felt sick.

Ian turned his head away.

"I'm going to try to make up—" No. He couldn't belittle the people Ian had loved by saying he wanted to make up for the time the Springs had been the boy's family. "Would you like it if I could be around?"

Thin shoulders rose and dropped.

"It isn't that I don't think Miss Cadwen is a good person. She is."

"Did you tell her?"

"Yes."

"When?"

"A few days ago."

"Figures," Ian said. "She's been funny."

"She—"

"She's okay, y'know. It's gotta be weird suddenly having a kid around, but she's okay."

Byron's eyes suddenly stung. He pressed his lips together. The shaft of feeling that went through him was unfamiliar but not completely forgotten: intense, protective tenderness. The sweetest thing he remembered of Lori was her loyal honesty and this son of hers could almost be speaking from his mother's heart.

"Sure she's okay," Byron agreed. "But it would be all right if I was there for you, wouldn't it?"

"That's why I'm not supposed to say I've seen you? Because Aunt Muriel didn't want me to?"

"Yes," Jade said. "I should have explained what was going on to you, Ian. I'm sorry."

"It's not your fault," Byron told her. "You won't have to pretend, Ian. I'll go to your Aunt Muriel and tell her this is all my doing. She'll probably be grateful everything's in the open."

"She's kind to me. She tries to be."

Hope began to shrivel in Byron. "I'm glad. I don't want to do anything you'd rather I didn't. Maybe it would be best if I stayed away—at least for a little while—until you decide you want to see me again."

Ian looked at him fully then. "I like my family here. They're different, but I'm getting used to them."

"Of course." Nothing had prepared him for the almost physical blow he felt. Ian was rejecting him.

"Uncle Art's teaching me a lot of things about working with wood. Auntie May's—" He glanced at Jade. "Auntie May's okay, too."

"Of course."

"When we met in the churchyard. You knew I was going to be there, didn't you?"

"Yes," Byron said simply. "I knew. I went there to find you."

The boy looked at him with eyes that glittered. "It was great when you knew about the Vikings and the Twins."

Jade made a strangled sound and bowed her head.

"Geez," Ian whispered. "I knew there was something about you."

Byron made a miserable attempt at a smile. "This is too much for you. It'd be too much for anyone."

"Yeah. But I'm glad. My dad . . . My real *dad*. Geez. Dad used to say my real dad was a good guy. He said he was someone I should be proud of because he did what was best for me. When I was little and Dad and Mom said prayers with me—like people do with little kids—they used to say thank you because my real—because my other . . . ." The boy was struggling but Byron knew he mustn't intervene. "They said thank you for me and they asked for . . . for you to be happy."

Jade sniffed. Tears coursed silently down her cheeks.

"I'm grateful you got the right parents," Byron said, meaning every word.

Ian got up. "Can we go back now?"

"If you want to."

"Yes." He walked to the river's edge, picked up a pebble, and shied it high into the air. In an instant it dropped into the water, causing not a ripple in the swift flow.

Turning back to Byron, Ian scrubbed his palms up and down the sides of his jeans. "Don't," he said, and his face began to crumple.

"I won't." Byron jumped to his feet. "I won't do anything you don't want me to do. If you'd feel better, I'll pack up and get out." His breath came in great gulps.

"No," Ian said. "Don't make Aunt Muriel sad . . . But don't go away."

Jade had persuaded him to let her be the one to tell Muriel Cadwen what had happened at Lanhydrock.

By then he'd felt too drained to attempt an argument and he'd given in to her gentle insistence that he keep the Martin for Ian regardless.

He let himself into the kitchen at Ferryneath and set the case on the table. ". . . *don't go away.*"

Byron arched his back, pulled up a chair, and sat down. However hard the next weeks might be. Whatever came of his attempt to gain custody of Ian, the decision to come here had been the right one. ". . . *don't go away.*"

He didn't want to remember the day of his eleventh birthday.

Hot. Yellow dust rising off parched, northern Californian earth. He'd smelled that dust through the screen door to the back porch. Mellie had been crying . . . so had his mother. That was when his father threw the iron skillet through the kitchen window . . .

Byron crossed his arms on the table and rested his forehead. *"Don't, Dad! Don't hit Mom!"*

He didn't want to remember.

"Shut your goddamn mouth, you whining apology for a son, or I'll shut it for you." Dad swayed and tipped up his can of beer, then tossed it, empty, across the room.

Mellie screamed and screamed and screamed.

"And shut that sniveling brat's mouth." Dad hefted a chair above his head and brought it down on the counter. The legs splintered and flew off. "Shut up!"

"Byrie, Byrie!" Mellie screamed. Trapped in her highchair, where she spent too many hours of her two-year-old life, she reached splayed fingers for Byron. Her nose ran and her cheeks were drenched. Sweat-damp curls clung around her flushed face.

"Don't go out tonight, Sam." His mother's voice broke. She had remained on the floor by the sink—where his father had pushed her. "Not on Byron's birthday. Stay tonight. I can't—"

"Shut your goddamn mouth!" Sam Frazer's thin face turned red. He spread his arms along the counter behind him and his chest heaved. "I'm not staying here with this mess and that's that. I'm going where a man's word means something."

"At the tavern, Sam? With the rest of the drunks?"

He swung from his height and slapped her—open-handed—across the face.

Byron heard the crack of big, male force on his fragile mother's tired face.

She didn't cry out.

"Goddamn it!" his father shouted, slurring the words. "Damn you all! You all want something from me. Bloodsuckers!"

"Stay, Sam," his mother whispered. "Don't go away. I need you."

"Will you shut your whining?"

Yet again the great hand rose.

"Don't hit Mom!" Byron threw himself at his father, clung to his sweat-stained shirt when he straight-armed him. "Mom's sick. She's real sick." Still clinging, Byron kicked and kicked while breath sobbed from burning lungs.

"Ungrateful sonovabitch," Sam Frazer said through his teeth. "I married her, didn't I? She's always been sick. Never lookin' after me like a man's got a right."

Byron kicked again and screwed up his eyes against the pain in his bare feet.

"You've turned my son into a momma's boy," Byron's father yelled. And Mellie hiccupped—choking, dry hiccups—and she wailed afresh.

Then the screen door slammed open, just as Byron had known it would. And just as he'd expected, there stood Aunt Dot. Mom must have called her sister, like she always did when she was going to try to keep Dad home.

Aunt Dot stood, her heavy legs planted apart, a shapeless floral dress stretched around her body. "A fine mess, I must say. As if I didn't have enough to do with my own family. Cal and me're trying to bring up four kids. Why you can't manage two, I'll never figure."

Sam Frazer crossed his arms. "Called her as usual," he said to his wife. "Might have known she'd be showing up any minute."

"You should have left him years ago," Aunt Dot said to her sister. She'd never been afraid of Dad and Byron liked her for that. It was all he liked her for. "Stopped at one, you should have," she muttered, hauling Mellie from the high chair.

"We're all right," Byron said, as loudly and firmly as he could. "You don't need to take Mellie and me."

"That'll be enough from you," Aunt Dot told him. "Ungrateful is what you are. Your mother's my sister and it's up to me to do my best for her in her times of trouble."

"No," Byron said, his desperation growing. "We'll be all right, won't we, Mom? Dad?"

"Get your things," Aunt Dot said, taking Mellie to the sink and sponging her face with the dish cloth. "And be quick about it. Your cousin Arthur's got a softball game. I'll have to leave you there with the little ones while Cal and me go."

His mother scrambled up and stood, hugging her middle. Wisps of her dark hair had pulled free of her ponytail to drape her neck. She looked at his dad. He stared back like he hated her.

"Mom," Byron said. "I'll help here. We can do it. I'll help. Don't send me off with her."

"Do what your aunt tells you," his father said.

His aunt, who invariably showed up when things got bad and who always said she was doing her duty even though she already had too much to do with her own "brood." His aunt, who never missed an opportunity to say how grateful he should be to have family to go to.

"Get going," his father said, scuffing to the refrigerator for another beer. He popped the top and sent a stream pouring down his throat.

"You can use some of your cousin's things for tonight," Aunt Dot said. "We'll pick some stuff up here in the morning."

She took a look at her sister's cheek where red welts were already bruising. "I don't know what you're coming to, Anne. I don't. What Mom and Pop would have said about the way you carry on, I don't know."

With that she hitched Mellie higher on her hip and marched to open the door. "I got things to do. Come on."

Byron looked at the birthday cake his mother had made. She'd been putting candles on the top when Dad came home. Byron had hoped it would be different this time, that because his mom was trying to do stuff other moms did, his dad might be pleased. Just this once.

"Well," Sam Frazer said. "I've got places to go. So if you'll excuse me, I'll be on my way."

"No," Byron's mother said. "Don't go, Sam."

He walked across the room as if she hadn't spoken. When he reached the table, he paused—and then he cupped a hand under the cake plate and sent it crashing to the linoleum. In an explosion of blue and white frosting, Anne Frazer's attempt at something normal for a change was spread over every surface.

"Well!" Aunt Dot marched outside. "Come on, Byron."

His father beat him through the door and set off toward the pickup.

"Let me stay, Mom," Byron begged. "I'll look after you."

"Go," she said through rapidly swelling lips. "I don't want you. Don't you understand that. Go!" She started shaking, and rocking herself, and pacing.

She was going away again, like she did when things got too bad.

He hesitated before going out onto the porch and down steps to the rough stone pathway between scraggly patches of brown grass.

Aunt Dot was already getting into her station wagon. "Get over here, Byron. And be quick about it."

He couldn't go; he wouldn't.

"Dad!" Byron started running toward the pickup. "Dad, wait up!"

The pickup's engine roared.

"Dad!" Byron drew level and caught at the rim of the driver's window. "Dad, don't make me go with her. I'll do all the stuff around here. You won't have to. I can do everything."

"Scat!" His father pried Byron's fingers loose.

"Please—"

The engine, gunned by a heavy boot, drowned Byron's voice.

"Please, Dad . . . don't go away."

Sam Frazer looked at Byron through the window of the pickup and his lip curled. He reached to give one last, vicious shove and drove off.

That had been the last time he'd been together with his father and mother and Mellie. Byron and Mellie never got to leave Aunt Dot's. Sam Frazer drank until, with the help of a dark night and a slick road, the booze killed him. Anne Frazer came to visit—Aunt Dot got her from the place where she'd been sent and brought her to visit. She would rock and smile at Mellie, and stoke her like she was a baby. Mom stroked Mellie like that when she was eight. When his mom looked at him, she cried without tears and said, "Sam, oh, Sam. Take me home." And she'd died in that place Byron never saw. Later he learned that in a state-run institution, his destitute mother died by drowning. She lay facedown in a tub, in water too shallow to cover her, and breathed in until she went away.

When Byron raised his face, he made no attempt to wipe away the tears. These tears were good. Tears that should have been shed a long time ago, the same tears he urged his patients to shed on their road to becoming whole.

Because of Mellie, he hadn't run away from Aunt Dot's. Then, when she was ten, she'd beaten him to it. She'd asked him to go with her, but he didn't believe she meant any of it. Ever since that night Byron had wondered how long she'd waited for him to meet her by the truck stop. After several months, when she didn't come back, and wasn't found, Byron left, too. He never heard from his sister again, but he still prayed she'd survived and was happy somewhere.

"You'll be a good psychologist one day," Lori had told him many times. "First you'll have to find yourself. Then you'll help others do the same thing."

And he'd thought his own healing was complete—until today. Today he'd looked into another boy's eyes and heard an echo of his own voice across the years.

"Don't go away," Ian had said, just as Byron had asked his father not to go away.

Sam Frazer had ignored his son's plea.

Byron would not ignore Ian's.

Chapter Eighteen

"Hello, Dad." Jade approached her father, who stood on the front steps of New to You. "How long have you been here?"

"Muriel called. I came right over."

"Ah." Jade's stomach took a nosedive. "She didn't waste any time." After dropping Ian off and dealing with Aunt Muriel's tearful reproaches, she'd been to Perron's shop to check in supplies, but that hadn't taken more than an hour.

"This isn't only about Ian," Art Perron said, waiting while she unlocked the shop door and then following her inside. "I've got other things on my mind and it's time I spoke my piece."

"Great," Jade said, unable to stop herself. "I've had a hard day, Dad. Couldn't this other thing wait?"

"No. This other thing, as you call it, could be affected by your shenanigans with that Frazer fellow."

Shenanigans. Wonderful. Now would come the third-degree followed by a bunch of orders she had no intention of obeying. This promised to be the perfect end to a perfectly awful day.

Jade kept silent while going to retrieve Dog from the tiny yard behind the shop. When she returned and climbed the stairs to her flat, Art Perron was already perched awkwardly on the edge of a straight-backed chair, his battered tweed hat swinging between his knees.

"I've got to feed Dog," Jade said. "Maybe we should get together tomorrow instead."

"It's time for this now. Your mother and I worry about you."

"Oh, no." Shaking her head, Jade made for the kitchen. "Not that. How many times do I have to tell you *not* to worry about me?" She stalked to the kitchen sink and jerked the faucet on.

"I was over at the shop this morning," Dad said. "Gavin and Bert were in for a pickup. They reckon they're close to being done."

She watched water gush into the white sink. "I know the status, Dad. Of everything. That's part of my job. Remember?"

"I remember. Could be that's where the mistake is."

"Meaning?" Jade turned off the water and faced him. "Perron's does very well. I see to that."

"Your mother always said we shouldn't have let you grow up to be a woman in a man's job."

"Damn it, Dad!" She leaned over the sink. "I told you this wasn't a good time for the kind of discussion you've got in mind. Nothing's changed. I'm doing what I like to do most. I know there aren't many women who see a freshly papered wall as an accomplishment. I do. I'm working at what I was trained to do. End of discussion."

"You almost done over at Ferryneath?"

Darn the gossip mongers in this little town. "No. I'm not almost finished. Everything I touch there turns into a major job. I decided to move outside and get the exterior paint done. I've got rotten wood to replace. There's loose window glass. The whole lot had to be burned off to nothing. I'm going to be there for a while, Dad. So what? We're charging for every minute."

Art Perron prowled, opening and shutting cupboards, not to look inside but to check hinges. "Send Bert or Gavin over to finish."

She stared at her father. "No."

"I said send Bert or Gavin."

"And I said no. Dad, I'm the boss now."

"And I own Perron's."

"All right. That's true. Are you sacking me?"

"I want you to stay away from Byron Frazer."

"I . . ." Jade took a deep breath that did nothing to calm her and—very deliberately—filled Dog's dish. "There, girl."

"The man's trouble."

"You don't know what you're talking about. You don't know Byron."

"Byron is it now? That man is dividing your family."

She would not argue about this. "I will be continuing with my work as planned. That's it, Dad."

He pulled out a chair, sat down, and slumped. "Doug Lyman made a bad mistake."

"That's another off-limits subject."

"Takes a big person to forgive a real mistake like that."

"Isn't Mom waiting tea for you? It's after six."

"He's sorry now. He's been sorry for a long time. You're the only one he wants. That little Rose needs a mother—with her own taking off like she did."

Jade looked at him with total disbelief. "Doug Lyman is a subject I won't discuss—with anyone. I will try to be there for Rose when she needs me. I'm very fond of her. Doug's a good dad. That's it."

"He was too young when you married. A man needs time to sow his wild oats."

Jade's pulse beat loud enough to thump in her brain.

"He's all over that now. With you back where you belong, he'd do well enough—you both would."

"You're making excuses for the man who was my husband and who found himself a lover while we were married." She scarcely dared to move. An alien desire to break something shook her.

"I'm asking you to give Doug another chance. For both of you. He needs a wife and you're the only one he's interested in. And you need a husband. It's not right for a woman to be without purpose, the way you are."

"I'm *not* without purpose. I can't believe what you just said."

"Well, I said it, girlie. And now I'm going to say something else. You always were headstrong. It's the man that's meant to wear the trousers in the family. You remember that. Then ask yourself if you ever allowed Doug to be the man of the house. A bloke doesn't turn elsewhere the way he did if he's got all he needs at home. You always were trying to prove you were as good as any man."

Jade clamped her mouth shut and willed the rage to subside. *He's an old man.* Her father was from another generation. He'd never change.

"Doug's a hard worker. He doesn't always make his plans the way I would. But he's a trier and he'll do well in the end, you see if he doesn't."

Something banged downstairs and Art immediately got up.

"Good grief," Jade said. "The shop door wasn't shut."

"You be open-minded," Dad said. "Tomorrow we'll talk more about why you set out to upset your aunt today. And keep away from Frazer. We're going to deal with him. He thinks we're so simple he can come in here and shove us aside. Well, he's got another think coming. He didn't want the boy before and he's not getting him now."

Jade massaged the space between her brows. What kind of joker-like fate set a woman up to fall in love with the man her family was sworn to drive away?

Love. God help her, she did love Byron and she could never have more than a little piece of him, the piece he chose to offer her until he either did or didn't get what he'd come here to get. Then he'd leave and she'd never be the same.

The sound of footsteps on the stairs jolted her onto alert. "Dad! There's someone coming."

Art Perron did something Jade never remembered seeing him do before. He turned red.

"Dad, what?"

The door to the flat opened. Dog, already bristling, growled low and steady.

"Reckon it's time I got on home. Your mother's in a fine state, I can tell you. Damn fool Muriel's there, and the boy. He's the one I feel sorriest for."

Jade could only stare, eyes wide, at the open kitchen door.

"Hello!" Doug Lyman's voice, calling from the living room, sent first a rush of annoyance, then a swell of rage into Jade.

"Art! I'm here."

She glowered at her father, whose eyes immediately shifted away. "How could you?" she murmured.

"Time you settled down again," Art muttered. "Give him another chance, I say. You'll both benefit."

"Over my dead body," Jade said through her teeth. Doug appeared in the kitchen doorway and she turned her back.

"All right then," her father said. "This is where I make myself scarce. I've done my bit, boy. The rest is up to you, but I think you'll find her more open now we've had a chat."

With something near amazement, Jade listened to Art Perron clumping across kitchen tile and, seconds later, closing the door to the flat behind him.

"This is what I've been hoping for," Doug said.

That her own father would sell out on her?

"You won't regret it. I promise you that. What I did was a rotten mistake, but I've paid for it."

"*You've* paid for it?" She bowed her head. "I'm *so* sorry you've had such a hard time."

"Harder than you know," Doug said, oozing sincerity. "But we can put all that behind us now."

Jade rubbed her eyes. Her father had set her up for this.

At Doug's touch on her shoulder, muscles all over her body locked. He smoothed strands of hair that had worked loose from her ponytail. "We were always good together, Jade."

"*Were.* You chose the right tense."

Doug tried to turn her toward him. When she resisted, he half lifted her to stand facing him.

Blood roared in Jade's ears. "*Don't* touch me," she told him, furious at the wobble in her voice.

"You're going to need a bit of convincing is all," he said, still gripping her right shoulder hard. With his free hand, he forced up her chin. "You're one of those women who only gets better-looking. Just seeing you turns me on."

She began to tremble. "Let me go, please."

His answer was to bring his mouth down on hers.

Jade struggled, but she couldn't begin to match his strength. His eyes had closed. He drew her against his body and she didn't have to guess how ready he was for what he'd obviously come to accomplish.

In the seconds that followed, his breathing grew labored, and if he heard the sobbing in her throat, or felt her desperate clawing at his back, he gave no sign.

"Stop it," she gasped when he drew back to breathe. "Don't do this, Doug."

Once again his eyes glazed and closed. He held her as he might a rag doll. And with his hard lips, he forced hers wide open to reach his tongue deep into her mouth.

Jade's stomach turned. Sweat broke out on her face and back.

"Come on," Doug whispered hoarsely. "We were good together, Jay. You haven't forgotten how. Let me in."

His mouth cut off her denial. And his hand moved from her jaw to her breast. He kneaded her flesh without finesse and his hips ground against her.

In an instant of utter clarity, Jade knew that struggling would only excite him more. She remembered that there had been an edge of violence to Doug's lovemaking and on occasions when she'd resisted, he'd taken that resistance as her way of saying she liked rough loving.

"Jay," he said against her ear, panting. "I want you. I've waited so long. I've got to have you."

She held absolutely still.

"God, you're so beautiful." Fumbling, he undid the buttons on her shirt and pushed his way inside her bra. "I never forgot these, sweetheart. You always had the best . . . the best."

Willing herself not to scream, not to fight, Jade fixed her gaze on his chest and locked her knees.

"Oh, yes," Doug said. "Oh, *yes.*"

She screwed up her eyes.

Roughly pushing at her breast, he bent to fasten lips and teeth over her nipple.

Jade grasped his ear and twisted.

"What the?"

She twisted some more and jerked—and Doug grabbed for her hand.

"I told you *no*," Jade said. Fury made her strong. "I told you to stop, damn you."

Her fingernails dug into the skin. He yelped and lost his balance. And Jade kicked him where the result was a bellow of pain.

"Get out!" Her yell joined Doug's.

He crouched, doubled over, apparently oblivious to his scarlet right ear. "Damn you," he said on a hissing breath. "Your dad's going to hear all about what his dear little girl's learned since she hasn't had a man around. You need taking down a peg and I'm the one to do it."

As determinedly as her shaking legs would allow, Jade walked into the living room and picked up the phone. She dialed the local police station and waited for Marjorie Feldon's pleasant voice to inquire, "Is this an emergency?"

"It may be, Marjorie," Jade said, grateful her old school chum was the dispatcher on duty. Still hunched, Doug staggered from the kitchen. "This is Jade. I'm at my flat. You know where that is. Give me a moment. I'm just waiting to see if I need help."

"What is it?" Normally unflappable, Marjorie sounded alarmed. "Jade?"

"Just keep me on the line."

Doug hovered, glaring, and Jade knew he was calculating his next move.

She stared back at him, unflinching.

"Jade?"

"I'm here, Marjorie. Busy night?"

"No. What—"

"I'll tell you all about it later. Right now I'm dealing with something as safely as I can. Is that okay?"

"Yes." Marjorie was a capable, sensible woman.

"Damn you," Doug said in a whisper. "Art's meeting me at the Preacher. He isn't going to like what I'm going to tell him. That yank's changed you."

"If explaining what you just tried to my father makes you feel good, then do it. Be my guest."

Drawing himself up, wincing, Doug left the flat with a less assured step than when he'd arrived.

"Will you tell me what's going on there?" Marjorie asked.

Jade carried the phone to the window and looked down on the street. Soon Doug's big, shadowy form emerged from the building and he set off in the direction of Town Quay.

"Oh, Marjorie," Jade said, letting out her breath. "Men can be such asses."

"Were they ever anything else?" Marjorie had not been lucky in love. "Are you all right, Jade? Or should I send someone over?"

"I'm okay, thanks to you. Just a brush with Doug. He's trying to get back into my life and it isn't going to work."

Marjorie said something that attested to the hours she spent in bad company. Jade laughed before hanging up. She sat on the closest chair and tried to calm her jumping stomach. Her father would get a very much edited version of what had occurred, but nevertheless, she had no doubt that the subject wasn't closed.

A knock on the door shocked Jade so badly she dropped the phone. "Go away!" She shot to her feet. "I told you to go away, Doug. If you come in here again, I *will* get the police."

The door was flung open. "What the hell's the problem?" Byron stood, framed against light on the landing. "The shop door was wide open. For God's sake, you've got to be more careful."

"Didn't you see Doug?" Her resolve faltered. Stinging in her eyes felt infuriatingly like the start of tears.

"Someone was walking farther up the street. But I didn't see who it was."

The phone receiver began to drone. Byron walked swiftly to pick it up and replace the instrument on a table. "What's wrong, Jade?"

She looked up at him, and to her horror, her teeth chattered so badly she couldn't respond.

"He did something to you." Byron took in her disheveled hair and rumpled, unbuttoned shirt. "Did that bastard? . . . Jade?" He dropped to one knee beside her and gently stroked back her hair. "Tell me what just happened here."

"It's over. Doug . . . Forget it."

"You're shaking and I want to know why. Did he try to force himself on you?"

She looked into narrowed eyes that glittered like green glass, green glass with sharp edges.

Very carefully, Byron eased her forward until her face pressed against his neck. Rhythmically, he continued to smooth her hair, but beneath the tenderness, she felt pure, tough tension that made his muscles rock hard.

"Tell me."

"It's over."

"Where was he going?"

"The Bell and Preacher. Where else?"

"He tried . . . Jade, he tried to force you, didn't he?"

"He thinks I should let him back into my life."

"So the answer to my question is yes."

What difference did it make if Byron knew her ex-husband thought she should want to climb into bed with him. "Yes." She was tired.

Everything about Byron became very still. He set her from him and rested a hand on the side of her face. Without speaking, he kissed her forehead then stood up, and for the first time she noticed that he, too, was disheveled.

"Byron?" She reached for him and he caught her hands between both of his. "What's wrong with you? Tell me."

He laughed and the sound was frightening. "Not now. I came face to face with an old enemy I never wanted to confront again, but I don't want to talk about it. There's something I need to do now. I'll lock the door on the way out."

A shaft of apprehension flashed goosebumps over her skin. "Where are you going?"

"Stay where you are. Don't move a muscle."

Jade stood up. "Where are you going?"

There was a subtle change in his eyes. Possessiveness? Possessiveness overlaid with fury? Watching her mouth, he framed her face. "No one hurts you, Jade. Not without dealing with me."

"Byron—"

His kiss, fierce enough to force her head back, silenced Jade.

As abruptly as he'd kissed her, Byron stepped away. "I'll be back."

"Byron, don't do anything—"

"Sh." He placed his fingers on her lips. "I'll only do what someone should have done a long time ago."

The rage was foreign. Frustration was an old friend. Byron shoved his way into the public bar at the Bell and Preacher. Smoke mingled with the scent of old, warm beer, and feminine laughter rose amid the rumble of male voices.

He squinted to see over the loud crush.

The sonovabitch had . . . The desire to inflict pain was also foreign. In Jade's flat, when he'd looked at the evidence of Lyman's advances, Byron had known an instant of murderous anger.

"Byron." A tap on his shoulder startled him.

He turned to see his neighbor, Harry Hancock. "Hi, Harry." The elderly man held a pipe in one hand and a glass of beer in the other.

"Recruited you to the Preacher, too, have they?"

Byron heard another voice he remembered. Raised above the babble, Lyman's words came clearly: "Bloody yank. Thinks he can buy whatever he wants."

"No, they haven't recruited me," Byron said to Harry. "I'm here on business."

The man's bushy gray brows drew down. "What's wrong, lad?"

"Nothing you need trouble yourself about. I'll deal with it and buy you another beer."

Harry glanced in the direction of the bar. Lyman's loud voice had moved on from general insult to plain threats as to what he intended to do to "that bloody Yank."

"If I were you," Harry said, trying to insert himself between Byron and the rest of the assembly, "I'd just step out and head for Bodinnick. There's some here can get nasty. You aren't the kind of bloke to deal with the likes of Doug Lyman and Sam Hill. Come on."

Byron firmly, but kindly, removed Harry's hand from his arm. "Don't worry. I can handle this." He'd learned not to be afraid of bullies.

Shouldering his way forward, he reached what felt like the inner circle, a group that held court before the bar. He recognized Doug Lyman's drink-reddened face, but the rest of the men were strangers to him.

To one side sat the woman who owned the building Jade lived in. She looked at him with something close to panic.

Byron nodded pleasantly at her. "Good evening, Shirley. May I buy you a drink?"

She tugged on a braid and glanced nervously at a big, ruddy-faced man with an imposing gut encased in a navy blue sweater. "No, thank you," she said.

Slowly, a tall, thin man turned toward him. He appeared to be approximately in his late sixties. With hard eyes, he assessed Byron. "You Frazer?"

"The same."

"I don't think you want to be here."

That was when Lyman fell silent. With one arm, he pushed the man aside. "That's him, Art," he said. "That's the bastard who's pushing poor Muriel around. And he's . . . He's not good for Jade. Giving her ideas she's got no business having if you ask me."

"*I* didn't ask you," Byron said, taking a step that brought him within beer-laden breath range of Lyman. "But there are a few other things I'm going to ask you."

"Like what?"

"Like why you went to your ex-wife's flat and tried to rape her."

Silence fell in the immediate vicinity and steadily spread until no one in the bar spoke. Doug Lyman's flush drained, leaving him putty pale and with a sweating brow.

"What's he talking about?" the man named Art asked. He looked at Byron. "Is something wrong with my Jade?"

Jade's father. The man's choice of words, together with a real view of dark blue eyes, left no doubt.

"Be careful what you say," Harry Hancock murmured. He'd come to stand at Byron's elbow. "You're not on your own turf here."

"You bet he's not," Lyman suddenly blustered. "Coming here with his money and his flash. Trying to take away our Ian."

"*Your* Ian?"

"I'm part of the family," Lyman said, shouting now. "Jade was my wife and she will be again once you stop putting fancy ideas in her head."

"Jade will never be your wife again," Byron said quietly. "You're history. When you committed adultery, you did her a favor. You'd already wasted more of her life than any piece of scum like you could possibly be worth."

There was a shifting of the crowd, a sense of a communal indrawn breath.

"What did you say?" Lyman came close enough for Byron to see the other man's pupils dilate.

"You heard me. And you tried to force yourself on Jade earlier this evening."

Lyman's Adam's apple jerked. He swallowed beer without taking his eyes from Byron. "You're not getting that boy. He belongs here now. No man who abandons his kid deserves to get a second chance with him."

"Ian's welfare isn't your affair," Byron said. "Neither is Jade. Stay away from her."

Shirley slid from her stool and stood behind the big, dark-haired man.

"Did you hear what he said?" Lyman asked, curling his lip and looking to his companions for support. "He's telling us what to do about our own. He came here to interfere in the Perrons' business and he's turning Jade's head with his big talk."

"Ian isn't the Perrons' business," Byron said very distinctly. "He's in Miss Cadwen's care. And what does or doesn't happen in that regard doesn't concern you."

"We're not letting you take that boy," Lyman said.

Under different circumstances Byron might have laughed at the man's clumsy attempt to divert attention from himself. "The decision about who brings up Ian will be decided by the law."

Fingers curling into the sleeve of his shirt broke his concentration. He turned and looked down into Jade's troubled face.

"Come away," she said. "This won't accomplish anything."

"I told you to stay put."

"I couldn't."

"See what I mean, Art?" Lyman said loudly. "He's got her eating out of his hand."

Byron swung back.

"Take off," Lyman ordered. "Get back where you came from. We aren't your kind of people. Isn't that right?" He sought about for agreement.

"Right enough," a burly, red-haired man said, muscling forward. "We don't want your sort in Fowey. We don't want you messing with our people."

"Clear out," another voice suggested.

A rumble of indistinct comments swelled.

"Please," Jade said, pulling on his arm.

"You'd best leave," Harry put in. "Before they get nasty."

"Come here, Jade," Art Perron said.

Lyman reached for her and Byron shot out a hand to ward him off.

"Damn Yank," Lyman said. "You with me, Bert?" He acknowledged the red-haired man, who nodded grimly. "Sam?" This time he looked to the man behind whom Shirley had taken cover.

"Think, Doug," the big man said. "Don't bite off more than you can chew."

Lyman's jaw jutted. "I don't see anything here I can't manage. This is your last chance, Frazer. Take yourself off, or we'll have to help you on your way."

"Go home, Jade," Byron said. "Harry, you take her."

"That's it," Jade announced. "I'm not leaving you people to brawl like bullies on the playground."

Lyman rolled up his sleeves. "This isn't woman's business, Jade. I'll talk to you later."

Byron narrowed his eyes. "I came here to do something and I'm going to make sure I do it. Why don't we go outside, Lyman?"

"Here will do just fine."

"Why? Afraid to face me without your cronies?"

Lyman lunged. Byron stepped aside. The man stumbled and barely kept from falling.

"Sod," Lyman hissed through his teeth. "Get him!"

"Stay put," the big man called Sam said, almost serenely. "All of you."

"Hell if I will. Come on Bert. Let's get him."

Bert took a step forward and stopped. "Doesn't look like Jade wants us to get him." He smiled. Not a pretty sight. "Looks to me like she's sweet on him. That right, Jade?"

Lyman's face turned a shade paler and he drew back his lips. "He's turned her head is all. Art, take Jade home."

"Take me home!" Jade's voice rose. *Take me home?* For God's sake. When did I turn into a little kid again? And when did I turn into someone *you* could order around again, Doug? Byron *is* my friend. I'm not afraid to say as much."

An ugly male titter broke out. "Looks like your old lady found a replacement for you, Doug," one man said. "Reckon as how you'd better give up on what you had planned."

Lyman drew himself up. "We'll see about that." He caught Jade's wrist and yanked her toward him. "You're coming with me."

"Don't!"

Byron's arm, snaking around her waist, interrupted Jade's cry. He lifted her from the floor and swung her from Lyman's grasp—and jackknifed over the fist the other man sent into his belly.

Before he could catch a breath, a chop to the back of his neck flung him down on rough oak boards.

"Byron!" Jade's voice came to him, but dimly. Keeping his head down, he focused on Lyman's booted feet.

Then he launched himself at the man's ankles. Wrapping his arms in a tackle, he felled Doug Lyman.

"Bloody hell." A grunt of pain accompanied the thud of the other's heavy body. "Get him. Get the bloody sod."

"Stop it! Stop them!" He didn't recognize a woman's shriek.

Lyman scrambled, but Byron held on.

Clinging, rolling, he turned them both over and worked his way up to pin Lyman beneath him. "All right," he said, for his quarry's ears only. "We can do this with as little damage as possible—to either of us. Or we can do it with a whole lot of damage to you."

Lyman's body jerked and Byron heard the sound of wood dragging on wood. "You don't give the orders around here," Lyman said, gasping. With a heave, he hefted something and Byron braced for impact.

The chair that smashed down missed Byron's back and shattered against the bar.

" 'Ere, 'ere! Watch that!" a male voice shouted. "I'm calling the coppers."

"Hold your horses, Albert. Lads will be lads."

Byron jammed a forearm across Lyman's throat, hitched himself up, and clamped the other's powerful arms beneath his own knees. "I'm not asking you for anything," he said, fighting for breath. "I'm telling you. Stay away from Jade. And don't meddle in anything to do with Ian."

"You—"

Byron's arm, jerking harder into the windpipe, cut off whatever Lyman had intended to say. "You heard me. Now get up." He sprang to his feet and waited until he once again looked directly into his opponent's angry eyes.

"You're going to regret this, Frazer."

"Not nearly as much as you're going to regret it." Byron pulled Jade to his side. "The next time you feel like pushing a woman around, remember the message I'm giving you." His right fist, connecting with Lyman's jaw, made the sharp crack of bone on bone. "That was for Jade."

The last thing he noticed before walking out was the big man, Sam. Sam's grin was accompanied by a salute.

Chapter Nineteen

The night was blessedly cool.

"Are you okay?" Jade asked Byron. "Do you hurt anywhere?"

"I'm fine."

Holding her hand, he walked away from the Preacher. Jade made no comment when, instead of turning toward Lostwithiel Street, he headed for the path above the water's edge. Bathed by the gentle breeze off the Channel, they walked in silence to the hushed slapping of water against rock.

"Did Lyman hurt you?" Byron asked suddenly.

"No."

"I hope I hurt him. A man who forces himself on a woman deserves to get the crap beaten out of him."

"You hurt him, Byron." And she knew a fierce pleasure at his desire to defend her.

A bird flapped suddenly upward from a low bush and soared a path across a white moon.

"So quiet," Jade said. "But so full of sounds." She laughed. "Does that make sense?"

"Everything you say makes perfect sense to me."

"Why did you come here tonight?"

"To see you. That's why. I just had to see you."

"Aunt Muriel was upset with me."

"I'm sorry. That was my fault."

"I didn't have to bring Ian to you."

"I'm glad you did."

Something skittered across the path. Jade faltered, then let Byron pull her onward. "He's such a nice boy."

"I know."

"He's doing okay here."

"Okay isn't enough."

She'd known what he would say. "I hope you don't make things unbearable—for everyone."

"I won't let that happen, Jade."

From the open sea came the muted wail of a ship's horn. Not far away, a small craft's running lights bobbed across the mouth of the inlet.

Byron walked doggedly on and Jade was happy to walk with him. *She would walk anywhere with Byron.* Her spine prickled and she swallowed deliberately. This way led to whatever a broken heart might mean.

They strolled from the outskirts of the town toward the deserted coastland. With the final smattering of lights obscured behind them, civilization felt far away and irrelevant.

At Readymoney Cove, Byron led the way onto coarse sand turned gray-silver by the moon. Their feet crunched as they approached the softly running surf. Jade took off her shoes and squealed when cold water slithered over her toes.

"Serves you right," Byron said, laughing and pulling her back. "The tide's going out. Let's find somewhere to sit and watch."

What he found was a smooth rock nestled amid a jumble of neighbors close to the shore. Side by side, they sat and looked toward the darkly swelling ebb and flow of the English Channel.

Jade sandwiched her hands between her knees. The breeze flirted with her full, cotton skirt. Byron stretched out his legs and leaned back to brace his weight on his arms.

When he left, he'd take part of her with him—the best part—the part capable of unselfish love. She tipped her face up to the sky and held her bottom lip tightly between her teeth.

"What are you thinking?"

She'd never been a good liar. "That nothing stays the same for very long."

For several seconds Byron seemed to wait, then he said, "Most things shouldn't stay the same. But I do believe that everything has a purpose—everything that happens."

Jade twisted to look at him. "Everything? How can you say that?" Moonlight painted the clear lines of his straight nose and cheekbones, the sharp angle of his jaw.

"We come to wherever we are because of what's gone before. If I hadn't been the child of an alcoholic father and an enabling mother—with all that meant—my life would have been different."

It was Jade's turn to wait and she did so gladly. The moment was precious, this moment of feeling him draw her into the very private places in his life.

"Some people would pity me for having lived through the hell of a dysfunctional family. I'd have pitied myself once. Now I know that in a very important way, my childhood was perfect. It was what it was and it set me on a path to a place where I could help other people trying to fight their way out."

Jade found Byron's hand and slipped her fingers into his. "You like what you do. You're good at it."

He laughed. "You only have my word for it, but yes, I'm very good at it. And I'm lucky. It's true that when I set out for Cornwall I was tired, and maybe disillusioned. Partly because I'd realized that although I do a good job with other people's wavy paths, I haven't done so well straightening myself out. Being here's been good for me. I feel filled up again."

She wanted to ask him why. "I'm glad." Not for the first time tonight, tears stung her eyes.

"Sorry to unload on you," he said.

"Feel free," Jade told him.

"I must feel safe with you. I don't remember that happening before."

Not even with Ian's mother? Not even with your wife?

"This may be the most beautiful place in the world."

But it wouldn't hold him for long. "It is to me. Ian likes it, too." He couldn't know how desperately she wanted him to stay.

"Jade."

"Yes."

He took her hand to his lips. "I can't seem to sleep anymore."

"What?" His breath warmed her skin. "What do you mean?"

"I mean that every time I try to sleep I think about you and bam! . . . I might as well give up."

"Oh."

"Oh? Is that all you can say?"

"I'm sorry you can't sleep."

"What I do when I should be sleeping and can't is a whole lot more fun."

Jade swallowed. In this great big airy night she couldn't fill her lungs.

"Aren't you going to ask me what I do?" He paused, and when she didn't respond, he said, "No? Well, I'll tell you anyway. There are two scenarios. I seduce you or you seduce me. Which one do you want first?"

"Byron."

"Byron," he echoed and she heard his smile. "I've shocked you. Good. Which one?"

"Byron!"

He let his head drop back and he laughed. His teeth glinted in the darkness.

Jade pulled her hand away and crossed her arms. "I'm glad I'm so funny." A purely sexual thrill did shock her then—shock and excite her. "Let's start with how I seduce you."

The way his laugh immediately died brought her intense satisfaction. With one finger, she lightly drew a line along the top of his jean-clad thigh, close enough to his groin to make him jerk and grab for her.

Too easily, Byron managed to sit up and haul Jade into his lap. "How you seduce me, huh?"

"I ought to know . . . Just in case."

Locked in his embrace, Jade wiggled—and Byron's breath hissed between his teeth. "Don't do that, sweetheart, not if you don't want a graphic demonstration of what I'm going to tell you."

She wiggled some more.

"I see." Scooting forward, he stood up and walked toward the sea with Jade in his arms. "I like being close to the water. It sharpens my imagination."

Jade heard her own heartbeat.

"In my fantasy, you come to me by moonlight."

She looked at the sky. "Yes, that's what I do."

"You come toward me and stand close enough for me to touch, but you don't let me touch you."

"Put me down, Byron."

He did as she asked.

Facing the sea, Jade stood in front of him. "What do I do then?"

"You drive me to the edge. And that's where I'm heading right now."

She shuddered. "Then you'll just have to let me go right ahead and seduce you, won't you?"

"Oh, yes, Jade." Byron spread the fingers of one hand on the side of her neck.

"You aren't supposed to touch me," she reminded him.

Jade turned toward Byron. He'd never seemed bigger, never felt bigger than he did now. Staring up into his shadowed eyes, she undid his shirt, pulled it from his jeans, and flattened her palms on his chest. The hair there was thick and soft, the beat of his heart steady beneath her hand.

His clean scent became one with the salt air. "You undress me, Jade." There was a break in his deep voice. "You strip me naked while I tell you how badly I want to be inside you."

Jade's stomach contracted. She pushed the shirt back from his shoulders and pulled it down his arms. "Tell me, Byron." The shirt fell to the sand.

"I want to feel myself just touching you. I want to press inside a little and wait, and press some more."

She opened her mouth to breathe. He wore no belt and the snap of his jeans came apart with a sharp click—before his zipper slid open. Standing on tiptoe, Jade sought his mouth. "This is where I kiss you," she whispered. He embraced her. The kiss was long and slow, and hot—and it left Jade weak-kneed.

Byron traced her ear with the tip of his tongue and nipped the lobe. Jade began to tremble violently. "Keep on telling me, Byron. I'm falling apart."

"That's how I want you. Falling apart—with me buried in you."

Her own cry became another night sound. His jeans were tight and soft. Her fingers fumbled to work them down. He stood still then, and everywhere she touched him, muscle and sinew jolted steel hard.

"You're falling apart," he murmured. "And I'm shattering."

Dropping to her knees was a relief. Smoothing the jeans to his feet made her weak enough to wish she could lie down—with Byron.

"We play now, Jade," he said when he stood naked before her. "You undress for me and you smile. It's a smile that says you want me, too."

She did smile, before she let herself study his body. The moon was a friend to both of them. Broad and powerful shoulders and chest, well-defined over ribcage and belly, lean hips and such strong legs.

Jade wrapped her arms around his hips, stroked his hard buttocks, pressed her lips into the tight, hair-rough, skin beneath his navel. And Byron groaned.

Tugging, she urged him to kneel, his thighs trapping hers. While they kissed again, Jade forced her hands between them to undo her shirt. The thought came that she'd never seduced a man before. Then there was only feeling again, feeling and instinct that sent her fingers searching downward to surround him.

"Jade. You're killing me."

She laughed. "And you hate it?"

"And I love it. But even strong men have limits."

"So do strong women. Lie down."

Shifting, he stretched out on the hard sand with Jade astride his hips. Her skirt spread over him but only thin satin panties separated them.

When she struggled free of her shirt, Byron's hands were on her bare thighs, stroking all the way to narrow lace edging on smooth satin—and beneath. She quivered and set her teeth.

"You're not telling me what I do anymore, Byron."

He shook his head and reached for her breasts. Jade caught his wrists. "I'm doing the seducing, remember."

"I remember," he said faintly.

Hitching herself up, she settled to sit on his middle. She slipped black straps from her shoulders and eased the bra down, gradually revealing her breasts. Without embarrassment, Jade looked at herself. Silvery light made her skin luminously pale against the black lace.

"Let me kiss you," Byron said.

Understanding him, she rocked forward. He released the center fastening on her bra and pressed her breasts together—and when he kissed them, Jade caught at his hair.

"When you come to me and do this," Byron said, nestling his face between her breasts and gently pinching her nipples between his fingers. "Then I can't seem to wait anymore. And then I'm the one who decides what we do next."

Air seared Jade's throat. Byron felt between her legs and she moaned.

"You are ready, Jade," he said, chuckling softly.

"I've never felt like this before." It didn't seem to matter how vulnerable she made herself. "Decide what we do next, Byron. Decide and do it."

"Your wish is my command." He sat and pushed her to sit between his legs. "Dawn becomes you, Jade. So does moonlight. Ah, hell—I'm a lousy poet. And I can't wait any longer."

Byron gripped her hips and Jade forgot the night, and the beach, and sweet sad fears of loneliness to come. He was with her now.

"You're quiet," Byron said.

Jade sighed. "I'm happy."

"Are you always quiet when you're happy?"

"I don't know. I've never felt this kind of happiness before."

He didn't answer. They walked slowly back along the Esplanade this time. Darkened windows, like silently shuttered eyes, glistened in the brick facades of guest houses facing the inlet.

Saying anything that suggested she wanted to tie him was a mistake. "I didn't mean—"

"I hope you did mean it," he interrupted. "I don't know how to tell you what it feels like being with you. You're something, Jade. Sexy as hell. Sweet as hell. I wasn't joking about insomnia and I do need sleep now and then. You know what that means."

She warned herself not to hope for too much. "I'm very forward, Byron." She giggled, then laughed. "Listen to me. I sound like a naughty kid. But seriously, I've decided I'm a wanton woman."

"*Good.* Wanton is very good on you."

"I'm glad you like it because I'm about to proposition you."

"Again?"

Jade batted his shoulder. "You've made me what I am. Now, let me proposition you. Stay with me tonight, Byron."

He stopped so suddenly she almost tripped over his feet. "How come you can do this to me? You make an innocent request and I'm hard. Just like that."

"Ssh." She looked around at the empty street before telling him in a husky whisper, "That was no innocent request."

"You enjoy danger, my girl." Holding her close, Byron backed her to a wall. He slid his tongue along the edge of her lower lip and darted inside. Spreading his legs, he made sure she felt the effect of her invitation. Seconds passed and the kisses became urgent.

Her bra was stuffed into his jeans pocket and Byron's hand went inside her shirt to cover a naked breast. She tugged on his wrist and pushed him firmly with both hands. Undaunted, he dipped to hike up her skirt and smooth her hips. How easily he slipped up inside the legs of her panties to knead her bottom.

Jade's knees had begun to sag when reason sneaked in. "Not here," she told him. "Let's go home."

"Chicken," he said. But he straightened her clothes, took a deep breath, offered a wicked smile, and set off at a brisk clip, pulling her with him. "It's time for the other scenario."

"Other—" She stopped, turning burning hot all over.

"The one where I seduce you—until you seduce me again."

Before she could protest, he broke into a run. Gasping and laughing, Jade kept up as best she could all the way to Lostwithiel Street.

"I want you with me all night," she told him between pants.

"You've got me."

He didn't slow down until they were within yards of the shop.

Something moved and Jade drew back on Byron's hand. "There's someone there," she said, her heart turning over. "Byron—"

"Byron?" The moving shape became a woman and she came toward them. "Oh, thank God it's you, darling. I didn't know what I was going to do next." A drawling American voice.

"What are you doing here?" Byron asked in a voice Jade had never heard him use before.

"I'd have thought that was obvious."

They were separated by only a few feet now. The woman was tall, dressed in a suit of some pale fabric, and her blond hair shimmered. When she came even closer, Jade saw that she was beautiful, with huge eyes and a face with fine bones any model would kill for.

"I had to find you, Byron. You've got to come with me to London tomorrow."

"I'm not hearing you," Byron said.

"You're hearing me very well, darling. Denning's taking us to lunch. He wants to talk about an English series, Byron. Six parts and the biggest money you've ever seen. I'm not letting . . . I've worked hard for this and we're not throwing it away on some little whim you've found in this hole."

Jade smarted. She longed to be safely inside her flat and away from this exotic creature who looked at her as if she were an alien. She silently exhorted Byron to tell the woman to leave.

"Denning?" Byron said at last. "Denning's offering me a six-part series?"

"Isn't it delicious? Even as he was naming a perfectly outrageous figure, he said he could be flexible if we weren't satisfied. Can you imagine?" She sniggered. "We'll have to make sure he knows how dissatisfied we can be!"

Byron released Jade's hand. "We'll drive up to London. Do we have a hotel?"

"What do you think?"

"I think we have a hotel. And I think you've probably thought of everything. We'll get away early. There's room at the cottage. You can stay there tonight."

Jade felt sick. Her palms sweated and she pressed them into her skirt.

"That sounds great," the woman said. "We should get there and sleep. We'll need to be bright-eyed tomorrow."

"You bet, oh"—he turned to Jade and put an arm around her shoulders—"forgive me, ladies. Celeste, this is my friend, Jade Perron. Jade, this is Celeste Daily. Celeste makes sure I never get too far off-track."

Chapter Twenty

Early morning sunlight bounced over ripples fanning from the ferry's hull. Jade rolled down the driver's window in the van and blinked against a cool, salty breeze. The distance to Bodinnick narrowed rapidly.

The sitting room windows at Ferryneath, clearly visible from the river, gleamed, revealing no hint of what went on inside the cottage.

Had Byron already left?

Ferrymen readied lines. In a moment she'd drive off and up the hill to the cottage.

Coming to work this morning had taken courage—so much courage. True, his kiss had been softly intimate before he left her the previous evening. But he *had* left her. "I'll call you," he'd said with a lopsided smile that suggested he'd rather stay.

But he had left her.

With a thud, and the scrape of metal on concrete, the ferry slid into dock and the gates swung open. First off, Jade waved to each familiar face she passed and drove the short distance that took her to the yard beside Ferryneath.

Wiggling all over, Dog shot to stick her head out the window.

She'd taken to deserting Jade in favor of following Byron around, and sleeping at his feet while he wrote. "You could be out of luck today, girl," Jade said. "Your new champion may not be in residence." *Would* not be in residence. The faint hope that he'd changed his mind about leaving couldn't force the miracle she longed for.

The Land Rover was in the yard again.

Jade brought the van to a halt and switched off the ignition. A jumpy sensation attacked her stomach. Celeste Daily would probably be there.

To hell with Celeste Daily. At least Byron was still here and that meant the woman hadn't managed to sweep him as completely back "on track" as Jade had thought last night.

As she climbed from the van, a familiar voice hailed, "Jade Perron!" and she shaded her eyes. Hand raised in a wave, Harry Hancock ambled along the path from his cottage.

"Morning," Jade said, and smiled when he drew close. Since she'd worked regularly at Ferryneath, she'd come to know and like Harry. "Lovely morning, too."

"Aye, it is that. I was wondering if Perron's would be the people to do a spot of bricking for me. Wall at the bottom of the garden. Wind did damage last winter. Ought to see to it before my daughter comes for her holiday. Nothing she likes more'n picking at what her old dad doesn't keep up."

Jade laughed. "Daughters are tyrants. Ask my dad." She remembered last evening's debacle at the Preacher and glanced away. "Will's our bricklayer. I'll have him come over and take a look." Byron usually came out when he heard her arrive. Heat crept over her body. He must have been tired by the time he got home last night.

"Did you talk to your dad?"

She frowned blankly.

"After . . . Well, y'know—after what happened at the Preacher."

"No."

"Ah." Harry took a pipe from the pocket of his saggy tweed waistcoat and absently tamped down the contents of the bowl with a blunt thumb. "That young Lyman wasn't long for the company after you left."

Jade breathed in through her nose, slow and deep, and watched a cabbage butterfly flitter its powdery white wings in the young sun's wash.

Harry's square, seamed face set seriously. "Your dad gave him a piece of his mind, I can tell you. But then the fool—sorry, I shouldn't speak of your husband that way."

"He hasn't been my husband for some years." Again her attention went to the kitchen door.

Harry flexed his shoulders. "Well, anyway, pushing his luck wasn't clever. He said what he thought of you for . . . for having anything to do with Byron. That's when your dad told him he'd as well pick his opponents more carefully the next time. Said Byron was more a man." He laughed shortly. "Then Lyman . . . He had other insights into your character, and Byron's. Sam Hill chucked him out. Reckon there's probably a man who's not feeling his best this morning."

Speechless, Jade stared at him. Her father *defended* Byron? And Sam threw Doug out of the Preacher?

"You're fond of Byron, aren't you, lass?"

Yet again she glanced at the cottage.

"I reckon he's fond of you, too. He's a nice chap, Jade—and he's got a pretty pile on his plate, hasn't he?"

Slowly, she pushed the van door shut. "Did he tell you about . . ."

"The lad? Aye. If he hadn't, someone else would have. It's all over the area. I told him once he started into it, there'd be no putting things back the way they were."

"No." But he'd gone ahead anyway.

Harry poked at short gray hair. "Got to admire him, though. He thinks he's got to do what he can for the lad."

"People have to do what they think is right." Jade walked around to the back doors of the van and pulled out the dolly. She paused. She was tempted to abandon outside repairs in favor of working on something inside. Byron would know she was deliberately making an excuse to see him. "How's the paint job on your place, Harry?"

"It'll do for a year or two more."

Jade inclined her head to Ferryneath. "This should have been done several years ago." She unhooked a ladder from the side of the van. Let Byron come out and find her. "People think they save money by putting jobs off. All they do is cause the kind of damage that costs even more."

Harry stood by, tapping his pipe stem against his teeth, while Jade armed herself with putty. "It's still early," she said, aware that he already knew what time it was. "I was working on the front, but I'll start this side for a while."

"Sun's full on the front," Harry remarked, following her to the cottage.

"Yes." She set about patching around the kitchen window. "Puttying makes a racket. I don't like to bother people."

"Oh, you won't bother me," Harry said.

"No." Jade worked the putty. "But Byron's probably sleeping in. Last night . . . Well, last night must have been hard on him."

Harry wrinkled his nose. "Wouldn't have known it this morning."

Jade turned to him. "This morning?"

"Aye. Took off more than an hour ago. In that fancy Rolls-Royce that American friend of his came in."

Hubert Denning draped a sinuous arm across Byron's shoulders. "Now don't tell me you've ever had a pistachio nut soufflé to equal that one." The arm shifted and Byron was thumped hard enough to make him wish he hadn't eaten the exquisite dessert—or the pig's trotters stuffed with morels.

"Pig's trotters," Denning said on cue. "Not a gastronome in London who doesn't rave about the trotters at La Tante Claire."

They walked through the sumptuous birchwood and chrome interior of La Tante Claire. Exuding barely restrained excitement, Celeste clung to Byron's right hand.

With discreet deference, an employee appeared to usher Denning and his guests through a door in the restaurant's blue-and-white facade and onto the busy sidewalk.

"I'll have Len drop you off," Denning said as his navy blue Bentley limousine slid obligingly to a stop beside them.

"No," Byron said hastily, ignoring Celeste's urgent squeeze on his hand. "No, thanks. I like to walk off a good meal."

An agreeable smile split Denning's aristocratically hawk-nosed face. "Quite. But I will hear from you before the day's out? We'll want to capitalize on the momentum gained from this current American series of yours. It'll work well to put you on live here while the taped segments are airing in the States."

"You'll hear from us, Hubert," Celeste said quickly, executing a meat-grinding maneuver on Byron's hand.

Byron smiled and nodded while the other man slid into the Bentley's pristine leather interior and whisked away into the heavy traffic of southwest London on a weekday afternoon.

"God!" Celeste said explosively. "He's so innovative. Why didn't we ever think of showing group counseling sessions live?"

"We have shown them."

"Not *actually* live. And not with call-ins."

"No."

"You do like it, don't you, Byron? God, this is *it*."

"I doubt if God's that interested."

She poked his ribs. "You can be such a sonavabitch, Byron. Such a—Well, you're overwhelmed and I don't blame you. We'd better get back to Claridges and go over the numbers. He's in a hurry, but we've still got a lot of work to do. He's hungry and that means we still haven't seen the bottom of the bank."

Byron really did have to walk.

Celeste crossed her arms and he finally looked straight into her very lovely gray eyes. He raised his brows.

"It's this ridiculous *boy* thing, isn't it?" she said.

He had no choice but to talk about Ian. "A son isn't something you can sweep away just because someone offers you a multimillion-dollar contract."

A faint flush dusted her smooth cheeks. "You managed to forget him very nicely for thirteen years."

"How right you are." He turned away and began walking.

Celeste caught up. "I'm sorry. That was bitchy. But I'm still reeling, darling. A kid. A thirteen-year-old kid produced like a rabbit from a hat, for God's sake."

"Maybe God *would* be interested in that."

"When did you get religion?"

"We're being flip. We're both edgy, so why don't you go back to your cozy little lair at Claridges and take a nice long, hot bubble bath or something?"

She threaded a hand beneath his elbow and pulled him to a stop. "You *can't* produce the son you gave away. Do you understand what I'm saying? If you do, your career's down the tube. Famed behavioral psychiatrist—expert on the family—reveals he gave away his son and took thirteen years to decide he'd made a mistake. How would you like to read *that* on the front of every rag in London—and New York—and anywhere else where I've worked my fanny off to get you where you are?"

Anger was what she hoped for. Anger was supposed to shake him back onto safe ground. "Take that bath, Celeste."

"We've got to get back to Hubert by this evening so he can take our response to his people. There's a time limit here."

"Yeah. I'm going for a walk."

"Byron—"

"Taxi!" He flagged the next free vehicle.

"If we don't get back to him by tonight, there's a chance he'll decide to rattle chains, Byron. He's a happy man now. Let's not do anything to spoil that."

"Get in." He held the taxi door for her.

Celeste got in and he slammed the door shut. Through the window, she said, "We've *got* to make contact."

"Don't worry," Byron said. "I know what's at stake."

After the cab swept away, he walked on, not seeing the faces he passed, or the buildings. Street noises melded together into a drone and he barely noticed the acrid scent of gas fumes.

A Pekingese dog with flowing fur, followed by a taut leash and an ancient lady with blue hair, crossed his path, and Byron paused while they passed.

What Celeste had said twisted like a knife in his gut, but she had a right. And she was also right when she said this Denning deal was better than anything they'd ever dreamed of.

He stood on the curb. Celeste was right yet again when she reminded him that Denning had made his time limitations clear. If they delayed going under contract, the terms might be just as good—but there were no guarantees.

Highly respected psychologists didn't suddenly produce discarded offspring—that had been Celeste's message. Not if they wanted to keep their credibility. If he'd told his story at the outset, he'd have had nothing but sympathy, she'd informed him. And he'd reminded her that Ian used to be part of a happy adoptive family, to which Celeste had responded that as far as she could see, Ian was still part of a happy adoptive family.

Byron Frazer was the man who had once been a boy with no luck—no chances—no one who put him first or gave a damn about what he wanted.

The upward climb had been long and tough.

A taxi approached with its yellow FOR HIRE sign on. Byron signaled and the cabby pulled over. "Where to, guv'nor?" the man asked.

"Claridges."

Jade heard her father's familiar footsteps behind her in the shop, and wielded a broom with more force than necessary, sending clouds of plaster dust swirling into the air.

He coughed and she grimaced guiltily.

"Hello, girl. Will told me you'd knocked off early at Ferryneath and come here. You work too hard."

She stopped brushing and faced him. "Hello, Dad."

"We need a chat."

"Not now."

"Your mother's coming in. She had an errand to do first."

"Let it alone for now," Jade said. She discarded the broom and began straightening bins of nails and screws. "It is getting late. I'll be going home soon. I think you should head Mum off and take her home, too."

"A boy needs a man's guidance."

She stopped in the act of filling a bin of washers from a nearby box.

"That Byron fellow of yours is all right." Dad chuckled. "Too bad you didn't stick around to see Doug's face when Sam hauled him out of the Preacher."

Jade smiled thinly. "You were wrong to trick me into seeing Doug."

He shuffled uncomfortably. "Did he . . . Well, did he really try to force himself on you?"

"Yes." She faced him squarely. "Yes, he did. I had to fight him off, Dad. And I got lucky."

Art Perron's brow furrowed. "I should have known better. That lad always did have a way of smooth talking his way into whatever he wanted. It's too bad little Rose is his daughter."

"No, it's not." Jade shook her head emphatically. "Rose will be Doug's reason for making something of himself. And he loves her very much. Rose will be fine with him."

The door to the shop opened and Jade's mother stepped inside. Dressed in a blue cotton suit and pumps that matched, she looked fresh and Jade was reminded of photographs of the pretty girl her father had married.

"There you are," May Perron said, puffing, as if finding Jade in the shop were a surprise. "I'd have come in with Mr. Perron but I stopped to pick this up." She presented Jade with a square box.

"It's not my birthday," she said, tugging off the top. Inside lay a kitchen clock encased in bright yellow.

"That's for that place where you live," Mum said. "Every little bit helps to make a place feel more like home."

"It's great," Jade said, unsure how to react to the first sign that her mother was finally accepting her daughter's determination to live alone. "Thank you both." She also knew she was looking at a peace offering.

Her mother bridled. "Wait till I set eyes on that Doug—"

"We've dealt with that," Dad interrupted quickly. "What I want you to know, Jade, is that I think Byron Frazer's a good man. And if he's what you want, then it's all right with us, isn't it, Mother?"

Jade's mother pulled her chin back. "I suppose so."

"And if the courts decide Ian's better off with Byron, I'm going to insist this family gets behind him."

Jade gaped.

"Oh, Art," May Perron said, her eyes round. "How can you say that? What about poor Muriel?"

"Poor Muriel will just have to lump it. The woman's a fool."

"No she isn't, Dad," Jade said quietly. "Not at all. And she's become very fond of Ian." She didn't add that she thought Ian was becoming quite fond of Aunt Muriel.

"Well, anyway, I've said my piece, not that what I think's likely to make a difference at this hearing or conference or whatever they're holding."

Jade became quite still. "I hadn't heard about any conference."

"Oh yes," her mother said, lacing her fingers together. "Poor Muriel's solicitor telephoned this afternoon. He said he's heard from Byron's solicitor—some London man—and the two of them want a chat the day after tomorrow. That's what he told poor Muriel. A chat, he said."

"Just with Muriel?"

"Oh, no. Muriel and Dr. Frazer. And Ian's got to be there, too. The London solicitor's agreed to come to Muriel's in St. Austell—so's not to make it too frightening for Ian. They think having him taken to London would be too much for him."

Byron had known nothing of this yesterday—Jade would swear to it. "I suppose they know what they're doing," she said. Byron must know about the meeting by now. He'd have to come back to Cornwall for it, but he could bypass Fowey if he chose.

"Are you all right, dear?" Mum asked. "You look pale."

"I'm fine." That was it. That was what nagged at her—Byron could do whatever he chose to do about Ian and never return to Ferryneath—except to pick up his possessions. And if he really didn't want to return, getting someone in to pack up for him wouldn't be a problem.

"Well," Dad said. "Nothing to be gained by empty chit-chat. We'd best be getting on, May."

Before either of her parents could make a move, there was a rap on the door.

"Darn," Jade said, looking at her watch. "That'll be Wentworths. They haven't made their delivery yet."

She hurried to press the button that raised one of two doors big enough to allow van entry.

"Did you miss me?"

Jade sucked in a breath and raised her eyes to meet Byron's. "You're in London."

He tapped her nose. "Am I?"

She swallowed and caught his hand. From behind came the sound of her father clearing his throat, but she didn't care. "I thought you had important business to deal with."

"I did. I still do. My most important business is right here, Jade. Going to London wasn't a good idea, but it helped me make a decision."

Not asking what his decision had been was easy. Jade couldn't think how to form the question.

"I know what I want now, sweetheart. I want everything. I want Ian—and I want you."

Chapter Twenty-one

Byron turned from contemplating an artificial log fire—an orange-and-black plastic contraption with a rotating light behind—and studied his companions.

Muriel Cadwen snapped and unsnapped the clasp of the boxy black purse she held on her lap. Ian stared at the cover of the magazine Muriel had handed him when they'd arrived and which he still hadn't opened.

Jade looked steadily back at Byron. Her heart was in her troubled eyes.

Byron's heart was on his sleeve.

"I've just decided I know what hell's like." The crack in his own voice startled him.

The clasp on Muriel Cadwen's purse snapped shut with something close to rifle shot force.

"It's like a waiting room," Byron continued. "Probably an endless series of waiting rooms with people sitting around trying not to look worried about anything."

Jade nibbled her bottom lip. Muriel nodded in fierce agreement. Ian continued to stare at the magazine but his fingers rolled in the edges.

"Doctors. Dentists. *Lawyers.* Or solicitors rather. About now I'd swear solicitors' waiting rooms are the worst."

"Difficult," Muriel murmured.

He regarded the woman thoughtfully. She really wasn't so bad and she definitely had protective feelings toward Ian.

"What do you think they're doing?" Jade asked. She hadn't wanted to come to St. Austell but he'd persuaded her that he needed her, and so did her aunt and Ian.

"Oh, it's all part of some ritual. They're probably comparing golf handicaps. Then they'll call us in for a frosty face-off and we'll finally get down to business."

Failure to gain custody of Ian had been, and always was, a possibility. Until today, right now, Byron had convinced himself he would win in the end. He couldn't be sure anymore.

There had been blocks of time, months, even a year or more, when he had been so involved with his career that he had felt comfortable just accepting bulletins that Ian was thriving. Rather than grow longer, those periods had shortened. Two lines converging. Two lives on a collision course.

Byron would never again be involved enough in anything to forget the boy who had become real, more real than for the short time they'd touched when Ian was an infant.

Whatever happened, Byron's life would never be the same.

"They're in there deciding what's best for me," Ian said abruptly, and in a too loud, too high voice.

"They're going to try to help us all decide what's best for you," Muriel said immediately and to Byron's astonishment. "Whatever happens, you'll be properly looked after."

Jade averted her face and Byron saw the sheen of tears in her eyes. He would never regret deciding to come to Cornwall.

"Ian's very bright," Muriel said. "But you know that. At the school, Mr. Bowles says Ian's exceptional."

"I do know." Byron watched the predictable red stain climb Ian's fair-skinned face.

"I'm thinking of ways to make sure he's challenged," Muriel continued.

Byron paced to the window. "He should be." The gray morning seemed appropriate.

"The other day I was talking to Reverend Alvaston. He said he might consider tutoring Ian in theology if we wanted him to—since Ian's so bright."

Jade made an unintelligible sound.

"I need to go to the bathroom," Ian said, getting up and making for the door.

"Run along then, dear," Muriel said, and when he'd left, she continued, "He really is such a nice boy. Polite. I didn't think so at first but he must have been shy . . . awkward. Everything would seem so strange here at first, I should imagine."

"Very different," Byron said.

"Yes." Again the purse clicked open and shut, open and shut. "I was engaged, you know."

Jade's head snapped up. "Engaged? You never told me that. No one did."

Muriel hunched her shoulders. "The family didn't approve. Then they preferred for me not to talk about Nigel afterwards so I didn't."

"That was cruel," Jade said, leaning toward Muriel.

"We wanted to have children. Nigel said we should get started as soon as we were married, and . . . Well . . ." She smiled and looked away. "World War II happened. He was a tail gunner in one of those fighter planes. Such a horrible job. Shot down over the Channel."

In the utter silence that followed, Byron decided what he wanted to tell Muriel. "I'm sorry. That's the hardest thing that can ever happen—to lose the person you love most. When my wife died, I thought for a while that I'd died with her."

Muriel nodded sadly. "That's how it feels."

An almost companionable air settled on them, only to be broken

by the arrival of Ian, followed by the shiny-faced man who was secretary to Muriel's lawyer. "Mr. Reed," the man announced, "will see
you now." They followed along a hall carpeted in threadbare red
and gray and into a darkly paneled room of handsome proportions.

Carson Lloyd-Summers came forward to greet Byron with a
hearty handshake. In contrast to Muriel's comfortably tweeded Mr.
Reed, Lloyd-Summers wore success in his chosen profession as
surely as he wore a bespoke Savile Row suit.

"Morning, Byron," Lloyd-Summers said. "Glad this worked out
for all of us. This must be Ian."

Ian endured his handshake with barely a flinch before the solicitor waved Jade and Muriel into chairs. Ian also sat, but Byron chose
to remain standing.

"I wasn't eager for this type of meeting," Reed said from behind
his well-waxed mahogany desk. "Mr. Lloyd-Summers persuaded
me and now I think it may be to everyone's advantage—it may
eliminate a great deal of pointless inconvenience."

Instinctively, Byron disliked Mr. Reed. "I think I can speak for
Miss Cadwen when I say we are both prepared to go through any
amount of what you term inconvenience to come to the right solution for Ian."

"Quite." Reed opened a folder. "Are you sure you wish to pursue
this action, Dr. Frazer?"

Byron frowned. Lawyers could be bloody infuriating. "I'm quite
sure. I wouldn't be here if I weren't." The man was only going
through the required motions.

"You came to this certainty rather late, didn't you, Dr. Frazer?
Thirteen years late?"

"Come now, Ted," Lloyd-Summers said congenially. "We all
know the facts presented so far. My client has intervened because
he considers it his duty now. While Ian's adoptive parents were
alive, there was no need—in Dr. Frazer's view—to interfere. More
than that, he decided any such interference would be unfair. Now
that picture has changed."

Reed appeared to consider. "Let's get to the heart of this. Dr. Frazer, we're dealing here with a finalized adoption. This boy"—he referred to the file—"Ian Spring, is in the care of his aunt by adoption, the woman designated to assume his guardianship in the event of his adoptive parents' deaths."

Law must attract a very particular type of mind—one that enjoyed endlessly reviewing already known facts. "We're all aware of this," Byron said.

"Bear with us, Byron." Lloyd-Summers's narrow head, with its smooth sandy hair, was vaguely ferret-like.

"What you've chosen to undertake, Dr. Frazer, is by no means clear-cut. You have chosen to engage the judicial systems of two countries—the United States and Great Britain."

"As a United States citizen"—Lloyd-Summers took up the monologue—"Ian, in theory, might be assumed to come under United States law, but we in Britain are not forced to acknowledge United States jurisdiction."

Byron looked to Mr. Reed, who slowly turned a page. "If a petition were filed in the United States and the courts there found for you, Dr. Frazer, there would still be the issue of dealing with the boy being handed over. We might, naturally, lean heavily on the fact that you gave up your rights when you gave up the child and—"

"*Don't* talk about Ian as if he weren't here," Byron interrupted explosively.

"I should think not." Muriel sat very straight in her leather wing chair. She sent a tight smile from Ian to Byron and he nodded.

"Yes, well," Reed said, evidently unperturbed. "All of this is almost undoubtedly academic, wouldn't you agree, Carson?"

"It may be," Lloyd-Summers allowed serenely.

Amazed, Byron approached his solicitor. "What is this? I agreed to this meeting although you admitted it was unorthodox."

"The case is unorthodox."

"Whose side are you on?" Byron took another step closer.

"Oh, come, come now, Byron. Let's not get emotional."

"This *is* emotional—for all of us." He indicated Jade, Muriel, and Ian. "We came here ready to attempt to find a workable solution, but we're *very* emotional about the issue."

Lloyd-Summers pushed back his jacket and slid beautifully manicured hands into his trouser pockets. "Of course. Unfortunately, something has developed since I spoke to you yesterday. Had I been in possession of certain information earlier, we probably wouldn't be having this meeting. In light of the potential problems—which were bound to become a matter of public record—I had no choice but to be open with Ted."

"I wish you'd be open with me," Byron muttered.

"It was necessary to check into the records of Ian's adoption," Lloyd-Summers said. For the first time, he appeared edgy.

Byron shifted uneasily. "I think Ian should be spared all this. He should be asked to state his preference—if he can. That's a heavy burden for a boy—particularly a sensitive boy—but ultimately I think the choice has to be his."

"Not at this point," Reed said brusquely. He peered at Ian and cracked a fierce smile. "In fact, I think Ian would be better off having milk and biscuits with my secretary. No need for him to be involved in all this boring grown-up stuff yet."

Byron smothered a groan, but instinct stopped him from arguing.

When the door had closed behind Ian, Ted Reed produced a handkerchief and mopped his face. "Nice boy," he said. "If you agree, I'll take it from here, Carson." Without waiting for a response, he continued. "These adoption records would be available to Ian when he's eighteen anyway. Your people were very reasonable. They agreed to let us see copies of them now since the boy's immediate welfare is involved."

"Good," Byron said, beginning to pace. Good God, what had they found? *Nothing.* There wasn't anything negative to find.

"Do you remember the interviews you went through after—er—the death of your wife, Lori Frazer?"

"Yes."

"A difficult time, I'm sure."

"Awful," Muriel said in a squeak.

Byron raised his chin. "I don't think any of this is relevant."

"It's relevant." Reed jabbed the paper before him. "But it is possible that we need not go into it now. What do you think, Carson?"

Lloyd-Summers chose that moment to sit in one of the leather wing chairs. Sliding back, hitching his trouser legs, settling his elbows on the chair arms, and steepling his fingers all appeared to Byron to happen in slow motion. The man swiveled his eyes toward Jade. "Perhaps we should continue without the ladies present—for the moment?"

Byron's mind felt vacant and fuzzy. "I can't see why."

"Mm. Yes, I think I advise we do that."

"No." There couldn't be anything Jade and Muriel shouldn't hear and Byron wasn't interested in dramatic maneuvers. "No, we'll remain as we are."

Lloyd-Summers tapped his fingertips together. "As you wish. But Ted has a point. We can make this much simpler if we just ask you to undergo testing."

Confused, Byron narrowed his eyes. "For what?"

"To establish paternity."

He heard the words but they didn't compute.

"Simple these days," Lloyd-Summers continued.

"No." *No!*

Ted Reed rolled his chair back a few inches. "Why not? As Carson says, it's simple." Byron felt how intently the man watched him.

"Why should I be tested to find out what we already know?"

"Byron," Lloyd-Summers said, "are you sure you still want to go on with this?"

Cold climbed his spine, vertebra by vertebra. "We came here to decide what's best for Ian. That hasn't changed."

"Very well." Ted Reed rolled close to his desk once more. "I have here a copy of notes made during an interview shortly after your wife's death. You had decided you didn't have room in your life for a child."

"Damn you!" Byron made fists at his sides. "I had *room*. I just didn't have anything else. And . . . I panicked."

"So you say. However, you made a number of remarks the interviewer thought to record. I'm not sure how much credence they'd be afforded at this late date, but they do raise question, and as Miss Cadwen's solicitor, I would certainly request that they be brought into evidence."

"Things I said"—he squeezed his eyes shut and focused again—"what the hell could I have said that anyone would take notice of? I'd just—"

"Lost your wife," Reed interrupted. "Quite. Shall I read you the comment I would be forced to pursue, Dr. Frazer?"

Byron nodded slowly.

"Very well. Speaking of your wife, the now deceased Lori Frazer, you said: 'She died for that little bastard.' "

He hadn't protested. He'd said nothing. Byron had listened to the horrible thing Mr. Reed said and then simply walked out. Aunt Muriel had been the first to react. She pushed to her feet, shock written in her eyes, and plucked at Jade's sleeve.

"Does that mean Ian isn't Dr. Frazer's son?" she'd asked. "I suppose it does. Poor Dr. Frazer. Such a good man."

Jade had got up, too, bemused by her aunt's comments.

"Don't you see," Aunt Muriel continued. "If he isn't Ian's father, but he still wants to make sure . . . For his dead wife's sake he wants to be sure her child is safe. I think that's so unusual—and brave."

Jade stared at the open door. "Please, Aunt, don't say anything about this to anyone. Definitely not to Ian. And not to Mum and Dad, not to anyone. All right?"

Aunt Muriel had nodded.

"Take Ian back to Fowey. I'll be in touch as soon as I can. Tell Ian I love him—that we all love him."

Then she'd run after Byron, reaching the Land Rover as he gunned the engine to life. When he noticed her, Jade saw him struggle to decide whether or not to drive away.

He'd killed the engine and rested his brow on the steering wheel while Jade got in.

The drive back to Bodinnick—he'd showed no sign of going anywhere else—had been accomplished in absolute silence. As he drove off the ferry, Jade touched his arm lightly. "I don't know what to say, Byron."

"Just be with me. I've got to think, but I need you, Jade."

"You've got me."

"I'm going to tell you something, but I'm not sure how—or if I'm ready."

He started into the cottage yard and slammed on the brakes. "Damn. *Celeste*. Damn it to hell. *Not now.*"

A silver-and-tan Rolls-Royce flanked the honeysuckle-draped wall.

"I can walk on the ferry and go back to Fowey," Jade said quickly. "Don't worry—"

"I want you with me." The Land Rover was too long to pull in behind the Rolls, so he parked beside the street.

The kitchen door opened and Celeste Daily rushed out. In an oversized dusty blue silk shirt and jeans that showed off very long, very good legs, she achieved an air of casual elegance that wasn't lost on Jade.

His jaw set, Byron got out of the Land Rover and started around the bonnet. Brandishing a rolled newspaper, Celeste headed him off. Jade hesitated before climbing down herself.

"Thank God you're here," Celeste said. She glanced at Jade but showed no sign of recognition. "Darling, this is terrible, but we can handle it. I want you to let me do the talking. That's what you pay me for and—as I'm sure you remember—I'm very, very good at it."

Jade shut the Land Rover door with both hands and hovered awkwardly beside the vehicle.

"I don't know what you're talking about," Byron told Celeste.

"I tried to warn you. You wouldn't listen. You *insisted* on going through with this whole ridiculous custody thing. Now we're going to have to work our way out of it together."

Byron held a hand out to Jade and waited until she stood at his side before saying, "Go home, Celeste. And *I'll* call you."

"I don't think so." She slapped the newspaper against his chest. "Look at the front page. We'll have to move fast, but we can turn this to our advantage."

The paper rattled as Byron unrolled it. For a moment he stared, and while he did, his features became rigid—all but the muscle that flickered in his jaw.

"Of course you're shocked," Celeste said in a soothing voice that set Jade's nerves on edge. "Take an hour or two to get used to what's happened, then we'll go out with a press release."

"How did they find out?" Byron said, almost to himself. "No one here would be likely to think of doing this. I'm almost sure they wouldn't. No one else knew, but . . . *You. You* told the papers? Holy hell—you did, didn't you? You told them about Ian because you decided that if I was going to go ahead with my plans, you'd find a way to use them."

Jade took a step backward.

Celeste fiddled with a shirt button. "You don't know I did."

"But it's true, isn't it?"

Celeste tried to turn away. Byron's large hand, yanking her around by the elbow, brought her face to face with him, and in close proximity. "Isn't it?"

"All right. *Yes!* Yes, damn it. I leaked it because I know how to orchestrate this mess into something useful to you—and to me. We're going to let the world know how sorry you are you gave up your son. We're going to dole out the details piece by poignant piece. Your painful childhood. Your fight to get the education you needed in order to help people who'd suffered the way you did to find themselves. How your mission is to save others from entering into the kind of destructive relationship you had yourself when you married. How—"

"*Shut* up." He jerked Celeste so close she had to raise her chin to look at him. "You're fired, lady."

Jade drew back against the Land Rover and watched Byron march Celeste to the Rolls and shove her inside. The woman said something through the window and Byron went into the cottage to return with a purse, which he tossed through the window.

The Rolls shot from the yard and disappeared around the corner with the screech of breaks.

Byron held out the paper. "I don't want Ian to see this."

Huge headlines announced: AMERICAN FAMILY EXPERT A FRAUD— HOW GURU DR. BYRON FRAZER DUMPED BABY SON. "Oh, Byron, I am so sorry. But all you'll have to do is explain the truth, isn't it?"

His short laugh turned her heart. "Come on in, sweetheart. It's time to tell you that story."

Rather than talk, Byron walked into the cottage and directly upstairs. Expecting him to return, Jade waited in the kitchen.

When half an hour had passed, she followed.

The door to his bedroom stood open and she saw him standing in front of the window.

"Byron?"

He didn't answer.

Jade advanced slowly until she stood a few feet from him. "If it'll help, I wish you'd tell me what happened."

He let out a breath and dropped back his head. "I'm so tired. I've made a mistake, an awful mistake, but I never meant to. I thought I was doing the right thing."

"Maybe you should sleep."

"Come here."

Her heart turned yet again. She went to stand beside him, to stare with him over the pewter waters of the Fowey estuary late on an overcast afternoon.

Byron looked down at her. "If I believed there was some mighty, omniscient plan, I'd have to think the real reason I came here—the one I didn't know about—was to meet you."

Reaching up, Jade rested her hand on the side of his face. She smoothed his jaw and gently rubbed his neck. Rising to her toes, leaning, Jade kissed him.

At last he touched her, skimmed his fingertips along her collarbones, and loosely circled her throat.

Jade shivered. They kissed for a long time.

Silvered light patterns flickered across the ceiling. Lying in the darkness, Jade nestled into the hollow of Byron's shoulder and savored his closeness and strength.

Closing her eyes, she drifted again. He hadn't told her his story.

Just remembering their lovemaking made her nerves feel open.

He breathed evenly. Curling over him, she shifted until her face rested against his neck. Very gently, she made circles in the hair on his broad chest.

"I love the way you feel." His voice rumbled beneath her cheek.

Startled, Jade leaned far enough back to see the glint of his eyes. "Me, too."

"My father was an alcoholic."

She waited.

"A crazy, mean, violent drunk who beat my mother regularly. My story is your standard son-of-an-alcoholic-and-an-enabler routine. A childhood in hell, only I didn't know how much hell until I was old enough to think for myself and do something about it."

"I'm sorry."

"Yeah, thanks. It's over now. Lori and I met when I was a freshman in college. She'd left high school and gone to work to try and make enough money to carry on with her education. Her history was so much like mine it was scary. Anyway, one day, when we have lots of time and absolutely nothing to do, I'll fill in some of the gruesome details, if you like. For now, it's only the stuff about Ian that's important.

"My dad died in a wreck. He was drunk—naturally. My mother never got over it. She was probably bipolar and she couldn't cope. My sister and I—she was younger—we had to go to my Aunt Dot and her husband. My mother killed herself. Mellie ran away and I've never been able to find out what happened to her.

"I got away and went to school in San Francisco on loans and by working two jobs. I met Lori in my junior year and we were together every moment we could be. But I had my moods. I hadn't dealt with my own grief. We were starting our senior year when I quit handling things. It all broke loose. I hated the whole world and I took it out on the one person who really cared about me—Lori."

He fell silent and Jade realized the tears welling in her eyes were about to overflow. She managed to brush them away.

Byron tangled a hand in her hair and hugged her so tightly she could scarcely breathe.

"Lori did everything she could to reach me. She offered me all of herself, all of her time. Even when I shouted at her and told her to back off, she still stayed right with me—until I took it one step too far.

"One night I told her there was nothing she could do to help me because she was cut from the same cloth as my dysfunctional family. I told that gentle girl she was as wounded and twisted as they were and I didn't need more handicaps. I told her to get lost and not to bother to come back."

Jade heard her own small cry and turned her face against Byron's shoulder. He rubbed her back with the palms of his hands and she felt him press his lips into her hair.

"She didn't come back. She disappeared. When I found her almost two months later, she was broken. I broke her. And I caused everything rotten that happened to her. That's what I have to live with and I deserve it."

"What . . . What happened between you then?"

His chest expanded. "I asked her to marry me. I said neither of us had anything but we might as well have nothing together. She refused and I asked again, and again—until she told me why she wouldn't."

His swallow made a clicking sound. "She was pregnant."

"Oh, Byron."

"Yes. Oh, Byron. She was pregnant and she wasn't sure if I was the child's father—or the creep she got involved with for a lousy week when she started running from me. He was long gone and she didn't know where he was—didn't want to know. She was determined to go it alone.

"So, I asked her to marry me anyway. I wouldn't take no for an answer and eventually she gave in. But Lori always worried that although I kept saying I thought of the baby as mine, I might not be able to when the time came to prove it."

Abruptly, Byron pulled Jade on top of him as if he couldn't get close enough. "She was right. Neither of us guessed what was going to happen, but Lori was right. When the chips were down, I gave up. I couldn't figure out a way to make it on my own with a baby."

"But you didn't hate the baby, did you?"

He laughed shortly. "No, I sure as hell didn't. I loved him because he was the only part of Lori that was left. When I gave him up, I told myself what I was doing was the best thing. And in many ways I still think it was at the time."

"What they . . . in St. Austell. What that solicitor said you said . . ."

"She died for that little bastard? Not Ian. I was talking about the man who seduced a lonely girl."

Pushing up to brace her weight on locked arms, Jade looked down into his face. "You are good, Byron Frazer," she told him. "And I love you."

* * *

River sounds penetrated the thick, hazy warmth that blanketed Jade. Voices from the ferry dock rose and fell and the metal ramps clanked beneath the weight of passing vehicles.

She opened her eyes, but snuggled deeper in the bed. "I love you," she'd told Byron. He hadn't replied, but he'd shown her then how much he loved to make love with her.

Her eyes opened wide and she turned her head on the pillow. A dent marked the place where his head had rested, but he'd left the bed.

"Byron?" She scooted up, pulling the sheet under her arms. The cottage felt still. On the bedside table, a clock showed that it was already past nine.

Jade was sitting on the edge of the bed, looking around for something to put on, when she saw the folded piece of paper. It rested against a vase on a chest near the door. In the vase was a single wild yellow rose from the bushes in the front garden of the cottage.

She swathed herself in the sheet and shuffled to smooth the note and read:

Dearest Jade,

This is one of the toughest things I've faced in my life. I watched you sleeping and realized how much I owe you—and your family—for wanting, and loving Ian. Right now I'm so confused that all I can think about is getting through the roadblocks. I'm going ahead with the testing. I am advised to go to London for this.

I don't know what the future's going to bring for me. I do know I can never go back to what I was before I came to find Ian, and found you, too. You deserve a wonderful life and I'm certainly not good enough for you.

I don't know how long these things take. I will let you know the results of the tests. I'll call about them. And I'll be trying to figure out what I ought to do—*regardless of the outcome. You'll be thinking, too.*

I don't have any right to ask, but please forgive me for all the unhappiness I've caused you and your family. Tell Ian that whatever he hears about me, I never stopped caring about him. I never will.

Jade . . . I feel so helpless. I love you . . .

Chapter Twenty-two

"Jade! Ian's here."

Setting aside her book, Jade looked up to see Ian preceding Shirley along the path leading to the bottom of the garden behind New to You.

"Hi, Ian." She hitched straighter in the deckchair and shaded her eyes against a warm, afternoon sun. July had arrived.

Four days since Byron had left.

How long could a blood test take?

"What's wrong?" Ian asked.

"Nothing." She smiled at him. "I thought you were going swimming."

"I went. Then I got bored." He was dressed in khaki shorts and a T-shirt and was carrying his guitar case. His tanned face made his sun-bleached hair appear almost white.

She had learned that Ian invariably got bored being with the other boys. He'd finally started making friends but he continued to prefer his own company. She smiled at him. "I'm glad you decided to come here when you were bored." He was quickly becoming so much a part of her life she didn't like to think of not seeing him almost daily.

In one hand Shirley carried the post. In the other she held aloft three of the iced lollipops she made from fresh-squeezed juice frozen in paper cups. "Relief on the way," she said. "Sustenance for the sunstroked."

Jade looked not at the lollipops, but the bundle of post. Byron might have decided to write instead of telephone. But if he did that, it probably wouldn't be because he wanted to tell her good news.

What did she want him to tell her?

Just come back, Byron.

Shirley dropped the letters into Jade's lap and perched on fluted concrete blocks surrounding a bed of marigolds and daisies. "I saw something in your charts this morning," she remarked, handing out lollipops before tying her braids in a lumpy knot behind her neck. "I don't suppose you'd be interested in knowing what it was?"

Jade looked at a return address. *The telephone bill.* "Can I stop you from telling me?" The next buff folder was a notification of a citizens' meeting on something or other. Three more bills followed and, finally, a postcard from a friend on holiday in Barcelona.

She was relieved. But what was taking so long?

"I saw a tall, dark man"—Shirley paused and closed her eyes— "dark curly hair. Green eyes. Broad shoulders. Lean hips. Long legs. Powerful arms. One of those kiss-me-now-you-know-you-want-to mouths—"

"Shirley," Jade interrupted warningly, casting a significant glance in the direction of Ian's bent head.

"Anyway," Shirley continued, spreading her gauze print skirt. "He was trying to send a message. It wasn't clear, but I think I got the gist of it."

Ian set aside his melting lollipop, sat down cross-legged beside Dog, and opened the guitar case.

"Do you want to know what the gist of it was?"

"I don't think so." Jade scowled at Shirley. "We could discuss this later, perhaps?"

"I might forget later. I think he said your name, over and over. And he had that hypnotic quality—sensual, sexy. He was asking you to . . . to *find* him, I think. To *save* him."

"Save him from what?" Jade leaned forward and swung her feet to the ground.

"Oh"—Shirley waved her arms—"from something really terrifying, I think. Like emptiness and loneliness and sexual deprivation."

"*Shirley!*"

Ian appeared engrossed in tuning the guitar he now balanced in his lap.

"I know, I know. That's what I thought. A turn-on just to think about, right? So *seductive.*"

"Are you going to stay and listen to Ian play, or do you have to get back to the shop?"

Shirley popped up. "I can take a hint. You two want to be on your own. There are ways to hunt people down, you know. Particularly *famous* people."

"Bye, Shirley."

"The simplest thing to do first would be to try making some telephone calls. You could call—"

"Shirley, please."

"Yes, yes. I must get back into the shop. The crush of customers has exhausted me today." She started back along the path. "Love and lust and wild sexual passion. Ooh, it makes me *shiver.* Nothing like a Scorpio to turn a woman to willing jelly."

"Willing jelly?" Jade muttered.

Ian began to play and she recognized the bleached, summerlike strains of "Sunflower"—the boy's favorite—Byron's favorite. She sank back into the chair and rested her head. Colored spots, violet, magenta, emerald, danced in the sunlight.

Where was he?

She rocked her head to see Ian and breath caught in her throat. He finished the piece and paused, head bowed, the fingers of his left hand splayed—very flat—across the strings while his right hand hung over his knee.

Just like Byron.

Jade clenched her teeth and shut her eyes tightly. If he didn't come back, when would the healing begin? Would these visions and reminders ever stop their almost hourly haunting?

Ian began to play another piece, and to hum—and Jade's heart seemed to stop. She looked at the boy again and he looked back. So serious as his voice skated off into falsetto.

So serious. *Just like Byron.*

"It's been four days, Jade."

She jumped. "Yes." There was no need to ask what he meant. "I know."

"He went away because of me, didn't he?"

"No."

"Then why? He said he'd always be here for me." Ian tipped up his face—and Jade saw Byron tipping up his face in just the same way. "He told me why he couldn't keep me when I was little. I understand that. D'you think he doesn't believe I understand?"

"No. I'm sure he knows you do."

"Then why did Byron go away like that? Without speaking to me again? I wish he'd call us or something."

"So do I." She couldn't always be strong.

"Last night Aunt Muriel said he'd come back. She said she's praying he will and that's that." He smiled. "Aunt Muriel puts a lot of stock in her prayers. She says if you pray for good, good is what will come your way. I never was much for praying."

"Aunt Muriel's a special person."

"Yeah. She's told me a lot about my mom. It makes me miss her more, but I like hearing the stories."

"I'm sure you do."

"Jade."

"Yes."

"I want my dad to come back."

Jade gripped the chair's wooden sides. "Oh, Ian." She shifted her feet to the ground once more. "Your dad's dead. That can't be changed."

He set aside the guitar. "No. I know. And I miss him, too. But I meant my real dad. I want Byron to come back."

She went to her knees and gathered the boy into her arms. "So do I." There was no stopping the tears.

"I'm gonna pray," Ian murmured.

Harry and Muriel ambled ahead along Hall Walk. Their heads angled companionably toward one another as they talked, but Jade couldn't hear what they said.

The weather had been beautiful throughout June, and today, as July's second day approached middle age, the waters of the Fowey Estuary picked up glints of sun that turned its surface to scintillating gold. Toasted grass gave off its familiar aroma of warm hay. Cows crowded against an uphill fence and whipped their sinuous tails at audacious winged insects.

"And here," Ian called from a spot on the very edge of the path that ran along the cliffs above the inlet, "died a brave but unfortunate peasant."

Grinning, Jade stopped and planted her hands on her hips.

"There," Ian cried dramatically, pointing to Jade, "stood King Charles I, surveying the Parliamentarian Army of the Earl of Essex, trapped in the Fowey Valley below. The year, of course, was 1664 and for you, Sire, I died by the shot of a Puritan." He flung out his arms, twisted, and fell flat on his back.

Jade chuckled and went to haul him up. "Very good."

"Yeah. Impressive. They only mention it once a day in school."

"By the time school rolls around again, you'll probably look forward to it. Think that might come true?"

"What d'you think?" He grimaced. "At least Aunt Muriel's promised to keep me out of Reverend Alvaston's clutches. *Theology.*"

"Remember I was the one who saved you. My turn for needing a favor is bound to come."

Ian raised his chin. "You can rely on me, ma'am."

"Aunt Muriel!" Jade called. "We're going to sit here for a bit. You and Harry go on."

Harry and Muriel turned to wave, then plodded on their way. "I like watching Aunt Muriel and Harry. It's nice to see them getting friendly. He makes her laugh and she doesn't take herself so seriously with him."

Ian said nothing.

A bench overlooked the mouth of the estuary, and Jade walked around to sit down. She snagged a stick and poked at fine dust around a pile of stones. Ian picked his way downward from the path until he sank from sight.

A hand settled on Jade's shoulder. "Don't jump."

She did jump. Violently. Then she swiveled and looked up. "Oh." Opening her mouth, she dragged in a breath. "Oh, Byron."

He dropped to his haunches behind the bench and stacked his arms on the back. Inches separated their faces. "Is it okay? Am I welcome?"

Her fingers crept between his. "Are you all right?"

"I will be. Even a very short trip to hell tends to leave you rough around the edges."

Jade looked from his clear, green eyes to his mouth, and suddenly, she grinned.

With a long forefinger, he touched the end of her nose. "What's funny?"

"Your mouth."

"Really."

"Shirley called it a kiss-me-now-you-know-you-want-to mouth." Jade giggled and began to shake until her teeth jarred together. "Byron, Byron. What took so long?"

"Only four days." Looking toward the sky, he shook his head. "The longest four days of my life. I wanted everything absolutely done and finished. Then I found I didn't want the next time I talked to you to be on the phone. I wanted to be looking at you. If you won't let me be with you, I'm going to lie right here and wait to become a heap of dry bones."

Jade glanced at the edge of the path where Ian had disappeared. "Ian's down there. He'll be back any second. Aunt Muriel and Harry Hancock are farther on."

"So I'd better make the best of the moment." Not giving her a chance to protest, he half stood and pressed his lips to hers. While he kissed her, he splayed his fingers over the sides of her face and pushed into her hair. Jade stole her arms around him and turned, never breaking from him, to kneel on the bench and kiss him back until they both drew apart a fraction. Resting brow on brow, they fought for breath.

"I love you," Jade whispered.

"And I love loving you." Byron dropped to his knees once more but they clung together. "There are going to be a lot of things to work out, but Art seems to think they're all what he calls minor nonsense."

"My dad?" Jade pushed away to look at him.

"What did Art say?" Aunt Muriel spoke from nearby and Jade turned to see her a few feet away at Harry's side.

Byron didn't let Jade go. "Ian doesn't know what happened?" he asked.

"Of course not." Muriel sounded umbraged at the suggestion. "That boy wouldn't have listened anyway. He's convinced you're his father and I don't see anything to be gained by telling him otherwise. We can leave things as they are and work out—"

"I am."

"We can work out a way . . . What do you mean, Byron?"

"I am his father." Byron narrowed his eyes and looked toward the sea. "Lori was pregnant when she left. I'm so grateful."

"Me, too," Jade told him. "Did my dad tell you where to find us?"

"Yeah. He wanted to come with me but I persuaded him that if you hadn't changed your mind about wanting me, we'd go back to see him and May."

"Art Perron's a meddling old fool," Muriel announced, puffing up like an angry pigeon. "And my sister isn't any better. This is none of their affair."

"Muriel," Harry said mildly.

"No, don't try to stop me. I will have my say. I should have years ago. They never did appreciate this girl for the gem she is."

"I told Art—"

"*I'm* the one whose going to tell Art a thing or two," Muriel broke in, flapping Byron to silence. "Later. What are we going to do about Ian? A court case shouldn't be necessary."

"I don't think so—"

"No. All that does is put money into the pockets of the likes of that nasty, rumpled Mr. Reed and your smoothy, Mr. Lloyd-Summons."

Jade hid a grin.

"Lloyd-Summers," Byron put in.

Jade hardly trusted herself to meet his eyes.

Harry bobbed on his toes. "Muriel may have a point."

"Yes," Byron agreed. "When Ian's eighteen, he'll be his own boss—if that's what he wants to be. In the meantime, I thought—"

"He could live with me during the week when he's at school. Then come to you at the cottage on weekends. In the summers he could be wherever he wants to be."

A shaft of cold climbed Jade's spine. She looked up at Byron. "How do you think things will work out for you professionally?"

"They'll go up and down." He offered her his hand and she held it tightly. "I've got some bridges to mend, but I think I'll find Celeste wasn't entirely wrong about people's capacity for empathy."

"So the career will be full steam ahead?"

"I know what you're thinking," he told her. "That damn cottage will cost as much as a mansion in Beverly Hills."

At first she didn't comprehend.

"I've contacted the owners and they've agreed to sell. That way I can be where I want to be most. Where I live doesn't impact my career."

"Oh." There didn't seem to be anything else to say, but her heart swelled and she longed to be alone with Byron.

"I could have told you Ian was your son," Muriel said smugly. "He does ever so many things like you do."

"Yes, he does," Jade agreed softly. "I've been watching him play, Byron, and he might be you as a boy. It's uncanny."

"So my idea will work then?" Muriel asked. "We'll—swing with it as they say."

"Mm." Byron tugged in his bottom lip and glanced at Harry. Jade caught the twinkle in the older man's eyes. "Where is that boy of mine?" Byron asked.

As if he'd heard a summons, Ian's blond hair appeared at the edge of the pathway and he scrambled up. Instantly he stopped, his gaze unwaveringly on Byron. "You're back," he said, lifting his arms, then quickly crossing them over his chest.

"Yes . . . Yes, son."

Tears swam into Jade's eyes. She turned her face away and looked directly at Muriel. Her aunt fished for a handkerchief and pressed it to her eyes and nose before giving Jade a watery smile.

Ian said, "You gonna stay a bit?"

Byron nodded and took a step toward Ian. "If it's okay with you, I'd like to stay a long time—sort of forever. I'm buying Ferryneath."

Ian's fair face turned crimson as he fought to control the tears, and the trembling of his mouth. "I knew you wouldn't be away long. You just had to work some things out, right? It's gotta be tough suddenly having to think about a kid you never thought about before."

"I thought about you before, Ian," Byron said quietly. "I thought about you a lot. Thank you for letting me into your life. I'm not sure I deserve to be there. There aren't any guarantees that we'll make a big success out of trying to be a family, but we'll sure try."

Haltingly, Ian approached. Byron met him halfway.

"I want to try. Will you always be somewhere I can find you now?"

"Yes," Byron told him. "Always . . . my son."

They went into one another's arms and clung together, the man big and powerful, yet tender in his vulnerability—the boy taking the man's strength and growing strong himself.

Pulling away, laughing, Byron playfully poked Ian's belly and Ian ducked, coming up to jab at his father. "You're gonna have to get quicker—Dad?" He paused, hand raised. "Do I call you Dad, or Byron?"

"I'm old-fashioned. If you can handle Dad, so can I."

"That's that, then," Muriel said matter-of-factly. "Now Byron, what about you and Jade, it's—"

"Auntie," Jade said warningly.

"Leave this to me." Byron gave a wicked grin. "I'm getting into this masterful thing. I've decided we ought to take a shot at being married."

While her nerves warred between the urge to cry and the desire to laugh, Jade got up and straightened her back. "That's a very romantic idea. And so romantically suggested. You might consider asking me, Byron."

"Not at all. Art already gave me basic woman-handling instructions. Don't ask. They always argue. Tell 'em. That's what he said. And by the way, he is considering changing the company name."

Jade gaped. "He is?"

"I should think so," Muriel said explosively. "*Perron and Son*, of all things. When his son never as much as raised a paintbrush in his life while his daughter took over and ran the whole thing. Perron and Daughter at last. I should just think so."

"I kind of like that idea," Jade said, realizing that the anger at her father's stubborn insistence on excluding her from the masthead had lost its edge. Now it blossomed again, together with a deep sense of satisfaction. "Justice at last."

Byron cleared his throat. "Um, that isn't exactly what Art has in mind." When he had everyone's complete attention, he added, "Since Jade and I will be married—and Art was looking for a suitable wedding gift—he's decided on Perron and Son-in-law. He says the add-on to the logo won't take much."

Harry Hancock laughed until tears squeezed from the corners of his eyes.

Byron Frazer
Ferryneath Cottage
Bodinnick, Cornwall

September

When I first heard about Ada Spring's death and decided I had to see Ian for myself, I took out an old shoe box I hadn't touched for years. Inside were keepsakes from my time with Lori, who was my first wife—for a short time—and Ian's mother. Looking at the notes we'd written to each other, and the flowers Lori had kept because I gave them to her and which she pressed between the pages of her books, the bracelet she wove in colored thread with her name in it, and the handful of photographs, I was angry that our time together had produced so little to count as a record.

I wasn't sure what would happen when I got here to Cornwall, but I brought the photographs and a few other things with me. At the time I couldn't have told you why. Now I know I wanted them with me in case I got to know Ian and decided he'd like to see what his mother looked like, and to have something, no matter how small, that had been hers.

The only note from Lori that I have in England is the one she wrote after she'd told me she was pregnant and I'd said she was an angry woman. I said if she weren't, she'd agree to marry me.

This is a day I couldn't have dreamed about, or had nightmares about, because I never expected it to come. I'm worried in case I've done the wrong thing, but I can only do what seems best. I've given Ian what I took from the shoe box. I thought he'd go through it here in the sitting room, but he looked at a photograph, and when I told him it was of his mother, he left.

I can see him in the garden. He's sitting on the grass by the hydrangeas with his back to me.

He's alone out there and dealing with his first and only meeting with Lori. Ian has caught a lot of big waves in the last year. I don't want him to drown in this one. I've got to go to him.

"Ian, you okay?" He's nodding, but he won't look at me. "All right if I keep you company?" He's nodding again.

Maybe I should have waited to give him these things. I can't take them back now.

"Sit down, Dad. I'm sorry."

"Why sorry? Boy, you can feel winter in the air. But what a summer we've had."

He isn't ready to chat about the small stuff, but I've got to fill in the silences.

"I think I look like her." The photograph he's holding is one where Lori's playing her guitar on the couch in our apartment. "She was the one who helped you play better, wasn't she?"

"Yes. She was self-taught, too, but the difference between us was that she was a natural genius, like you, and I was just enthusiastic. You do look like her." There's also something of me in him—the determined posture, probably, and the way he looks at you when he's angry.

"She said she wanted me." He stabs a forefinger into the folded note. Is he angry now? "She said she was looking forward to the baby—that was me—I know it from the date. She says she wants her baby and she'd give her life for him."

I must not reach for him, but looking into his face is destroying me. He's breaking up.

"I expect you want all this back?"

"It's yours now, Ian. I brought it for you."

"Is this all there is?"

If I let the laugh out, he won't understand. "I have letters Lori sent to me, and some I sent to her. One day you can read them if you want to."

"I won't want to."

I think he will, but he can't think about hurting himself any more than he's hurting today.

"Would it look weird if I put this on?"

The bracelet. I never thought he might want to wear it. "It ties. Let me do it for you. Nothing weird about it. Everyone wears things like this sometimes." But I'd rather not have to look at Lori's bracelet on Ian's wrist. It's too much.

"She made it, didn't she?"

"Yes."

"Did she have a ring? You know—from when you were married?"

"Yes." Telling Ian all the details is my duty—to Lori, and to him. He won't look into my face. "Did you keep it?"

I can't hear for the noise in my head. "Lori . . . I didn't want to take it off her finger. And I didn't want a stranger to take it off. She would have wanted to keep it on anyway."

"So you buried her in it?"

"Yes."

"Where?"

"In a churchyard not far from Golden Gate Gardens. In San Francisco." Dr. Harrison helped me pay for the funeral. I wanted to refuse, but I needed the help. Later I paid him back and told him I was sorry for the way I'd treated him when Lori died. He just smiled.

Ian's stare is as intense as Lori's used to be. "I'd like to go there."

"You will. I chose it because we loved the gardens and I thought she would have liked the idea of being near them."

"I'll play for her."

And I'll listen, and when I can't stop myself any longer, I'll cry. There wasn't enough time for tears when I needed to shed them, and later I didn't take the time. If he'll let me, I'll grieve with my boy.

"I want to go to Mom and Dad's graves, too, and play for them.

Mom's favorite was 'You Are My Sunshine.' When I was a little kid, she sang it to me. Then she liked me to play it for her."

Getting used to hearing him speak about the Springs and call them Mom and Dad so naturally is something I'm going to have to get used to. "I'll take you there too, Ian. Do you think you need to go soon?" He's lost so much and he isn't even fourteen.

Lori's note seems to hold his attention more even than the photos. He's put the pressed flowers back into the envelope. "Not too soon. Not until we're settled here. Really settled. You do still like it, don't you, Dad?"

Do I like it? Oh, yeah, I like it more with every day. "This is where I want to be most of the time. This is where I'm hoping to have a life that counts for something."

"That's what I want." He sounds so old. "I'll know when I want to go to the States. I'll tell you then, but it can be when you're ready after that."

"I'll be ready when you're ready." I'll make myself ready.

"Is it okay for a boy to cry?"

I'm supposed to be good at this. "I've done my share of crying."

His eyes are red as if he's fighting the tears. "I've cried when I've been on my own, too, but . . . I just wondered what you thought about that."

"It takes guts for a man to cry and not be ashamed."

"She said she'd give her life for me. And she did. I wish I could have known her. Please don't leave, Dad. Don't leave me."

Those words are going to follow me forever. "I won't. I can't. Come on, it's okay for me to give you a hug, too."

Somewhere, somehow, I was gifted with chances I never expected to come my way. What I make of them is up to me, but I will fight to be what this son of mine needs.

"That's Jade's van." Ian recognizes the sound of the engine as well as I do. "We'd better put all this away."

"You don't have to."

His hands are a young man's hands, not a boy's. He's deft. "I'll show her when she'll want so see everything. She might be upset. That's not a good idea right now, is it?"

"Jade's not jealous."

"I didn't mean that. This wouldn't be the best time to make her think of—well, you know. Would it? She'd be sad for my mother, but she—well, you know."

"I know you're smarter than your old man." I want to see Jade, to hold her. "I wish she'd stop working so hard."

"Maybe you should just tell her to stop."

"Remind her who wears the trousers around here, you think?"

"Yeah. Tell her it's for her own sake and the baby, but put your foot down."

His hair feels warm beneath my hand. "You know much more than you should have to." He's right, of course, and I've got to get good at dealing with all the pieces of my life at once. "Do me a favor, Ian. Don't say anything along those lines to Jade. About me putting my foot down, or wearing the trousers."

It's great to laugh with this boy, and the best to hear Jade joining in before she's even reached us on the lawn.

F
CAM   Cameron, Stella

        Finding Ian

DUE DATE   M037 24.00
